We hope you enjoy this book.
Please return or renew it by the due date.
You can renew it at **www.norfolk.gov.uk/libraries**
or by using our free library app. Otherwise you can
phone **0344 800 8020** - please have your library
card and pin ready.
You can sign up for email reminders too.

D0808491

NORFOLK COUNTY COUNCIL
LIBRARY AND INFORMATION SERVICE

NORFOLK ITEM

30129 075 651 985

Copyright © Pauline Manders 2016
All rights reserved.

Pauline Manders has asserted her right under the
Copyright, Designs and Patent Act 1988 to be identified as
the author of this work.

This book is a work of fiction. Names, characters,
places and incidents either are the products of the author's
imagination or used fictitiously, and any resemblance to
actual persons living or dead, business establishments,
events, or locales is entirely coincidental.

Cover design Rebecca Moss Guyver.

ISBN – 13: 978 - 1539404101
ISBN – 10: 1539404102

Also by Pauline Manders

Utterly Explosive (2012)

Utterly Fuelled (2013)

Utterly Rafted (2013)

Utterly Reclaimed (2014)

Utterly Knotted (2015)

To Paul, Fiona, Alastair, Karen, Andrew, Katie and Mathew.

ACKNOWLEDGMENTS

My thanks to: Beth Wood for her positive advice, support and encouragement; Pat McHugh, my mentor and hardworking editor with a keen sense of humour, mastery of atmosphere and grasp of characters; Rebecca Moss Guyver for her boundless enthusiasm and inspired cover artwork and design; David Withnall for his proof reading skills; Richard Roebuck for his advice and knowledge relating to mobile phones; Maggie & Will Aggiss for inspiring the filming theme; Sue Southey for her cheerful reassurances and advice; the Write Now Bury writers' group for their support; and my husband and family, on both sides of the English Channel & the Atlantic, for their love and support.

CHAPTER 1

Nick leaned against a marble pillar, his tool kit at his feet. He gazed at the curve of the elegant staircase. It drew his eye from the promise of opulence on the first floor to the symmetry of the cool entrance hall below. It was a world of make-believe, and around him cameras rolled and spotlights blazed. A man stumbled down the steps, his leather coat open, the sheepskin lining billowing around his calf-gripping leather boots. Aviator goggles and a balaclava helmet dropped from his hand as light struck his face.

'Cut!'

'But–'

'Don't look away, Cooper, and don't drop anything. Remember you're supposed to be recovering from a rough landing and this is the first hint that something might be wrong with you. I want it more subtle. I need you to pause, look into the light shafting through that doorway and not be dazzled.'

The director turned. 'Give him a softer light. We'll make it glaringly bright in the editing later. Cooper, think setting sun with hints of pink grapefruit, touches of blood orange. You're doing splendidly. We're only trying to help you.'

'Oh, for God's sake. Not constantly changing things would be a start,' Cooper muttered.

Nick watched the lighting crew. Equipment on gantries spanned the vaulted ceiling from high above the first floor. A tripod-mounted spot stood directly in front of the actor.

'That's it. The front door is open. You can hear Emily outside. OK, take it again from the top. The light'll hit you when you reach the last three steps. That's when you pause.'

It was early morning and the front door was closed. Hardly a setting sun through an open front door, Nick thought. But who was he to have an opinion? He'd never been on a film set before and up until yesterday he hadn't even known Althorne House existed. Who'd have guessed a grand country house built on the proportions of a stately home and faced in sandstone was hiding near Moats Tye?

'Shit!' the props girl yelped as she caught her foot against his toolbox.

The director swiped out sideways in her direction, irritation and annoyance obvious from his gesture. Cooper, now on his second take, hurried down the stairs.

'Sorry,' Nick mouthed, his attention focussing on the girl.

She pulled a face. 'Where's Owen? He takes up less space than you,' she breathed.

He bent to catch her words, a professional whisper, barely audible above the rolling camera. 'He's–'

She put a finger to her lips, shook her head and then slowly drew a line across her throat. He guessed the slight nod in the direction of the passageway behind was an invitation to follow. It was his first day as stand-in jobbing carpenter, and despite the location site being only five miles from his home in Barking Tye, he felt completely at sea.

He trailed after her, thankful his trainers didn't squeak on the smooth marble. She stopped and turned to face him in the gloom of the unlit passage.

'Hi, I'm Priddy. You're new round here, aren't you? First rule – don't make a sound while they're filming. So where's Owen?'

'He's got food poisoning. He sounded pretty dire when he rang me last night. That's why I'm here. He asked me to fill in for him. I'm Nick, by the way.'

She smiled fleetingly. 'I was checking the walking sticks and canes by the mock-up wall. I leaned against it and, well it nearly came down. It's very flimsy, Nick.'

'Flimsy?'

'Yes, kind of shaky.'

'Unsteady? As in unsafe?'

She nodded and then shrugged.

'Thanks, Pretty. I'll go and take a look.'

'It's Priddy.' Her whisper followed him back down the passageway.

So how had Owen landed himself a job like this, Nick wondered. He'd hardly seen him in the two years since the carpentry course at Utterly Academy, probably because Owen never attended the apprentice release days. But Nick was surprised he hadn't said anything about his glamorous job on the occasions their paths had crossed. That is until yesterday when he'd phoned in the grip of galloping gut rot.

The director's voice cut through the air as Nick sidled back into the entrance hall.

'This time, more of a pause, Cooper. Just for a fraction of a second longer, and look straight into the light as it strikes you. Then hurry down the last few steps. Drag your foot slightly as you step onto the marble.'

While Cooper climbed the stairs, Nick retrieved his toolbox and slipped into the space behind the false wall. He moved carefully as his eyes adjusted to the gloom. It would have been pitch black if it hadn't been for the light seeping around the gap at one end and filtering down from the gantry high above. His hand brushed against something. He froze mid step.

'Bloody death trap,' he muttered and groped for his phone. Its torch flashed and diffused into the gloom, picking out a wooden four-by-two as it bridged the space. And then another and another. 'Of course, support struts.' They sloped between the wall's framework and the marble floor. He could have been inside the skeleton of a whale, each four-by-two a rib. And the marble - black oblong marks, like rubber-tread prints smudged the cool polished surface.

'Camera One, you're in front of him.'

While the director's voice resonated through the sham wall, Nick's footsteps smacked and tapped as he clambered through the space. 'Forget the inside of a whale. It's like a bloody sounding box in here,' he murmured.

He whistled softly as he looked at the struts again. There were only three, and there were no secondary supports or fixings – not enough to anchor the wall and not enough to dampen the sound as it ricocheted between the stretches of smooth flat surface. Why weren't there more four-by-twos?

'And sweep around as he reaches the bottom step. We want to see what he's seeing. Camera Three, focus on his feet!'

The director sounded inches from the false wall. For a moment the image of Pretty drawing a finger across her throat flashed into Nick's mind. This wasn't the moment to crash around while the cameras were rolling. He didn't want to distract from the focus on Cooper's manly feet.

Silently, he moved closer to the nearest strut and ran the torch light along it.

'What the hell?' he breathed, his thoughts racing in disbelief.

Dark holes pitted the surface of the wood where the strut had been peppered with extra drillings, weakening the structure and shedding fresh powdery shavings across the marble. Screws or bolts should have filled the shadowy depressions, fixing the angled wood to the floor support. So where were the screws and bolts? And how many holes did a bolt need?

He flashed the torch upwards, tracing the strut back to its connection with the wall frame. 'Oh God,' he murmured, 'no bolt.'

Bang! Something or someone collided with the wall.

Nick leapt back. The frame rocked towards him. The strut slipped. He watched, helpless as the structure tottered above him. Instinctively he shot out a hand, but the wall was too heavy, the momentum too great. The base began to slide away. Another strut moved. His stomach twisted.

'Watch out!' he yelled. 'Get back from the wall.'

'That's great Cooper. Real emotion! Keep the cameras rolling.'

'Get out of the way, the wall's going over,' he shrieked.

While the base scythed into the hallway, the rest of the wall started to pitch down on him.

With a crouching, hurdling leap he cleared a sliding strut. Watery light closed off from one end. He forced his way through vanishing space, brushing past the frame. He shouldered his way around the end and burst into the hallway. Daylight, spotlights, safety – they almost blinded him.

'Shit,' he gasped, as the wall crashed onto the marble, like a tray hitting the floor.

•

Nick sat on the stairs, gasping to catch his breath. Around him, suspicion, disbelief and shock radiated from the director, cameramen and lighting crew.

He explained again, 'Like I said, I'm Nick, Nick Cowley. It's my first day here. I'm standing in for Owen. The props girl told me the mock-up wall was unstable. An accident waiting to happen. I went to check it out. She said her name was Pretty.'

'You mean Priddy.'

'Yeah, something like that. Look, it's not my fault. A camera, or one of you bashed into the wall before I'd had a chance to–'

'Accident?' the director screamed. 'Incompetent shoddy work, you mean. It's a bloody disaster. We could have been killed, the cameras destroyed and Cooper injured. The whole schedule's messed up.'

'Yeah, but Cooper froze on the third step,' a cameraman muttered.

'So where the hell is Cooper then?'

'I don't know, Merlin. Probably being comforted by Prosecco,' a calm voice murmured.

'And you said the bolts were missing, right?'

'Yeah.' Nick guessed the words were directed at him. The suspicion was palpable, the hostility scorching.

'Like… sabotage?'

No one spoke for a moment. It felt as if they were closing in on him, like a pack for the kill.

The director broke the spell. 'Get me the construction manager. On the phone, now,' he roared.

'Yes, Mr Leob,' a young assistant squealed before scuttling away.

Nick rested his head in his hands and tried to make sense of it all. Had Owen set him up? He'd said no one would even know he wasn't official. 'Just stand around, there'll be nothing to do,' he'd said and now the construction manager was about to find out about him. And was it a coincidence that Owen's girlfriend was the one comforting Cooper? If he hadn't known better he'd have assumed Cooper was in the arms of a sparkling wine, not a make-up artist and Owen's current live–in.

'How long to get this mess cleared? I want the wall up and the cameras rolling. I don't care if you work through the night. Fix it.'

Merlin Leob's voice brought Nick back to the moment. He raised his head and scanned the chaos, taking in the detail for the first time. In front of him the mock wall lay on its back, the broken frame fissuring its paper finish and a segment of the base tilting on a strut. It had come to rest a few feet short of the staircase. Walking canes and a shattered decorative hall table littered the marble floor. Paper cups lay on their sides, splashes and pools of coffee staining the scene like blood. Clipboards, tripod stands and stools were strewn across the marble, as if flotsam left by a tide. And amongst it all, faint oblong rubber marks spotted the floor.

'I'll need help,' Nick said. He cast around.

'No, not you. This only happened since you've been here.'

He opened his mouth to protest but before he could splutter a word, the director's mobile burst into life.

'Lester?' Merlin yelled into the phone.

His heart sank. Perhaps he could slip away while Merlin bawled at the construction manager, somewhere across the airwaves. But there was a problem. Nick had said his real name. Stupid, stupid, stupid.

•

When the construction manager arrived twenty-five minutes later, Nick was surprised by how young he looked. He hadn't expected someone in his early-thirties, barely ten years older than himself. He burst into the entrance hall, red faced and sweating, words tumbling from his mouth.

'Oh my God,' he said, eyes darting around. 'I came as fast as I could. I was already on the A14 heading for Peterborough. It was lucky I'd only just left Ipswich, so I wasn't far away.'

Nick dropped a piece of decorative hall table on a pile by the base of a pillar and wiped his hands on his jeans.

'Hi, I'm Nick,' he said, stepping over a bin bag and holding out his hand.

'Yeah, yeah. After I'd spoken to Merlin I phoned Owen. He sounds as sick as a dog. Why the hell didn't he contact me first, you know, before he rang you yesterday? Shit what a mess.'

'Look, this really isn't my–'

'He said you were on a two week break. Yeah, I know - you're with Willows & Son. I've just rung them to check that you are who you say you are. Seems you come highly recommended. So what the hell happened here?'

Behind the agitated face, Nick glimpsed a steely, highly organised manager.

'If we can lift a section of this false wall, you can see for yourself. But we'll need–'

'I can't spare anyone. All my men are working elsewhere. But your boss said he'd send someone over from Willows. It'll cost me an arm and a leg, but they're only coming from Needham Market, and time is money.'

'Great, but what about the missing bolts and sabotaged struts–'

'Foul play? Get real. It's the film that's make-believe. It sounds like Owen wasn't up to the job. You've no experience with on-location set design and construction - directors constantly interfering and demanding modifications. Merlin probably had the wall moved a dozen times. It's a nightmare. Thank God no one was injured. We could have been up to our eyes in health and safety reports and huge insurance claims.'

'But–'

'Any concerns, report direct to me and not a word about this to anyone outside. Understand? I'll send in Kay to decorate the wall again and… yes, Priddy covers prop continuity. She'll be here somewhere. I need to speak to her.'

Nick caught the implied warning and dropped eye contact. He made a decision. If there was enough charge left in his phone, he'd use it to photograph the excessive drillings and the holes with missing bolts. He'd been around long enough to know it was always easier to blame the outsider, and boy, did he feel like an outsider.

'Merlin starts filming again tomorrow morning, six thirty. Kay will be here in a couple of hours. You should have the frame repaired by then. And this time, put the bloody wall up so it stays up.'

'But–'

'Yes, I know. You'll have to work through the night.'

CHAPTER 2

'Hey, have you read this? They're shooting a film somewhere near Stowmarket. Gavi Monterey and Cooper Brice are starring.' Chrissie ran her fingers along the fold, smoothing a page of the Eastern Anglia Daily Tribune as she spread it on her cramped kitchen table. She rather liked Cooper Brice; chiselled good looks and a hint of auburn in his hair.

She read on. *Set during the First World War, Brice plays the part of a test pilot in the Royal Flying Corps.*

'Hey, they'll be filming out at Orford Ness as well, Clive. Apparently the War Office bought the site in 1913 and,' she raised her voice as she read directly from the page, '*the Armament and Experimental Flight of the Royal Flying Corps was moved there in 1915.*'

'What?' Clive sounded distant. Her cottage was small and he was only next door in her living room, but she knew the tone. He'd be miles away, his mind on a case.

'They're filming near Stowmarket,' she repeated, but louder.

'Yes I heard. They're using Althorne House. It's in Moats Tye, but they'll be keeping that quiet. You did say Gavi Monterey, didn't you?' His voice sounded nearer, interested.

She looked up. It seemed he had been listening after all. Clive stood at the kitchen door, coffee mug in hand.

'I thought you couldn't hear me.'

'I couldn't. Well, not properly. She's the one who wears purple Lycra.'

'What?'

'Well so I've heard. Gavi Monterey. She's a keen cyclist. We had a memo last week about the filming. To put the police in the picture, so to speak. Keep us informed.'

'So how do you know about the purple...? Of course, the memo included a shot of her–'

'Cycling. Strangely you're right on the button, Chrissie.'

'I can't think how I guessed,' she mumbled, hiding her smile and turning her attention back to the newspaper. She moved her mug of tea to free up another column of print.

It had been a lazy start to the day. For once Clive wasn't on duty and they had the whole weekend ahead. He seemed more relaxed than usual. Perhaps it was something to do with the euphoria of the Olympic Games spreading from London and permeating across Suffolk for the last couple of months. She wondered if it suppressed people's baser instincts to kill, because the usual trickle of Suffolk murders had temporarily run dry with the warmth of competitive good will. And now it was over. They'd watched the closing ceremony on the TV together, the previous week.

'You look miles away,' he said from the doorway.

'No I wasn't. I was reading.'

She sipped her tea, almost expecting his mobile to ring, a shade of foreboding in the air.

'Hard to scan the lines without moving your eyes,' Clive murmured.

She smiled again. It was difficult to fool him. He was too good a detective inspector. Could he tell she felt a heady mix of excitement and apprehension? It had been fizzing inside her for weeks, alternating between her head and her stomach. She imagined it would have disappeared by now, that signing on the dotted line would magic it away. But legally committing herself to the Clegg Cabinet Making & Furniture Restoration business only two days ago had merely intensified the fizz. Of course investing her own money and vision of the future was part of the deal, but self-doubt kept creeping into her mind. Could she pull it off? Would she make a success of it?

She made a decision. 'I'm going to keep this newspaper.'

'Why? I didn't know you were a Gavi Monterey fan.'

She didn't answer for a moment, her thoughts still racing on. The newspaper would be like a good luck token. Something with August 16th 2012 printed on it. A memento from the fateful day. She remembered picking it up from the solicitor's waiting room before she'd gone through into his office. She'd held it, hoping it made her look both relaxed and business-like when she signed the contract.

'You seem to have forgotten Cooper Brice,' she said.

'Ah.'

Brrring brrring! Brrring brrring!

'Yours?' But she knew the ring. She patted across her kitchen table, searching out her mobile amongst the clutter of her laptop and newspaper. *Brrring brrring! Brrring brrring!* The strident noise resonated on the old scrubbed pine as she read the caller ID.

'Nick?' she said, frowning.

'Chrissie? Hi. Thank God I've got hold of you. Look, I've had a bit of a disaster and I've been up most of the night. No, just listen. Can you repair a decorative hall table that's been crushed?'

'Crushed? I suppose so....' She caught Clive's eye. Read his minutely raised brow.

'Can you collect it now? Althorne House. Please.'

'Althorne House? You mean at Moats Tye? Isn't that where they're filming–'

'Yeah.'

'You mean you're on the film set? Epic! But how–'

'I haven't got time. I'll explain when you get here.'

'OK, OK. But how big is this table? Will it fit in my car?'

'I don't know. Certainly it's not half as big as it used to be. From where I'm standing it looks more like a pile of kindling. Veneered kindling. Shit, just get here, Chrissie. Please, as soon as you can. Give me a bell when you arrive.'

'Is it one of a pair?'

Silence - Nick had ended the call.

What the hell had happened, she wondered, as the calm of her Saturday morning shattered.

'Well,' Clive said evenly. 'I heard crushed, Althorne House, how big is this table and will it fit in my car? Seems like an ambulance won't be needed, just the services of a bloke with room in his boot and a proper back seat.'

'What? Yes, oh thanks,' she said, distracted.

'You never know, I might get to see Gavi Monterey, as well.'

'What? What are you talking about, Clive?'

'I was working my way round to asking, what the hell has Nick been up to this time?'

'Now that's not fair. He doesn't go looking for trouble. It just seems to find him.'

'I know. I'm starting to think it's something to do with that course at Utterly. It follows all of you around. No, don't deny it. You as well.'

She didn't bother to argue. Clive offering his car had triggered a thought. Perhaps the small yellow 1980s sports car she loved so much wasn't practical now she was a partner in the Clegg carpentry firm. She would be transporting furniture herself. After all, she wasn't an apprentice any more. So, would Ron Clegg let her drive his old van?

'I wonder...,' she murmured under her breath.

'You see, you agree with me. I do have a point.'

'What? About the course at Utterly? Don't be ridiculous. Now come on, we're wasting time.' She smiled and tilted her head for a kiss.

The morning sun scorched the gently sloping fields as Clive drove his sleek Ford Mondeo along the back ways from her cottage in Woolpit. The wheat harvest had been particularly late due to earlier rain, and now the window of sunshine had triggered the combines in earnest. They moved across the fields, as if in a last chance dance, spewing plumes of grain and leaving trails of stubble.

Clive followed the road into the shallow Rattlesden Valley and then skirting around Stowmarket, away through Combs Ford.

'It's pretty here,' Clive said as he took the fork past the old Combs tannery.

The route narrowed and twisted, and the tarmac became looser as they neared Moats Tye. The entrance to Althorne House wasn't obvious. It was shrouded by trees, and if Chrissie hadn't spotted a lad sitting near an open gate and wearing a vest-style tee, they'd have sailed on past. She felt her pulse racing as Clive slowed. Anxiety or excitement? She didn't know. She'd never visited a film set before.

'Do you have a pass?' the lad asked.

'No. We've come to collect a piece of broken furniture.'

'A decorative hall table. I'm a furniture restorer,' Chrissie added, hoping she sounded professional.

The lad frowned. 'I'll have to phone the house. Names?'

'Chrissie Jax and Clive Merry.'

They waited, the sun roasting the car while he made the call. Chrissie couldn't hear what he was saying, but then he didn't appear to say much. He seemed to spend most of the time waiting for someone to answer.

'Oh for goodness sake,' she hissed and whipped out her phone, her fingers sweaty as she texted Nick. *Help – main gate proving an obstacle. Please ok us with someone.*

At last the lad lowered his mobile and nodded. 'OK, you can go in. Don't head for the front of the house, drive round to the side. It'll be obvious. Just park with the other cars, OK?'

'Thanks,' she said as Clive slipped the car into gear.

As they approached the house, Chrissie could see why it had been chosen as the film location. Flat lawns to one side merged into grazing parkland. It would be ideal for landing an open cockpit biplane, or at least pretending to. The house, built in an eighteenth century classical style, seemed modestly grand. The architect had used the trick of extending the walls upwards, hiding the pitched roof and increasing the apparent height to a full four storeys. Large elegant ground floor windows drew her eye. Wide steps led to an oversized front door. It all gave an illusion of scale. The greying and weathered sandstone exuded an air of permanency. It was a theatrical statement as well as a home.

'Designed to impress,' she murmured.

'Aren't all grand houses?'

They followed the gravel drive to the side of the house. She caught sight of Nick immediately. He stood, waving them into a space next to a refrigerated van, its cooling unit whirring and humming like a demented bee.

'You look hot.' She tried to keep her face neutral, but she was shocked by the contrast of his flushed cheeks with the shadows beneath his eyes. 'Are you OK?'

'Yeah, sure.' He rubbed his hand across the moisture beading his forehead, and then ran his fingers through his short dark hair. A kind of head massage of desperation.

'So where's the crushed table?' she said, avoiding asking the obvious questions as she got out of the Mondeo.

'Look, this was nothing to do with me. I kinda walked straight into this mess. Owen asked me to fill in for him yesterday and—'

'Do you mean Owen, the guy on our course?'

'Yeah.'

'Neat. So this is what he's been up to. But how come a crushed table?' She glanced at Clive who seemed to feign a lack of interest as he shaded his eyes and gazed at the side of the house.

'Come on inside and I'll show you, but we'll have to wait until they're between takes.' He walked as he talked, keeping his voice low. She struggled to catch his words as he described what he'd discovered before the wall toppled over.

'So does anyone else think it was sabotaged?' Clive asked.

'Only Dave. He came over yesterday evening from Willows. He thought it was strange when we couldn't find the missing bolts. He also made the comment that, if they knew they'd want to move the bloody wall, why hadn't they put casters into the frame?'

The cool air in the passageway chilled Chrissie's skin.

'But no one was hurt. Right?'

'Only the construction manager's pride. We've got the wall back up and if there was any evidence – well it'll be difficult to see now. The only person they're willing to blame is me.'

'Because you're the new guy, right?'

'Something like that. Look, I've had more than enough grief over this. I did Owen a favour but I don't want to get involved. It's not my place. So for God's sake, Clive, don't let on who you are. You're not here in an official capacity.'

'OK.'

'On another note, who pays for repairing the table?' She knew it sounded materialistic, but the question had been burning her tongue for several minutes.

'Sorry, I don't think my head's working straight anymore. I should have said the construction manager wants to talk to you, Chrissie. I think it'll be his firm, or rather on their insurance.' Nick ran his fingers through his hair again.

She didn't say anything. She'd just noticed a pile of broken wood lying in the passageway like road kill – a flattened table, with fractured legs, and veneer shed like feathers.

'I think it must be walnut,' she said, crouching to get a closer look, 'and French-style with kingwood and satinwood banding. This leg looks like a cabriole... no, a sabre shape.' She ran her hand over the wood. Something struck her as not adding up.

'There are only two legs, Nick.'

'Now what?' A voice seemed to boom along the passage. A youngish man in jeans and a charcoal tee shirt strode towards them. She sensed the animosity.

'Sorry?' she said, still holding the part-cabriole leg.

'I assume you're here to collect this table. What do you mean, two legs missing?'

'Sorry, I should have said. I'm from the Clegg Cabinet Making & Furniture Restoration business. Strictly speaking I'm looking at a console table. No back legs. There'd have been a bracket on the wall to support it instead. I'm Chrissie Jax, by the way.' She stood up and extended her free hand. She reckoned being in her early forties gained her gravitas points.

'Lester Loxton, Construction Manager.' His handshake was firm, the skin on his palm, calloused.

'I guess the front legs snapped when the wall started to slide. The damage to the inlaid top probably happened when the wall fell backwards. I would imagine most of it ended up above the false wall, not under it. So the top would have shattered, rather than been crushed.' She smiled. A professional *top that* kind of a smile.

'Most of the fragments skidded across the hall floor. Travelled yards,' Nick muttered.

'Just as long as we've got enough legs, and nothing's missing.' His tone changed, 'I believe Nick told me you're local.'

'Yes, the workshop is near Wattisham Airfield.'

He seemed to relax. She guessed she must have passed some test.

'We need to talk details.'

She scribbled down her email address and contact number for him. When she looked up she noticed Nick and Clive had vanished. The sneaky rats, she thought. They'd slipped away to catch a glimpse of Gavi and Cooper. She swallowed her irritation. Chiselled good looks and a promise of purple Lycra must have proved too much of a draw. Could she blame them for abandoning her to a heap of wood and the gloom of the back corridor? Yes she damn well could.

'You're frowning,' the construction manager said.

'No, no. I was concentrating. So the owners know about the accident, and they're happy for the repair?' She reined in her restless mind to talk costs, billing addresses, and time frames.

'Yes, yes. They've had a chance to see it. Obviously they're a bit upset, as you can imagine. Will you email me an estimate when you've had a chance to look…?' Lester's voice died as he stared at something behind Chrissie.

Down the passageway a door clicked shut, something rustled, and then she heard a giggle. Chrissie spun around, her eyes searching out the sounds. She understood immediately. At the far end, two people pressed close to each other. She took in the detail. A head with short curly hair. Blonde. A girl. The other, taller….

'Cooper?' she whispered.

Lester coughed. 'Perhaps,' he said loudly, 'I can help you get this to your car?'

The man looked up. Chrissie recognised the straight nose and high cheekbones. They matched pretty well the photo she'd seen in the newspaper earlier. Perhaps there was something to be said for a dimly lit passageway. Just wait till she told the others, she thought.

'Hurr - umph.' Lester cleared his throat.

'Yes, yes of course. Let's get the console table into the car.' She stopped gaping and turned to face the broken carcass and legs. 'Damn, I need a dustsheet.' A door opened, then closed somewhere back along the passageway. She stifled a laugh.

'I'm afraid the reality in this business is that–'

'There is no reality?' she said, struggling to regain her composure.

'Especially with the actors. But....'

'Discretion. No I won't be saying anything.' She tried to appear off-hand, as if she was used to rubbing shoulders with the glitterati, was unfazed by actors, and that secrets were safe in her hands.

'Good. I wouldn't want it to get out about the false wall. It wouldn't look good for the film and theatre construction company if word got out, you know.'

'Of course not.'

So he'd missed her point. Cooper's antics and the sexual tensions on and off set must be so common they weren't even worth a comment. What a place to work, she thought, thrilled by the sighting.

Lester produced an old tablecloth from somewhere, and with the air of conspirators, they wrapped the shattered console table. She thought it looked quite jolly in its colourful shroud, as he helped her carry it outside into the sunshine. Clive's car was locked, but she wasn't going to let on it wasn't hers, or at least that she didn't have the keys.

'Just leave it here on the grass. I'm going to sit out and enjoy the sun. Clive texted me a moment ago – he'll be here in a minute.'

'OK then, Chrissie. Email the estimate as soon as you can.'

'Of course. Just a thought, do you want me to speak to the owners about it?'

'No. At this stage I'd rather you dealt only with me. It's better this way. No muddles. Bye now.'

She smiled as he raised his hand in a vague salute, and then hurried away. She got the feeling he might prove a useful contact for her business if she made a good job of the console table. But the trouble was it might not be easy to repair. She wasn't too sure yet.

'So,' she asked herself as the sun's dry heat raised her spirits, 'do I tell Clive about the star sighting, or does the corridor kiss and fumble stay a secret between Cooper, Lester, the mystery blonde and me?'

CHAPTER 3

Matt rubbed his eyes. It didn't help. They still smarted. He rested an elbow on the computer desk and propped his head on one pink chubby hand.

'Ouch!' He'd forgotten about the sunburn blistering his ear.

'It must have been one hell of a festival,' Damon murmured.

Matt slumped further into the plastic stacker chair facing the blank computer screen. If the skin on his neck hadn't been so sore he'd have turned to say, 'Awesome.'

He grunted instead.

Damon Mora of Balcon & Mora, an internet based people tracing agency in Bury St Edmunds, sat at a trestle-table desk a few feet away. His shabby office chair squeaked as he leaned forwards.

'When you're ready, I'll send you the first batch of names from the debt collectors.'

'Cool,' Matt breathed, feeling anything but.

The air in the office was suffocating. The fans whirred in the hard drives stacked on the trestles. Matt hoped the sound would make him feel cooler, but like a lot of things in his life, disappointment was inevitable. He logged onto the computer and waited for the first batch of names to arrive while his skin prickled and smarted.

Perhaps it was the heat, or the cramped space, or even the whirring in his ears, but with a sinking, spinning feeling, he was back at the festival. Was it the music or the prospect of sharing a sleeping bag with Maisie that drove him to buy the two-day tickets? He reckoned it was both.

He'd made sure he chose the smallest possible tent, barely the size of a sardine tin, because for that one night he planned to get cosy. They'd even partly deflated the airbed to squeeze it in.

And then the sun struck. To the sounds of Snow Patrol, The Killers and Madness, Maisie and he had slowly roasted and blistered on the hottest day of the year.

'Ouch! Me back,' she'd squealed. 'Nah, don't touch me skin. I'm dyin'. I swear I'm dyin'.'

And so the journey back from the V Festival near Chelmsford had been agony yesterday; Maisie clinging to him as she sat, perched behind on his scooter, while his helmet rubbed and chafed his raw ears.

'Matt! We've loads of names to trace – hundreds of students churned out of uni last month. Leaving their flats, moving on, no forwarding addresses. Oi, are you even listening to me?'

'What? Oh yeah, sorry.' Matt returned to earth with a jolt.

'The names. Come on, get them up on your screen. What's with you today?'

'Maisie said 'eat stroke.' He opened the first batch of names.

'Then drink plenty of water and eat some salt. You're supposed to replace what you've sweated off.'

'Electrolytes. I read somethin' 'bout it somewhere. Sports rehydration drinks. It don't help the sunburn, though.' He pictured the tiny lettering on the side of a can.

'No, I know that look. Don't reel off the chemical names. Just get on with the batch I've just sent you.'

'Pain killers,' Matt groaned as he focused on the first name on Damon's list. His photographic memory would have to wait.

'Oh no-o-o-o.' It just wasn't fair. Why did the first name have to be Jones? The second most common surname in England after Smith. This was going to take for ever. He pulled a face, but it hurt his puffy crimson skin. Time to concentrate. *Priddy Jones – last known address: 84, Neet Road, Peterborough.*

Priddy? Unusual, he thought, that's if it really was a first name and not a nickname. He looked at the date of birth on the list. So Priddy was twenty-one.

A quick check on Google Maps, and he'd found the address. Neet Road ran past an art and design college, close to the edge of the University Centre campus in Peterborough. Was it a coincidence? Could the location mean Priddy Jones had something to do with the college? A student, perhaps. A quick check on a directory site, and he had a phone number for the address. It was as he'd expected – no longer registered to anyone named Jones, and it didn't match the number on the debt collectors' list. He knew if the numbers were still active, then the debt collectors usually managed to track down their targets themselves. But he'd had to check. He reached for the office handset and tapped in the latest number registered to 84 Neet Road. No Answer.

'OK, LinkedIn....' A few mouse moves, and the name popped up. No photo but someone with the right year of birth and listing theatre and film set design as their profession. *Alumna - Peterborough Art & Design.*

'Killer app,' he breathed. 'Fits with Neet Road. Now... Facebook. Cool.' He gazed at a recent post. A girl with shoulder length wavy brown hair stood in front of the Wolsey Theatre smiling and pointing at a billboard. It was too much of a coincidence. It had to be the same Priddy Jones he was tracing.

'Aint the Wolsey in Ipswich?'

'What?' Damon frowned.

'Sorry, mate. Thinkin' aloud.'

He squinted at the billboard in the photo. *The Waldringfield Wives*. It was time to dig deeper. His plump fingers keyed *stage set designer, The Waldringfield Wives, Wolsey Theatre, Ipswich* in the Goole search box.

'Spammin' hell,' he muttered as the search engine threw up website after website with only a single word in common with the nine he'd typed in the box. 'Narrow the flamin' search field,' he groaned.

'For God's sake, Matt. Cut the running commentary. I know your game – you're trying to wear me down. I'm not going to change my mind.'

'What?' Matt glanced up from a list of stage set designers who'd worked at the Wolsey Theatre.

'All that wilting heat stroke – it's just to get sympathy, isn't it?'

'But I aint well.'

'I'm still not letting you off.'

And then he guessed Damon's meaning. It was the thorny subject of working from home again. Damon had said it was about keeping the clients happy. The words security, confidentiality and professionalism had been tossed around. Damon might trust him, but the clients didn't even know Matt existed. They weren't going to risk names and details being passed on to a third party, someone working from home.

His brain fizzed. Too many changes of subject. Too many balls being juggled in the air. He hadn't told Damon, but if home meant his mother's modest semidetached bungalow in Stowmarket, then he didn't want to work from it. For him, the Utterly Academy library or the computer lab with its bank of computers was his emotional home. Even the Utterly canteen ranked higher than his mother's greasy kitchen and barren fridge. And anyway, while it was still summer he'd resigned himself to making the regular trip on his scooter to Balcon & Mora.

He listened as Damon's chair creaked. He knew all the moves. Damon would have lifted his arms, stretched and then clasped his hands behind his head. A kind of *this discussion is now closed* gesture. He'd always found that sort of thing easier to read than faces.

'I'll croak if I don't get water,' Matt mumbled as he turned his attention back to the list of stage set designers. He felt on safer ground with a screen full of names. 'Hey, I've got her.'

'Good. Who've you got?'

'Priddy Jones, the first name on me list. I reckon she works for a stage an' film set company based in Ipswich. I'm guessin' a quick call....'

He knew Damon controlled both computers in the office, could look at either screen, and see what Matt was seeing. He waited a couple of seconds.

'What you reckon, Damon?'

Damon read out the letters, 'IS & FSD & C Ltd. Seems it stands for Ipswich Stage & Film Set Design & Construction. What a mouthful. I bet you'll find it's a case of long name, small company. Give me a snappy oneworder and I'll give you a multinational. What are you waiting for? Make the call.'

Matt ran his tongue over dry lips. So how to play it, he wondered.

'Here, catch.' Damon tossed a plastic bottle of water across at Matt. 'Now don't say I don't care.'

'Youch,' he muttered as he stretched for the bottle, his tee shirt cutting across his armpit as he broke the bottle's flight and fumbled the catch. He tipped it into his mouth, gulping and spilling in equal measure, then brushing off the droplets as they tracked down his beard. Maisie had said if he shaved it off the straggly hair might grow back a different colour, lose the ginger tones. It might even match his head of dark sandy hair. But he liked it as it was. At least the sun hadn't burnt the skin on that bit of his face.

'Yeah, I got it,' he said.

He'd pretend he was writing a piece for a student magazine or webpage; a, *what are the latest set of graduates doing now* kind of thing. He tapped in the company's phone number and waited, oiling his Suffolk accent with more swigs of water. It was time to slip into an alter ego, in his mind he needed to be someone else.

'Yes?' a woman's reedy voice answered.

'Priddy Jones?'

'Er... let me see if she's on our books. Yes, she's working for us. Sorry, what did you say you wanted?'

His mind buzzed. 'Oh yeah, I'm from her old uni. I write stuff for the Student Chronicle. Yeah, for the students in Peterborough - it's great to know how the graduates are getti' on. It's a kinda boost to everyone, something to aim for.... Yeah, that's right. And you'll give her me message.... Yeah, I know you can't give out numbers, but you can give her mine, right?' He gave his mobile number.

And then finally, 'Well thanks.... Yeah.... My name? Felix Leiter. Yeah, I'm a student. Spelled LIGHTER, that's right. And if she can get back to me in the next couple of days.... Yeah, publishin' deadlines. Thanks.... Bye.' He punched the air. The trap was set. When Priddy Jones rang back he'd capture her latest mobile number on his readout. Sweet.

'Felix Leiter?' Damon breathed. 'Since when have you been an ex CIA agent? James Bond's best friend? Your hand and leg bitten off in a shark attack?'

'Yeah, well. It's spelled with an IGH, right?'

'Give me strength. OK, back to work.'

CHAPTER 4

'Oh hi, Prosecco.' Nick stood at the foot of the elegant staircase and eyed the false wall. All things considered, he'd done a pretty good job with Dave and Kay. As long as Merlin wasn't planning a close-up of where the console table previously stood, the cameras would be none the wiser.

'How's Owen?' he asked, keeping his voice casual. He felt tired. It had been another early morning start and now the crew were breaking for lunch.

'Nick? It is Nick isn't it?'

'Yeah. I thought everyone knew me by now. Friday, Saturday, Sunday – I was walking around like I had a target pinned to my back. You know, the new guy, the rogue carpenter, a bad luck charm. Now it's Monday, and it seems I've become invisible.'

'Well hi, Nick. Welcome to the world of film making.'

'Thanks, but about Owen?'

'If you want to know, why don't you phone him?'

'I have. Every day since the wall toppled over. I just get his answerphone. What's going on? I mean, is he getting better or is there something really wrong with him?'

He watched Prosecco's face. For a make-up artist, she wore remarkably little make-up. Or was it just her skill with the powders and creams of her trade? Could her fresh complexion, wide cheekbones and generous mouth be just an illusion? He glanced down at her hands. A bruise stained the back of one, the skin was grazed.

'That looks sore,' he said, momentarily distracted.

'Yes, it stung like hell when I did it. You know how it is. Nothing much to show at the time, but now it looks dreadful and it hardly hurts at all.' She turned as if to go, the conversation ended.

'But Owen? You haven't said.'

'I'd say on the mend. He texted me only a few minutes ago. Said he felt hungry. I guess that's a good sign.' She tossed the words over her shoulder.

He watched as she crossed the hallway, unhurried and graceful.

Irritation and frustration bubbled up as sympathy died. What the hell was Owen playing at? He whipped out his mobile and fired off a text: *Answer your bloody phone. We need to talk.*

So, Owen was blanking him. The bastard. He couldn't hide forever. It was inconceivable to think the construction manager hadn't already spoken to him. And Prosecco? Didn't they live together? She must have told Owen about the wall.

'Bastard,' he said under his breath.

What's more, because of Owen he'd abandoned his plans to sing with his guitarist friend Jake at the canoeing club barbeque on Sunday afternoon. It would have only been an open mic session, but that wasn't the point. For once the weather was good, and what better than to lounge in the sun, barbequing, drinking and chatting up Yvonne, the lithe canoeing instructor. Instead he'd been the on-site carpenter again. From where he was standing, all he could see was his fortnight's leave being swallowed up covering for Owen.

'The bastard,' he repeated, resentment taking a firmer hold.

'Hello, Nick. What's up with you?'

He looked up. 'Oh hiya, Dave. I didn't expect to see you here?'

For a moment he hoped Dave was going to send him away, say he and Willows were no longer wanted on set and he was free to take his leave. But Dave's kindly face told a different story. His thinning hair was neatly combed, his work trousers changed for a pair of upland trekkers, still tough enough to look as if he hadn't made an effort.

'I thought I'd pop over in my lunch hour. See how you're getting on. You know, just check if you'd had any more disasters.'

'Thanks, but....' He let his words drift. Dave had been his trainer at Willows for two years. During that time he'd learnt just about every expression, every nuance, every tortuous compliment, straight criticism or caring act Dave could deliver. But driving over to see how he was getting on wasn't one of them. He could have phoned instead.

'Dave, why don't you just say you're on celebrity watch?'

'Less lip, thank you. So – what's wrong?'

'If you must know, I'm pissed off. I keep phoning Owen and he won't bloody answer. And before you say anything about him being sick, his girlfriend just told me he's on the mend.'

'Hmm... I expect his ears are still burning from Lester's call. In fact I got the feeling he won't be coming back. I think he's been "let go". I guess it's easier for the construction team to blame someone who's not here.'

'What, you mean he's been fired?'

'I reckon so. But somebody took all those bolts out, and if it wasn't Owen, then maybe he thinks you–'

'What? Owen thinks I took the bolts out? So it's all my fault he's lost his job?'

'I don't know, Nick. It's only a suggestion, but it could be why he's not answering you.'

'But....' It was starting to make sense. The cast, the crew, Prosecco – he guessed they secretly blamed him because he was the new carpenter behind the fake wall when it toppled. And now Owen was lending his silent voice to the chorus of disapproval. No wonder he felt they were treating him as invisible.

'Come on, Nick. Let's go outside. There's nothing happening in here. A bit of fresh air might help.'

'Yeah, well they're taking a break from filming. I think they're setting up for Gavi Monterey.'

'Really?' Dave's voice brightened.

'Yeah. I heard someone say she's meant to be a volunteer. One of the very first Land Girls.'

'As in, The Women's Land Army? I thought that was Second World War?'

'I don't know – but I copped a glimpse of the script. Well I guess it was the script - only a page or two and mainly about costume. It said *wears Women's Land Army uniform. Breeches, boots and leggings* and… yeah there was a sketch of some kind of a smock.'

'Really? So when is the film meant to be set?'

'I don't know. Nineteen sixteen, seventeen… eighteen. Maybe earlier. They keep changing around when they're filming. At the moment we're doing staircase and hallway scenes from across the whole film.' He caught the flash of interest in Dave's face.

They walked along the passageway leading to the side entrance and car park. A huddle of people queued at a trailer, its side hatch open and serving food. The smell of freshly brewed coffee and frying chips filled the air. The refrigerated van whirred and buzzed nearby.

'Come on,' Dave said, 'let's take a tour of the garden.'

They ambled past manicured box hedges, clipped low and encompassing vibrant bedding plants. Circles, triangles and squares were laid out with geometric precision. It reminded Nick of a kid's algebra set scattered on the ground and filled with scarlet geraniums and crimson dwarf lilies. The formal beds gave way to a mown lawn, drawing Nick's eye to a swathe of green parkland bordering fields of wheat stubble.

'Wow,' Nick breathed. 'It seems pretty flat when you drive here, but actually standing now and gazing across it all, it's kinda rolling.'

'I wouldn't call it a hill though. We're hardly seventy metres high. Look, you can see Stowmarket and... Combs Wood. Did you know it's a coppice wood, very old? They say it's in the Doomsday Book.'

'Hmm....' As Nick soaked up the timelessness of the scene, the knot in his stomach and tense muscles seemed to melt away. Perhaps he should just relax, he thought. As long as he kept checking the bolts were still secure in the supports at the beginning of each shoot, what could possibly go wrong?

'Hey,' Dave said, looking at his watch. 'I want to see if Gavi's going to turn up on set.'

'Go on then. You go ahead. I'll be along in a moment.' He took his time, enjoying the gentle breeze. It played over his short brown hair, lightly fingered his neck and cooled his ears.

By the time Nick stepped through the side entrance and into the corridor, he'd regained his equilibrium. He felt at one with Althorne House and any ideas of grabbing his toolbox and quitting the job were quietly shelved for the time being. He took a deep breath. Traces of jasmine, rose and amber floated in the air. It seemed familiar, but he couldn't quite place it.

'Hi, Nick.'

He spun around. 'Pretty! I didn't realise you were behind me. Hey, where've you been?'

'What d'you mean? I haven't been anywhere.'

'But you weren't here on Friday night to help with the wall. And I don't think I saw you around on Saturday or Sunday either.'

'No, but Kay knew about that and covered for me. I'd got other things I was supposed to be doing. And anyway, what's it to do with you?'

'Nothing, it's just–'

'And it's Priddy, not Pretty. I've already told you.' She flicked her layered fringe back, combing it with her fingers and making it disappear into her wavy brown hair. She stared at him, her eyes and forehead no longer veiled by her hair. It struck Nick as a defiant gesture. Was she challenging him to not believe her?

'Hey sorry, Priddy. No offense meant. It's just that I think of you as–'

'Don't say pretty.'

'No, I wasn't going to say that.'

He caught the angry flash in her eyes and continued in a rush, 'Although I think you are… pretty. It's just that you're one of the few people round here who talks to me. I mean without me having to start up a conversation with them first.'

Her expression softened.

'Look, you must realise I've never been on a set before. This is all new to me, Pr–'

'A fish out of water, and all that. Yeah, it's pretty obvious.'

He tried not to smile.

'OK, OK. I said it this time. A truce on *pretty*.' She pulled a face.

'Agreed. So maybe some time, when you're not busy, you can tell me all about the secret world of props?'

'Yeah, sure. But this isn't the moment.' Her voice seemed to break. 'I'm afraid I've got to rush. Bye, Nick.' She pushed past him.

So now what had he said wrong? He watched as she hurried down the passageway. How strange, he thought. Was everyone in this business of creating make-believe so very touchy and easily offended? He glanced at his watch. Ten more minutes and then the afternoon shoot was scheduled to begin. There was still plenty of time to check the bolts in the false wall supports, but he knew he'd better get on with the job if he wanted to find a good spot to stand and observe the filming.

A group of camera and lighting crew ambled up behind him, filling the passageway with laughter and banter. They were the first wave in the small tide of film crew returning to the set. Someone slapped him on the shoulder as they reached him, the group surrounding and bearing him forward with them like flotsam.

'Hiya, Nick. Any surprises planned for this afternoon, mate?'

He caught the faint smell of chips and burgers as he walked.

'Yeah, I heard Special Effects are worried you're putting them out of a job,' another one jibed.

Nick laughed with them. 'If I didn't know better I'd think….'

His height gave him the advantage. At six foot three he could have hammered them down into the ground if he'd chosen. At least he hoped they'd imagine he could. It was time to blag confidence.

'Are you lot angling for an invite to one of my firework displays, then?'

'Stray rockets and stuff like that? No thanks mate.' The laughter sounded good-natured. Nick relaxed.

He sensed their professional anticipation, verging on excitement as they talked light meter readings and F-stops with each other. The buzz around him was infectious. His mood lightened. Perhaps he was graduating from invisible to sepia. If everything ran smoothly from here on in, he reckoned even a sepia on-site carpenter didn't have much to do beyond hanging around watching. He supposed it might suit him, as long as the sun kept shining and he was back at Willows after his leave ended.

He filed into the hallway with the crew.

'Hey about time, Nick. I thought you'd be back more or less straight after me. They want the wall moved a few feet that way.' Dave's face was flushed.

'Why?'

'For the front door scenes. To make sure the edge of the false wall isn't caught in some of the wider shots.'

'But if I'd known, we could have moved it before we went wandering around outside.'

'No point wasting time fretting about that now. Free up the casters, Nick. Out of the way everyone!'

A couple of the camera crew who'd filed in from the passageway leant a shoulder to the end of the frame, while Nick grasped onto a strut to help steady the wall as it was moved.

'Easy now.'

'That's enough.'

'Thanks, guys,' Dave said.

Nick locked down the casters and straightened up, feeling a hotter, sweatier shade of sepia. Even Priddy smiled, in a composed sort of a way, as she brushed past with a couple of Edwardian walking canes.

The front door had been opened and natural light flooded into the hallway. A cameraman moved with his camera into position on the stairs, while a sound assistant holding a microphone mounted like a dead wombat on a stick, stood to the side of the staircase. Now Nick got it. The director's trick was to make the hallway appear larger than it actually was, turn the orientation and create the illusion of distance to the front door. Neat.

Merlin appeared outside the front door with a flurry of his clipboard, and talking earnestly to Gavi.

'She's beautiful,' Dave whispered.

'Don't you need to get back to Willows?'

'OK, OK. I was just thinking, the front door tends to swing a bit. We could make a wedge to stop it moving. There's plenty of wood left from repairing the wall'

'I'll cut a door stop now,' Nick said, pleased to feel useful.

'Right, I'll be off then. If they're still shooting after four, let me know and I'll drop in on my way home.'

It didn't take Nick long, barely more than a couple of saw cuts on the portable workbench. He reckoned the door wedge would be well out of shot, just as long as the camera wasn't tracking Cooper's dragging foot again. And then a thought struck. It was going to take a bit of getting used to, this working alone now he wasn't an apprentice. And for a moment he felt the heady mix of excitement and regret. His life was moving on, but had he taken enough notice of Dave? Absorbed sufficient teaching? It was time to spread his wings and fly. Dave had been with him virtually every working day of the past two years, but something Dave had said was still playing on his mind.

He made a decision and slipped back along the passageway. He pulled his mobile from his jeans and called Owen's number once again.

'Hi?' Owen's voice sounded distant, thready.

'Owen? Is that you?' Surprise sharpened Nick's voice.

'Yeah. Who'd you think you were ringin' then?'

'Well you. I've been trying for days. Why the hell haven't you answered?'

'I've been ill. Any road, I'm answerin' now.'

'Right. You heard what happened here? You know the false wall came down in the middle of a shoot?'

'I heard.' The voice hardened. 'What the hell were you playin' at?'

'Me? It was nothing to do with me, Owen. All the bolts in the supports were missing.'

'What?'

'Didn't Prosecco tell you?'

'No.'

'Or Lester?' He chose his words, 'Were the bolts there on Thursday, you know, before you got ill?'

'Of course they were there. I was throwin' up when Lester rang. And now you say it, yeah he was gabbin' on about some bolts, but I couldn't follow him. Until you said about bolts just now, I'd forgotten he'd mentioned them.'

Silence hung in the air. 'I heard rumours you aren't coming back. Is it true?'

'Yeah. Lester said somethin' about *letting me go*. I'm self-employed. I thought he'd fired me cos of me sick record. But,' he whispered hoarsely, 'if it was about those bolts, I reckon... it was you wasn't it? You thought you'd get me into trouble. You're after me job, you twofaced piece of shit.'

'Don't be bloody ridiculous. Why would I want your job? I've got a permanent job at Willows when my leave ends. Listen, I didn't take out the bolts. And if you didn't either.... Well, think about it Owen, who did? And why?'

'What the hell are you on about?'

'I don't know... I suppose–'

'Then why bloody call me?'

'I wanted to have it out with you. I thought you'd taken the bolts as a stupid joke to make trouble for me. I was angry.'

'So now we're both angry.'

'Yeah well, just so you know it isn't me who's lost you your job.'

'Oh yeah?'

'Look, let's meet up for a pint. What do you say?' The words popped out before Nick could stop them. He supposed he felt sorry for the bloke, but however sympathetic, he wasn't going to be completely stupid. Nick made sure they settled on a time when he knew his mates would be around.

'OK, then. Friday evening, the Nags Head. Cheers.' Owen almost sounded matey.

'See you.' Nick ended the call. He felt professional. It was how Dave would have expected him to behave. He squared his shoulders, switched his mobile to silent and headed back into the hallway to watch the afternoon shoot.

CHAPTER 5

'What do you think? You haven't said much, Mr Clegg.'

Chrissie stood back and surveyed her workbench. The lively reds, blues and greens crisscrossing the pale linen were at odds with the subdued tones all around her in the barn workshop. The brightly coloured tablecloth cried out for cream cheese and cucumber sandwiches, pork pies and strawberries; a picnic fit for a summer's day, complete with a gentle breeze and scents of meadow flowers. Instead the air hung warm, dry and heavy with the smell of white spirit, linseed oil and beeswax.

She had unwrapped the console table, spreading out its tablecloth shroud. Then she'd examined each piece, laying it out carefully, like a post mortem.

'I still don't understand why it was attached to the scenery wall. They could've knocked up a cheap replica. This is a genuine antique.' Ron Clegg bent to look more closely at the veneer.

'I know. Nick thought they'd used it to give some kind of stability to the wall. I reckon it was pure laziness. They probably thought, why bother to make a replica when the real thing is standing here staring us in the face?'

'To avoid this happening.' Ron reached for a broken leg, his arthritic knuckles casting faint shadows. 'This Lester you keep mentioning, well he sounds a bit slapdash. Did you say he's the construction manager?'

'Hmm…,' but her thoughts were already racing along another track. 'Do you think it's the owners? Maybe they wanted their table to appear in the film. And if the film turns out to be successful, then their table gains provenance.

Suddenly it becomes more valuable, movie memorabilia even. You know the kind of thing... the table Cooper Brice hid his World War One revolver on, before blowing out his brains.'

'What? Does he do that in the film, Mrs Jax?'

'I don't know,' she said, shrugging, 'I was making it up. But you see what I'm trying to say.'

'Yes, yes. Everyone gains, until it goes wrong of course.'

'Which it did. Horribly. But you still haven't answered my question. What do you think, Mr Clegg?'

She watched his gnarled fingers as he tapped the tabletop, working his way methodically across its surface. She knew he was listening for the note to change from the deeper resonance of the attached veneer, to the lighter more papery sound of the loose veneer.

'It's not too bad. No, the main problems are the obvious ones. Like these areas, where the burr walnut veneer has come away from the curved rail. Here.' He pointed to where the two legs had broken from the curved rail support for the top.

'The legs are solid walnut,' Chrissie murmured.

'Yes, and they had T bridle joints to straddle the curved rail.'

'And both legs broke just below... and through some of the tenons.'

'Hmm, so do we make a new tenon section for each leg and scarf it onto the rest of the leg, or...?'

'Rout in two new pieces of wood as spines across the breaks? I'll go and have a search around, see what old walnut we've got with a similar grain.'

'And take a look through the veneers, while you're about it, Mrs Jax.'

She hurried across the barn, with its workbenches, band and table saws, sanders and router. Shelves sagged under pots of wood glue, polishes and stains. A rack of metal bar-cramps hung along one wall. It was all so familiar she hardly registered any of it. Her mind was too busy picturing Ron's store of salvaged old wood.

Outside, a light gust of easterly wind stole the sun's warmth, and for a moment the enormity of the barn workshop, clad in dark stained weatherboarding, dwarfed her spirit. Her steps faltered as she made the short journey along the side of the courtyard to a brick outhouse. It had once housed a still, the copper tank just about recognisable in the back of the disused fireplace. Now it was stockpiled with a hoard of saved but broken furniture, donor wood for restoration projects.

'Efficiency,' she muttered, as she rummaged through the pile, 'that's the word. Along with, professionalism, tradition, quality, business acumen... charm and luck.' And with each muttered attribute she delved and pulled out table legs, side panels, and broken chairs.

She was a believer in charm and luck. But, she told herself, as she lifted a mahogany-fronted drawer to one side, there was bad luck as well as good. And what about the saying, you made your own luck?

She thought back to Saturday afternoon. Clive had driven with her over to the Wattisham Airfield perimeter lane, and then down the rough track to Ron's workshop. Clive had helped her carry the tablecloth bundle into the barn. When he'd said they had the rest of the weekend ahead of them and couldn't she wait until Monday before starting work on it, she'd taken the hint and they'd left.

Ron hadn't been there at the time so there'd been no need for explanations. When she came in to work on Monday morning he had already arrived and was pretending to be unaware of the tablecloth package. She guessed it was his way of saying that what she chose now as her work projects was her business. He was treating her like a respected colleague but it felt uncomfortable, this knife sharp transition from apprentice to partner.

'Talk about an elephant in the room. A striped red, blue and green one,' she'd said, unable to contain herself any longer. And like an excited apprentice, she launched into her account of Saturday and the film shoot at Althorne House.

'You'd better unwrap it,' Ron had said.

It seemed like a long time ago now.

She dragged her mind back to the task in hand as dust floated in the storeroom air. Spiders, disturbed by the movement of broken cabinets and rickety chairs, scuttled across the pale, Suffolk brick floor. She shuddered, straightened up, and turned her attention to the wood stacked against one of the walls.

'Hey, that's more like it,' she said, spotting a thick flat walnut base to a pedestal table.

She eased it from the stack. The pedestal was missing, but the large base stood on small bun-shaped feet. It looked reasonably straight grained. 'Excellent, no splits,' she murmured, brushing her hand over the surface.

It didn't take her long to search through the neatly stored veneers, held flat between paper and boards on a shelf. She'd spent hours labelling and sorting them into

45

some kind of order, months ago on a slow rainy afternoon. Her system was alphabetical, so Walnut was easy to find. W was pretty much near the bottom of the pile.

Armed with her spoils, she hurried back to the barn workshop.

By lunchtime Chrissie had planned and priced up the repair. 'I promised I'd email Lester with the estimate, but–'

'It's a dead spot here.'

'We're only a couple of hundred yards from the helicopter base. I bet they get the internet OK.' It was an old chestnut and she knew she was never going to crack it. Fibre optic cables in rural Suffolk were as rare as hen's teeth, and the phone-mast broadband cover was as patchy as a nasty attack of moths.

'Use the landline, Mrs Jax.'

'Yes, you're right. I'll call him now. I can email the estimate when I get home.'

Lester answered after the second ring. 'Hello?' His voice sounded edgy, almost suspicious.

'Hi, Lester. This is Chrissie Jax – Clegg Cabinet Makers and Furniture Restorers.' She paused, barely long enough to hear his mumbled greeting, and then pressed on, determined to sound confident and business-like.

'I've had a chance to assess the damage to the console table....' The words flowed as she described the broken legs, tenons, and loose and missing veneer. He didn't say a word as she ran through her proposed repairs.

'And your price?'

She hesitated. 'You're happy with my assessment and suggested repairs?'

'If the price is right.'

'Three hundred and fifty pounds, that's including materials.' Her pulse thumped in her ear as she waited, slowing her breathing. She caught Ron's heavenward glance.

'Three hundred and twenty-five.'

'Three hundred and twenty-five?' She flipped the phone onto speaker.

'Yes. That's the most I'm willing to pay. We're trade, remember. Can you start on it straight away?'

'But...,' she hadn't expected to haggle. 'Don't you have to check with the insurers first? I mean–'

'Let me worry about the insurance, Chrissie. Get it done by the end of the week and you'll get your three hundred and twenty-five. Cash. I guarantee. And if you've done a good job, there'll be more work coming your way.'

She shot a querying glance at Ron, saw him nod.

'OK. Three hundred and twenty-five pounds. I'll email the estimate later today.'

'Don't forget – repaired and back at Althorne House on Friday. Bye Chrissie.' He ended the call.

'Wooah.' Chrissie let her breath escape, like a deflating balloon.

'He sounds a bit sharp,' Ron said quietly.

'Pushy, more like.'

'I must say, you were pretty slick, Mrs Jax. The walnut from our salvaged wood hasn't cost us anything. In fact it beats me how you managed to pluck that figure out of the air.'

'You're forgetting I was an accountant for twenty-two years. But cash? And he says it's OK without getting back to the insurers? He's....'

'Comfortable with cutting corners?'

'Yes, and maybe worse than that, which means I'll make doubly sure I put this through our books. Whatever he's up to, we keep our fingers clean.'

For a moment Chrissie remembered reading about insurance scams, and the advice regularly printed in newspaper columns from agony aunts spawned from the financial world. As far as she could make out, the insurance companies were pretty switched on to the possibility of fraud, often suspected it, and were generally sticklers for the small print in terms and conditions.

'Hmm... let's hope it's because he wants to avoid making an insurance claim,' she murmured. But there was still something niggling from the call. Now she was a partner in the business, shouldn't her name be included? Clegg and Jax, not just plain Clegg?

'I was thinking, Mr Clegg....'

'So was I, Mrs Jax. If Lester sends you more casualties, you could be making a habit of gathering up carcasses, you know furniture kill. Is your car large enough? I mean, Saturday it was a flattened console table, next week it could be a smashed double wardrobe.'

'Oh right, yes. I was thinking more about the name—'

'My decrepit old van? Well you're welcome to borrow it. But I don't have anything else. It's all I drive.'

'Then don't you think it's time we invested in a newer one, for the business? I can have a look around, see what's out there. What do you think?'

'I think you need to get stuck into repairing the console table. You haven't got time to waste searching out... I don't know, some stripped-out, thirty-year old, yellow VW Campervan. It would be totally impractical.'

'Yellow VW Campervan? Why do you say that? Have you seen one, Mr Clegg?'

'No I haven't, Mrs Jax.'

She didn't believe him. She'd heard his hesitation, saw him glance away.

'I'm not changing my yellow TR7 for a van, however yellow it is. Not even an old VW Campervan,' she said. 'It would be ridiculous.'

'Quite.'

She let the matter drop, but she was too intrigued to forget it. For the moment there were more pressing matters. It was time to get started on the console table repair.

CHAPTER 6

Matt slipped his arm around Maisie and pulled her closer as they walked past the flint church in the centre of Stowmarket. His brain ached from his day tracing names, but the ride back from the airless Balcon & Mora office, and the prospect of an evening with Maisie had cleared his mind and cheered his mood. He hadn't seen her for a couple of days.

'Ouch,' she squealed, 'me shoulders! It's been murder every time I move. Thank God me shift's over. Them blisters – I caught 'em with me nail yesterday. Now me skin's comin' off like a....'

Matt waited, wondering which creature she'd choose that shed its skin. 'Snake?' he suggested.

'Yeah... nah, that's sick. Why'd you say snake?'

'Cos snakes shed their skin. Anyway Mais, I like your skin.' He bent and caught the side of her forehead with a fleeting kiss. A mix of almond oil, jojoba oil, lavender and geranium soured his lips.

'Euhh. That tastes horrible. What you put on your skin?'

'I thought you liked me skin?'

'I do Mais, but lavender kinda makes me tongue go numb.'

'Lucky I didn't put oil of cloves on it, then.'

He ambled to a halt. 'Yeah, but I'd 've smelled it a mile off, wouldn't I.'

They stood, gazing up at a pale brick building. Three tall narrow windows stared down from the first floor.

'What we lookin' at, Matt?'

'The John Peel Centre.'

'Yeah, I know that. I meant, why are we lookin' at it? Weren't it the old corn exchange?'

'Yeah. I was lookin' at them windows. Last week someone smashed an upstairs window, broke in, stole some fire extinguishers and a toilet, and then left 'em on the roof of the cycle shed next door.'

'Wicked. Can't have been them front windows though. A toilet? How'd you know that?'

'Read it today when I was doin' some newspaper searches.'

She nestled closer to his side. He guessed harmony was restored, but he wasn't sure why.

'You aint goin' to put cloves on them blisters, are you, Mais?'

'Course not. What made you say that? Anyway, it's all raw now. I've heard you can absorb stuff through raw skin. And I aint got toothache, either. Where'd you park the scooter?'

They wandered along Church Walk, skirting the low hedge, and enjoying the early evening shade from mature ivy-clad lime and yew trees. A small area of park-like grass stretched away, criss-crossed by paths and broken by bench seats and the occasional tomb stone.

'Nice here, aint it?' Maisie murmured.

Matt had tucked the Piaggio almost out of sight between the hedge and some private access to a row of old cottages.

'It'll get all sticky under them limes,' she added. But it didn't seem to bother her as she climbed up behind him. He started the engine.

Later that evening and alone again, Matt yanked his pillow up behind his back and settled on the bed with his laptop. Around him, the gloom of the ill-lit room pressed close. It was always like this in his bedroom; the chaotic bed, the grubby blue walls like Mediterranean smog. The feeling of emptiness intensified as muffled sounds drifted from his mum's TV in the bungalow's living room. He opened his laptop, his mind still on Maisie. The screen glowed comfortingly.

For a moment he pictured Maisie, both arms thrust into the air and swaying to the music as they'd watched Ed Sheeran strumming his guitar, centre stage.

'Mais likes 'im,' he mumbled. He hadn't thought about Ed since the V Festival a couple of days ago but now he recalled it, he reckoned there was more than a passing resemblance between them. He ran a hand over his beard. It was straggly unkempt, not Sheeran-like, but it was a beard. They both had one. And his hair was reddish, like Ed's.

'And we're both from Suffolk.' If he was honest, that's where the similarities ended. He typed *Ed Sheeran T-shirt* into the search box. 'Yeah, she'll like that.'

Beep-itty-beep! Beep-itty-beep beep!

With his eyes still on the laptop screen, he pulled his mobile from his jeans pocket.

'Yeah?' he said, expecting to hear Maisie's voice.

'Hello? Is that Felix?'

He sat bolt upright and flipped his computer screen down. Frag, he thought, the debtor girl. He'd forgotten about her. A number showed on his caller ID. Great, he almost had what he needed. Just a few checks to be sure.

'Hello? Am I speaking to Felix Lighter? From the Student Chronicle?' Her voice sounded questioning, sharp.

'Yeah... yeah I'm Felix,' he said, his voice cracking, his mouth dry.

'Sorry to call so late, but I've only just got your message. I haven't missed the deadline, have I?'

'No,' he said too quickly, teetering on the brink of scammers' hell - the dreaded voice block, word jam and creative freeze of an imploding scam. Something he'd heard Damon talk about. He needed to get his act together, and fast.

'It's Priddy Jones. Peterborough, right?' He cleared his throat, and visualised her name. He'd read it enough times on his internet searches. He saw the complete typescript in his mind's eye.

'Yeah Priddy, you're one of this year's graduates. Art & Design,' he continued. 'Real interesting. And I heard you're already workin' for a stage and film set design & construction company. Cool.' His words came more easily as he read from his photographic memory.

'Yes, but I didn't think anyone would be interested.'

'Oh yeah, you'd be amazed. Hey wait a sec, let me get somethin' to write on.' He flipped up the screen on his laptop and opened the Utterly Academy webpage and the Past Students' Blog, something he'd never bothered to read before.

'See, students *need a role model*,' he said, his eyes scanning a blog now up on his screen. '*Someone who shows it's possible*, you know, an *inspiration*.'

'An inspiration? I'd hardly call myself that.'

'Well students want to hear 'bout that kinda stuff. Like *how I landed my first job*, you know – Peterborough to Ipswich, and how *making the most of my first break* can lead to *the job of your dreams*.'

'But props and props continuity isn't my dream.'

'Yeah well, maybe dream's a bit flowery, but somethin' like, *first step on the ladder*. I was seein' it as a headin' for me article.'

'Ye-e-s, I think I get it. So you want to know how I got my first break and how it led to this job?'

'Yeah. So, first question. How'd you get your job?'

'Through some work experience in my last year on my course. But strictly speaking, I wasn't paid, so it doesn't count as a job.'

'Yeah, but you were workin', so it counts for what I want to write.' Matt started to relax. He quite liked the sound of Priddy.

He listened as she told him about the production she'd helped with at the Wolsey Theatre. He already knew what she was going to say, but he had to check he'd got the right Priddy Jones.

'Did you get all that?' she asked.

'Yeah, yeah. But how'd it lead somewhere?'

'I asked the construction manager if I he thought I'd be allowed to keep any of the props. I mean I'd made some of them, so I reckoned it was OK to ask. Turned out he was a collector himself. He's into Star Wars memorabilia, that kind of thing.'

'So how…?'

'Stage set design, construction, props – there's a bit of a crossover. I spoke to lots of people and it seems they liked me. And I must have hit it off with the construction manager because... oh don't say that in your article.'

'Nah, course not. Go on.'

'I was offered a job in the company once I'd completed in Peterborough.'

'Cool. So how are you likin' Ipswich?'

'It's a bit different to Peterborough. I'll be happier, more settled once I'm in my own flat.'

'Yeah, some nice places in Ipswich near the waterfront.'

'You're joking. A bit too pricey for me. No, I'm afraid it's off the Norwich Road for me.'

'So were you somewhere nice in Peterborough?'

'Neet Road. Do you know it?'

'Yeah, walked along it enough times.' He pictured the Google map. 'Look, I think I've got enough. If you give me your email I'll send you what I'm goin' to write, if you like.'

'Yes, OK,' she said.

He keyed in her email as she dictated it over the phone.

'Before you go, Priddy – one last question. The prop you're proudest of?'

'A nutmeg grater. Bye Felix.' She ended the call.

He punched the air. 'Felix Lighter, you're a scammin' genius.' He'd got her mobile number and her email address. But a nutmeg grater? What in phishing hell was she on about, he wondered.

He closed his eyes and let himself drift into another world, one of CIA agents, James Bond and comic-strip super spies. A life where hidden weapons, cyanide capsules and toxic chemicals penetrating raw skin, were the norm. He was agent Matt Finch, code name Ed Sheeran....

CHAPTER 7

Nick settled on the bench seat and sipped his pint of Land Girl. He took his time, letting the golden ale linger in his mouth, savouring the mix of sweetness tempered with citrus hops and rounded off with a subtle dry finish as he swallowed. He leaned his head back, closed his eyes, and enjoyed the early evening atmosphere in the Nags Head. So far, it was turning out to be a damned sight better Friday than a week ago, when the scenery toppled over.

While muted voices mingled with the stale smell of spilt beer, Nick thought back over his week. It had been tiring. Tiring standing around doing nothing, and then out of the blue, stressfully exhausting as Merlin generated moments of frenetic activity.

'Steps for Cooper,' Merlin had shouted, and when nothing instantly appeared, 'Nick! Knock some up. Now!' Of course now had meant ten minutes before he'd asked.

Funny how he associated Cooper with steps. These ones were to help him get into the biplane. Cooper was supposed to step athletically up onto a strengthened point on the lower wing where it joined the fuselage, then swing his other leg into the cockpit. But the biplane was too old and too valuable for someone like Cooper to clamber over and throw his weight around. Nick made the top step like a small platform, and the same height as the lower wing. It hadn't been difficult, just another trick to keep out of shot.

'You seem happy.'

'What?' Nick opened his eyes. 'Hey Chrissie! I didn't notice you come in.'

She stood, holding a glass of ginger beer and watching him. An up-tempo number erupted from the jukebox.

'Did you get Ron's van back OK?' he asked, as the indie-rock number gathered volume.

'Of course. Thanks for helping me unload the console table.'

'No problem. You did a bloody good job on it. Lester was well impressed.'

'Thanks. He didn't say much.' She pulled up a chair and sat down.

'Only because he'd have seemed a mean bastard for not paying you more. I saw him looking at it after you left. Was it tricky sticking the veneer to the curved rail?'

'A bit awkward, but it's an antique, so it made sense to use traditional animal glue.'

'Hmm... so hide glue and hammer veneering? I suppose it meant you didn't have to make a curved caul and clamp it.'

'I thought about it because it's a burr veneer. But our walnut burr was tougher than it looked. I was ready with some pieces of flexi glass and band cramps, but Ron said to try with a veneering hammer first – and it was OK. Working it across in a zigzag motion got all the excess glue and air out, no problem.'

'Have you ever used a vacuum press? That's good for curved surfaces, you know, hand rails for staircases and things like that. Willows is buying a vacuum system.'

'Wow.' She sipped her ginger beer.

'Yeah.' He found himself tapping his foot to the music and softly hum-singing along with the catchy riff.

'I suppose I should be pleased Lester paid up, and with cash.'

'He's hard-nosed.'

'Tight fisted, more like. So, has it felt like you're on holiday?'

'Sort of. I wouldn't want to do it for too long, though. Have you heard Owen's been sacked?' He didn't wait for Chrissie to answer, but ploughed on, 'I felt sorry for him, so I said he was welcome to join us for a drink if he wanted.'

'Great.'

'He might not turn up, of course.' Secretly Nick hoped Owen would bottle out, but almost on cue the old pub door swung open and Matt sauntered in with... hell, he was with Owen.

'He's turned up,' Nick breathed, his words lost inside his beer glass. The up-tempo beats faded and the jukebox fell silent. Mellow babble filled the Nags Head again. Nick's stomach tightened.

He studied Matt and Owen as they waited at the bar to be served - Matt short, scruffy, and generously plump; Owen tall, with a well groomed centimetre beard, and a head of short dark hair to match. The faded jeans and black tee clung to the hint of his quads and biceps.

'Hi!' Chrissie called, and then quietly to Nick, 'Was it some kind of a tummy bug?'

'That's what he told me. I guess he's over it now,' he murmured as he watched Owen gulp at an overfull pint of beer before easing his way past a group of drinkers. Matt waved, slopping lager onto the rough floorboards and hurried over.

'Hi. Guess who I've just seen? He's right behind me. Hey Owen, over here, mate.' Matt gestured to Owen.

'Wow. You've caught the sun.' Nick took in Matt's crimson forehead and puffy eyelids more closely.

'Almost a dermal peel,' Chrissie added. 'Are you OK? Hey, and Owen, hi! I haven't seen you in a while.'

'Yeah well, on-site work takes you all over the place. Anyhow, cheers. Good to see you all again.' Owen lifted his glass and drank. Nick couldn't help noticing the shadows under his eyes.

'Your work sounds very glamorous. You must've met lots of famous actors,' Chrissie said.

Owen shrugged, in a sort of bored, *when you've met as many famous people as I have it's too tedious to talk about it*, kind of a way. He moved his eyes slowly, as if he knew it all, but then he'd always been a bit like that, Nick thought. The difference now was that the light behind the eyes seemed to have dulled. Was he depressed or on something? Or both? Nick couldn't tell.

'So are you feeling better? Have you recovered from whatever…?'

'I was as sick as a dog when I rang you. Whatever it was hit my guts like a twister. It worked its way through me like–'

'Spare us the details,' Chrissie muttered.

'It was bloody vicious. And I'm still feelin' pretty rough. Prosecco's bought some kind of oral supplement or cleanser on the internet. She reckons it might help get the rest of it out of me system.'

'Prosecco?' Chrissie queried.

'Me girlfriend.'

'Ah. And the cleanser? Has it helped?'

'The burning and tinglin' round me mouth's gone. And me eyes… they're better. And I don't feel so cold, but me guts, they're still a bit raw. The instructions say it's a cleanser so you have to stick with it even if it's painful. I'll skip the details.' He pulled a face, and then sipped his beer.

'What's your doctor say? You have seen one haven't you?' Nick asked.

'Yeah. Right when it kicked off. Asked me if I was takin' any drugs, then said to drink plenty of fluids and to go back if I'm not gettin' better. I reckon this counts as fluid.' He lifted his glass.

'So what's the miracle cleanser called?' Matt asked.

'Just that - a miracle mineral solution.'

'Yeah, but is it a name or a description? I mean do you drink it or rub it in? Would it help me sunburn?'

'I don't know. You'd have to read up about it. Prosecco might know. Mind you, she's probably got some cream or potion that'd help. She's into herbs and organics.'

Nick couldn't hold back any longer. 'Look Owen, I'm really sorry about Lester and your job,' he blurted.

'Get over it, Nick. I have. Anyway it was pretty boring. Time to move on, I guess.'

For a moment Nick searched Owen's face to read the lifeless eyes. Was Owen really over it? 'You missed seeing the biplane flying today. The pilot, not Cooper of course, did some touch landings.'

'Touch landin's?' Owen asked.

'Yeah, well touch and go. He flew past, coming down low enough for the wheels to touch the grass and then accelerated back up into the air.'

'Like a pretend landing?' Chrissie said.

'Yeah, it's all part of the illusion. The magic of film.'

Nick felt the atmosphere lighten. Owen laughed and Matt went to set the jukebox off again.

•

Saturday morning found Nick on set with an ache behind his eyes and a fragile stomach. Was it a surfeit of Land Girl, or had he caught Owen's gut bug, he wondered. Either way, it had turned into a late evening in the Nags Head. Matt had played air guitar to a Florence and the Machine track on the jukebox while at the same time pretending to be Ed Sheeran. In a flash of beer-infused kindness, Nick had invited Owen to come canoeing when he felt stronger. 'I might just take you up on that,' Owen had said.

Owen was too arrogant to be a good mate, but they'd parted on friendly enough terms.

'Awesome,' Nick murmured. He stood watching the film crew, his mind harking back to Matt on air guitar.

'Awesome,' he repeated.

Merlin moved across the hallway and blocked Nick's eye line. Camera lenses zoomed to catch Gavi's downcast glances, haunting smiles and hesitant lines while she stood at the front door. It was a cloudy day, but the lights were bright, full sunshine bright.

'She's pretty, isn't she?'

He barely caught the whisper, but the word pretty gave him a clue. It had to be Priddy who'd tiptoed close. She stood at his side. But why was she holding a small camera in her hand?

'What are you doing?' he mouthed and pointedly looked at her camera.

'This?' She held it up. 'It's for prop continuity.'

He bent closer to hear her words.

'Then I know exactly where everything's placed. And if Gavi looks good in my shots, I can always get her to sign them later. Win, win, wouldn't you say?'

'Neat,' he whispered. 'Look, I'm going to have to take a walk. I need to clear my head. Do you want to come?'

She waggled her camera, by way of an answer.

'OK, I'll leave you to it. Heavy night, last night,' he muttered and then gestured as if holding a beer glass and drinking. He guessed she must have picked up the faint smell of Friday evening's alcohol on his breath because she grinned and turned her attention back to her camera.

He left Priddy to her task and sneaked along the passageway leading out of the rear of the hallway. The ache behind his eyes grew to a pounding as he quickened his pace, anxious to quit the building. Outside in the gravelled parking area, the smell of coffee brewing and fried bacon drew him to the refreshment trailer. His stomach grumbled. Had he caught Owen's gut bug? He hoped not. The gentle nausea and unsettled gripe was more likely a legacy of too much Land Girl the night before, he reckoned. And he was pretty sure it was the overcast day that made him shiver in his short sleeved tee, not a toxic bug behind a soaring temperature. He knew from past experience that fluids and eating would help. He'd be fine. He'd escaped Owen's gut bug, and in a few days' time his leave would be over and he'd be back at Willows.

While he waited for an acned man in a paper hat to serve him a bacon bap, he weighed up his chances with Priddy. He liked her, or rather he liked her irreverent approach, but he suspected she wasn't interested. She came across as chummy, not flirty. And all her mysterious hinting of having more important things to do than help when the scenery toppled over was odd. He guessed she probably had a boyfriend somewhere, but wanted to appear interesting. And of course it made him curious.

The more he thought about it, the more he realised he didn't know much about the rest of the film crew, the actors or the people behind the scenes. He'd barely grasped their names. During the week he'd been on the location site, he'd never even taken a hike past the area where their trailers were parked. But now, with his bacon bap in his hand, and a shoot in full swing, this would be the time, he decided. There'd be nobody to bump into, no one to make him feel like an outsider.

He ambled past the manicured box hedges encircling scarlet geraniums and crimson dwarf lilies, and followed a path short-cutting into a courtyard. Space was limited and the vans and trailers had been drawn into neat rows. He read the names as he strolled past: *Mr Leob, Mr Brice, Ms Monterey*; a row further back had more general labels like *Tech Editing, Actors, Make-up, Costumes & Props*; and at the rear he found a row of portable toilet cubicles.

Chewing the last mouthful of salty bacon and soft sweetened bread, Nick walked back to the *Costumes & Props* trailer. He peeped through the curved sloping window at the front, but the smoked acrylic glass meant he saw only a faint reflection of himself, nothing beyond the net voiles inside. He knocked on the trailer's door.

'Hey, what are you doing?'

He twisted around. 'Oh hiya, Priddy. Did you get the photos you wanted?'

'Yeah, but why are you here? I thought you said you were taking a walk.'

'I am, but I was curious. The secret world of props, and all that?'

She brushed past and opened the door. When she turned to face him she blocked his path. 'Secrets? Well there aren't any. And not many hero props here either, only standard ones.'

'OK then, so tell me about the biplane. I expect there's a mock-up one back in the studio – for trick action shots, right?'

'Yes, and I guess you could call that one a hero prop.'

'Awesome. Did you make it?'

'Sure, along with the carpentry guys.'

'Carpentry guys? Do you mean Owen?'

'No, Lester. Why all the questions?'

'I was just wondering, that's all. It's like a different world for me. I mean, what happens when the film's completed?'

'What do you mean?'

'To all the props – where do they go? I mean it's pricey to store stuff. And like the photos you've just taken, you must have hundreds. What do you do with them all?'

He caught her sideway glance.

'Is there something you want to buy? Are you angling for a particular prop?' she asked, dropping her voice.

'No, I-I....' He wasn't sure where this was leading. Was she expecting him to make an offer for Cooper's flying goggles or something? He didn't want to appear rude by not wanting a souvenir, so he smiled.

'If you're after hero props,' she said slowly, 'you mentioned the mock-up biplane, just now. Is that what you want?'

Nick gaped. 'What? Are you serious?'

'Yeah. I could be. Why not? I'd have to run it past Lester though.'

CHAPTER 8

'What's a nutmeg grater, Chrissie?'

'You're the second person to ask me that. Why do you ask?' Chrissie grabbed Clive's arm as she wobbled on some rough boughs and small trunks strewn across the path. They must have been laid as a walkway when the ground was wet and muddy, because the weight of passing tread had half-pushed them into the dark loamy topsoil.

'The second person? I didn't know there was such a thing as a nutmeg grater till I saw you looking on your laptop,' Clive said.

'What? Before I printed out this walk? Not much gets past you.' She waved a sheet of paper as she swung her arm to get her balance.

They were five minutes into Coombs Wood, now a nature reserve but recorded many centuries earlier in the Doomsday book as *a wood for 16 swine*. They'd reached a point where some coppiced hornbeam had been cut and piled into rough stacks. It was a perfect spot to pause on a Sunday afternoon walk.

'Come on Chrissie, nutmeg graters. You still haven't said.'

'Well, as the name implies, they're graters, and often incorporated into a container which was also used to store your nutmeg. This was in the days when nutmegs were exotic and expensive. I suddenly remembered Matt asking me about them, so I thought I'd do a quick bit of research before it slipped my mind again. And then I looked up Coombs Wood.'

'Matt asked about nutmeg graters? Don't tell me it's going to be the next craze. Smoking weed with ground nutmeg?'

'Trust you to think like a policeman. Of course Matt isn't. He doesn't do drugs. Mind you, it's not the sort of thing I'd have expected him to ask about. I was a bit surprised myself. I suppose I should have delved a bit, but we were in the Nags Head. He was full of the V festival and Nick was describing the biplane. Oh yes, Owen was there as well.'

'Owen? Isn't he the one…? Althorne House? The missing bolts?'

'Hmm. But nothing was said. Owen's been sacked and I think Nick feels awkward about it.'

'It's Nick who feels awkward?'

'Well according to Owen, it wasn't Owen.'

'Now don't tell me I'm being a detective, but–'

'Let it drop, Clive. Nick's only there for a few more days and then, well it's water under the bridge. Anyway, I hoped I might catch a glimpse of the biplane in the air. Nick said they were flying it on Friday. We should be able to hear it from here if it's in the air again today.'

'But we're surrounded by trees, Chrissie.'

'Yes, good point.' She gazed up at the leafy green canopy. 'If we take one of these tracks,' she pointed to her printout, 'then we get to the edge of the wood. Apparently there's a ditch and banks around the edge. It's meant to be a sign of how ancient it is.'

They took their time, following the path through the trees.

'I think that southern hawker,' he pointed at a long delicate, mostly black dragonfly, 'is the nearest thing to a primitive plane that we're going to see today.'

She had to admit he was probably right.

Back in her cottage in Woolpit that evening, a sports commentator spoke excitedly on the TV about the Paralympics, due to begin in three days' time. Would the present calm and goodwill that had flooded Suffolk since the Olympics, trend through the Paralympics as well, she wondered. She'd grown used to Clive finishing work on time, nights unbroken by emergency call-outs, and weekends free from overtime. In fact she was surprised how quickly she'd slipped into a domestic routine. But something niggled. She missed hearing about his cases, or rather the ones troubling him. She feared boredom, or more accurately, mental stagnation.

She flipped open her laptop. Perhaps Clive had a point, she thought as she typed *uses for nutmeg graters* into the search box. Within moments she was immersed in her mission, no longer conscious of the TV or Clive lounging on the sofa next to her.

She opened a webpage promising *another use for the nutmeg grater* and browsed her screen. What did a stage production called The Waldringfield Wives, have to do with nutmegs or graters, she wondered. At first she couldn't find any connection but as she read on, the words *a nutmeg grater was used to hide the poison* leapt from the text. The article enthused about the plot and the haunting presence of a nineteenth century wooden nutmeg grater painted to look like the Brighton Pavilion, and appearing in each scene. It was always on stage but seemed to move to different places with each scene change, such as onto a side table, a shelf, or a writing bureau.

'Wow, wooden and like the Brighton Pavilion. I wonder if there's a picture,' she murmured as she typed the description in the search box.

'A film and memorabilia site?' She was surprised, but of course it made sense when the page opened.

And there it was for sale. The dimensions were bigger than Chrissie would have expected for a genuine nutmeg grater, but she reasoned it was a stage prop and therefore had to be large, so as to be seen from the back of the dress circle. 'And to think, someone made it to look so realistic, just as a prop?'

Lower on her screen, a notification caught her eye. *People who searched for nutmeg graters like Brighton Pavilion also searched for....* She clicked without much thought.

A nutmeg grater like the Ickworth House Rotunda, she read. It was an item on an online auction site, and the seller's address indicated Warwickshire. 'Ickworth House?' she repeated. Was it the same Ickworth House as the one near Bury St Edmunds? Suffolk's Ickworth House?

She took a closer look at the photos of the grater. It was made of boxwood, with a circular base and a domed top. A mid-nineteenth century piece. 'Six inches tall and painted to look like the Rotunda,' she whispered.

She scrutinised the bidding history. So far there was only one bid of ten pounds, and no reserve price. The bidding was due to close on Sunday at nine o'clock.

'But that's today and there's less than an hour to go.' Her calm began to evaporate.

'Less than an hour to go? What are you talking about?' Clive asked mildly.

'I'm really excited. I've found an online auction site selling an antique nutmeg grater. Here, take a look. It's kind of Suffolk and it'll be a good talking point. Something to net the punters in, don't you think? It'll be great for our stand at the next antiques and fine furniture fair.' She turned her laptop towards him.

'It's the Rotunda, isn't it? So what's it doing in Warwickshire?'

'I think it was made, I don't know, like a souvenir. So I'm hoping no one outside Suffolk will want it and, if I'm lucky, it'll go for a song.' Excitement fluttered in her stomach.

'And if you're lucky, it won't be a scam, it'll actually arrive through the post, and it'll be genuine.'

'What? You think I might get ripped off? I've just checked the seller's history and it seems OK.' She caught his smile, saw he was laughing. 'Oh stop it, Clive. You're just winding me up.'

By one second past nine o'clock, Chrissie's knew her winning bid had been accepted.

'Yes,' she said, and punched the air. 'Mine, and for forty pounds.'

•

Chrissie braked gently, checked the road was clear and turned onto the Wattisham Airfield perimeter lane. At eight o'clock on a Monday morning, all was quiet. To one side, the grass verge merged into the brambles and shrubby hawthorn of a chaotic hedge. The height varied like a ragged haircut, with an occasional crab apple tree, small beech or birch. Wild hedge rose and blackthorn peppered the brambles and hawthorn, and behind stood the silent authority of a tall wire link fence and the Wattisham Airfield.

She barely registered the airfield perimeter, her eyes were too busy tracing the other side of the lane. In a moment she knew the Clegg workshop notice would come into view. She slowed, ready to swing her TR7 onto the uneven track leading to the old barn. The car rocked and pitched as she steered between the potholes, missing some but catching others. Her tyres spat gravel and stones, rattling and volleying into the wheel arches while the 2 litre engine burbled gently under the yellow wedge-shaped bonnet.

Ron's van was already parked outside. She drew up next to it and hurried in, eager to tell him about her internet buy.

'Good morning, Mr Clegg. You'll never guess what I found on the internet yesterday.'

'Good morning, Mrs Jax.' He looked up from his workbench, where he'd been repairing a drawer base. 'Will I need to sit down first?'

'No, but I'm going to put the kettle on for some tea. Do you want a refill?' She slung her soft leather bag down and picked up his mug.

'Yes, that would be nice. Now come on, Mrs Jax. Don't keep me in suspense. Tell me.'

'An old nutmeg grater. I bid for it and... now it's mine.'

'A nutmeg grater? I didn't know you were interested in antique silver.'

'Silver? Why do you say that?'

'Because I remember old Mr Prout, the auctioneer, had a collection. He said the ones most people collected were made of silver. They were a bit like snuff boxes - small enough to slip into an eighteenth century gentleman's pocket.'

'Yes, I've read about those - for the man about town who wanted to grate nutmeg onto his hot punch, coffee or chocolate. Well this one is six inches tall and stands.'

'Hmm, then I guess it'll be a later one. Nineteenth century, and part of a gentleman's travelling canteen.'

'And it's wood, Mr Clegg.'

'Ah, now this is starting to make sense. More your style, I'd have said.'

While the kettle boiled, Chrissie rummaged through her bag.

'Here,' she said, 'I've printed a picture of it from the website.' She watched him frown.

'It looks very much like–'

'The Rotunda. At Ickworth House, Mr Clegg. I've looked it up and the Rotunda was completed in1829.'

'So the grater was made,' he bent to read the printout, 'sometime in the *mid-nineteenth century*, Mrs Jax.'

'Exciting, isn't it.'

'Hmm. I'll tell you what is exciting though. I've had a call from someone in Aldeburgh. They want you to make a pair of Arts & Crafts-style plant stands, like the one you made for our display at the Snape Maltings Antiques and Fine Arts Fair in June.'

'Wow, really? That's fantastic news.' A wave of optimism swept through her. At this rate, if the orders and work kept coming in, then the business was going to be OK.

By Thursday she was starting to wonder when her parcel from Warwickshire was going to arrive. She'd already contacted her client in Aldeburgh and ordered the American black cherry he'd selected for the plant stands. She approved of his choice and rather liked the way its pinkish coloured sapwood contrasted with the reddish brown darker-flecked heartwood. The straight grain and fine texture meant it was going to be easy to work.

In the meantime she was waxing and polishing a corner cupboard. The old pine was buffing into a warm colour, more a milky coffee than buttery beige. She had replaced the broken and missing shelves, and refitted its door. Now it swung true on its original hinges, and closed on the worn lock. She stepped back to admire her work.

'Sounds like we have a visitor,' Ron said.

'Isn't that a helicopter, Mr Clegg?' She listened to the rhythmical hum of a rotary engine quickly build to a harsh vibrating rumble as it passed overhead. Then she caught the lighter sound of a van's engine.

'A customer or my nutmeg grater?' she murmured, as tyres scrunched on the rough courtyard outside. She'd given the seller in Warwickshire the workshop address, rather than her home address. That way she knew there'd be someone in for parcel deliveries during the day.

Moments later, and hopeful, she heaved the old door open. Her excitement grew as she stepped outside and watched a delivery man sort through a pile of cartons and boxes in the back of his transit van.

'Yes. Ah, here it is. Mrs Jax? *Clegg Cabinet Making and Furniture Restorers.*' He handed her a package the size of a shoebox.

'Is it your grater?' Ron asked when she hurried back inside, eager to tear open the packaging.

'I hope so.' She cut through the outer sticky tape and prised the box open. Layers of newspaper and bubble wrap fell away, and then her fingers brushed against the pale wood of the Rotunda. She looked more carefully.

'You're frowning, Mrs Jax. Is something wrong?'

'I-I don't think this is....' A knot tightened in her stomach.

Ron put down his smoothing plane and walked over to her bench.

'The paint....' Her eyes took in more detail. She shook her head in disbelief as she added, 'And the base isn't worn.' She felt so stupid.

'Here, let me see.'

She almost threw the nutmeg grater into his hands, her pulse racing and her face on fire. She watched him examine it, slowly running his fingers over the exterior and removing the lid to look inside.

'Well it certainly isn't a mid-nineteenth century nutmeg grater, Mrs Jax. It doesn't show any real signs of age or having been used. If you look closely, even the grater doesn't appear worn. Someone might have dipped the metal in acid to make it look old, but....'

'And the wood's not even been hand painted under the varnish. Someone's applied photographic transfer paper. It's a damn fake.'

'But the printout you showed me looked genuine.'

'I know. How can I have been such a bloody fool?'

'If you've still got it with you, let's take another look, Mrs Jax.'

Anger replaced humiliation as she rummaged in her bag and pulled out a dog-eared sheet of paper. She smoothed it flat on the workbench and scrutinised it. Superficially the nutmeg grater looked pretty much the same as the one she'd been sent, but the detail was different. The close-up showed markings in the wood that didn't match hers. And she could see it had been hand painted.

'The varnish has yellowed and the colours look more muted through it,' she murmured.

'Another sign of age,' Ron added.

'Yes, I agree. I think the printout is of an authentic grater from the mid-nineteenth century. The one I've been sent isn't the one in this picture. It's a copy. You know, it reminds me of something I've seen before.'

A mental image of the stage prop, a nutmeg grater made to look like the Brighton Pavilion, flashed into her mind. She could have sworn it was the same hand at work. Of course she knew she'd have to go back and compare on the memorabilia site. But she was pretty sure she could see the similarities, just as an art expert could recognise the same brush strokes, use of colour and individual style of an artist's painting on a canvas.

'I've been had. Bloody scammed, Mr Clegg.' She felt as if her world had come crashing down around her head.

CHAPTER 9

Matt headed along the back roads, threading his way from Stowmarket to Bury St Edmunds. The Piaggio 49cc two-stroke engine babbled and prattled like a skittish lawnmower, while a warm breeze worried his denim jacket. He wasn't in a hurry; after all, Damon didn't demand an early morning start.

'You're paid by results, not the hour. Just as long as you trace the names,' he'd said, and Matt took him literally. He knew by ten o'clock the earlier crush of cars filtering through the ancient grid of streets near Bury's centre would have melted to a trickle.

He wove his way to the Balcon & Mora office stacked close to an alley behind the Buttermarket, and pushed his scooter onto its parking stand. Flakes of peeling skin took flight as he pulled off his helmet and plodded up a staircase to the pint-sized waiting room. Already his forehead felt moist. He pushed the office bell and waited. It was ten minutes past ten, Thursday morning.

'Hi,' he said as Damon swung the door open, then hurried back to his desk.

Just being in the presence of Damon's fast moving energy sapped Matt's strength and he slumped onto a plastic stacker chair.

'Are you OK, Matt? Your face has gone a kind of–'

'It's peelin', mate. Underneath this,' he vaguely indicated his face, 'I'm bronzed. It just aint obvious yet.'

'Well at the moment it looks very red. Even under where it's peeled. Honestly, you'll be lucky if it just fades.

It's been almost two weeks. Have you put anything on it, or taken something to get rid of the swelling?'

'It's the shape of me face, and me beard.'

'Right.'

'Me girlfriend said I should use some cream, but it makes me all sticky. An' someone was talkin' 'bout some miracle mineral supplement last week, so I looked it up. It's meant to be mega brilliant, but I'm not convinced. There's loads of warnin's 'bout it. I reckoned it couldn't help me cos it's only for drinkin' and if I splashed it all over me, well I don't want bleach on me skin. That aint what I'm after.'

'Bleach? On your skin? You'd be in an even worse state. Why are you talking about bleach?'

'Well, I read this miracle stuff contained sodium chlorite. You're supposed to drink it mixed with fruit juice. That way the fruit acids react with the chlorite and boom, your guts are full of chlorine dioxide solution – well that's a kinda bleach, aint it?'

'Shit, that sounds dangerous. And people swallow the stuff?'

'Yeah, I read it could be like swallowin' industrial-strength bleach if you get the doses wrong. Corrosive.'

'What? So this stuff's for sale?'

'Yeah, on the internet.'

'And this person who's taking it, are they OK?' Damon asked as he typed something on his keyboard.

'I don't know. He weren't feelin' too great before he started, so how'd you tell?'

A flash of conscience burned Matt's cheeks. Owen hadn't crossed his mind for days, and now, spilling all this miracle mineral stuff out to Damon brought it into sharp focus. He should have said something. He should have thought of Owen sooner.

He watched Damon as he studied the computer screen, his hazel eyes unblinking like a sepia bird of prey in pursuit, his pasty face topped with stone-washed mousey hair. To Matt he seemed so computer skilled and so single-minded, sometimes it was difficult to believe he was still in his twenties.

'What've you found, Damon?'

'I think you should tell your friend to stop taking this stuff. There've been deaths reported.'

'Frag. He aint me friend but I'll text now.'

He didn't know Owen's number, but he was sure Nick would. He shot off a message: *Hi Nick. Just discovered miracle mineral stuff is bleach. I aint got Owen's number. Cd u warn him bleach can kill. Thx.*

'Right,' Damon said. 'Now you've done your good deed for the day, time to start work. Get logged on and I'll send you the latest batch of names.'

Matt settled at his computer, satisfied he done the right thing. He glowed with a feeling of inner warmth. Not the coolest answer to the rising temperature in the airless office, but degrees better than a flaming face, he told himself.

He was two names into his list when his mobile rang.

'It's OK, Damon, it could be about the bleach,' he lied as Chrissie's name came up on the caller ID.

'Yeah well, social calls you take outside the office, remember?'

'Sure, Damon,' he said and mumbled, 'Hi,' into his mobile, careful not to use Chrissie's name.

'Matt? I don't know what to do. I've just been scammed. I bought what I thought was an antique nutmeg grater on an internet auction site on Sunday, and today–'

'Your account's been emptied?'

'No. I've been sent a fake. Not the one displayed on the site. Shit, I'm angry. I'm so hopping mad I can't think straight. If I give you the details, can you trace the seller for me? I mean a real name, a real address. Someone I can get hold of.'

'Can't you just send it back? Get a refund?'

'I could if I had an address. But it's worse than that. The seller wasn't using a secure payment site like PayPal, so no buyer protection on the auction site.'

'Spammin' hell. How much were you stung for?'

'Forty pounds, but even the credit card people would need authentication it's not an antique if they were going to give me a refund - and that'd probably cost me forty pounds. No, these bastards carefully priced it to make it not worth my while. And it's too small for Clive to pass on to his cybercrime colleagues.'

'That's pretty shit. So you think we're talkin' professionals?'

'I reckon so, Matt. Look, I've no internet connection here, so I'll text you some details. OK?'

'Yeah, I'll call you later if I've anythin'. Bye.'

Matt felt the hazel-eyed unblinking stare centre on the back of his head. 'OK, Damon. It weren't about bleach,' he muttered.

'So I gathered. It sounded from here like you were picking up a request to trace someone. A job for yourself? You know it doesn't work like that.'

'But it were only Chrissie. She's an old mate from the Academy. I aint chargin' a fee.' The warm self-righteous feeling twisted into a tight knot behind his V Festival tee shirt.

'I think we need to get a few things straight, Matt. You work for me. All work is channelled through this office. All charging is channelled through this office. Got it?'

'Yeah, but favours are OK for mates, right? And in return... a pint? A meal? She's a mega cook. She could cook us both a meal. What d'you think?'

'I think you should tell me what you've got so far. Let me decide. Some of the stuff you come up with can be quite... unusual. If it needs me cracking into websites, well we may charge money. And if I uncover something very criminal, I may take it to the police. Deal?'

'Yeah, thanks Damon.'

When Chrissie's text pinged onto his mobile seconds later, he handed it to Damon.

'So we've got links to an auction site, a stage production review and a memorabilia site. Interesting,' Damon murmured as he keyed the links onto his screen.

'The Waldringfield Wives? Haven't I heard you mention that play? Wasn't it something to do with tracing a girl last week?'

'Priddy Jones, yeah.'

'She never got back to you, right? Hmm I've got her details as far as you got, and then the trail went cold. I think you should try leaving another message for her, otherwise I might have a trawl myself.'

'Right.' Matt turned back to his computer, sweat beading on his forehead. Now he'd lied twice to Damon.

'You get on with the names on your list, Matt. If I have to break into a website on this one, you can come and watch and learn,' he said, looking up and smiling.

CHAPTER 10

Nick drove into Needham Market on Saturday morning. The narrow High Street, with its mix of old brick and timber framed shops and houses, was choking with traffic. He pulled across the slow stream of cars and into the station yard.

'Where the hell is Jake?' he muttered.

So far Nick's week hadn't turned out as he'd expected. Yes, he was pleased to be back at Willows since Thursday, but already he missed the drama and glamour associated with the film shoot. He kept wondering what they'd be doing, Cooper, Gavi, Priddy and the rest. When old Mr Willows said he was still wanted by Lester whenever he could spare the time, part of him was secretly pleased.

And there'd been Matt's text. Bleach? It was unbelievable. He wasn't surprised Owen replied so quickly to his warning. But why didn't he make some comment when he answered? It was just a text asking to be taken for a taster session canoeing, nothing about the miracle mineral stuff. *Come about 10:30 ish. Will hv changed oil on van by then.* It could only mean he'd recovered.

Nick had arranged to go along with Jake. He was keen to go canoeing again, and who better than with a band mate. The pair of them planned to drive over to Grundisburgh in Nick's car and pick up Owen. If they followed the cross-country B roads, the route took them pretty much directly through Grundisburgh and then on to Woodbridge and the canoeing club.

'Come on, Jake. It's nine forty-five. Where are you?' Nick mumbled.

He swallowed his frustration. This was the first Saturday he'd had off in three weeks, and he wasn't going to spoil it by getting cross.

'Hiya,' he shouted through his open window as he spotted Jake, a canvas sports bag by his feet and wraparound sunglasses covering the upper third of his face. 'Poser,' he added for good measure, and laughed.

He swung the old Ford Fiesta in a wide arc in front of the redbrick station building and drew up near the taxi ramp. While Jake opened the hatchback and slung in his sports bag, Nick selected a CD. 'Florence and the Machine OK for you?' he said by way of a greeting.

'Say My Name? It's on that CD. Yeah I like that one. So what's the rush?' Jake said as he settled into the passenger seat.

'There isn't a rush. It's just that Owen said to be there for half past ten. Something about changing the oil on his van earlier.'

'So remind me about Owen. Another of your friends from Utterly?'

'I wouldn't call him a friend exactly, but yeah, he was on the same carpentry course. He's the reason I was helping out on the film shoot. Remember I told you?'

'Oh yeah. So what's the lowdown on Gavi Monterey? She's starring right? Come on, dish the dirt.'

'Gavi? Well, she's a keen cyclist. And of course she's stunning, but I haven't seen her in the infamous Lycra yet. Dave from work's a big fan.'

While Florence demonstrated her impressive vocal range to an up-tempo beat, Nick eased the Fiesta through the bottleneck road out of Needham Market. Soon they were under the low railway bridge and heading east of the

A14. Nick tried to explain why he felt uncomfortable with Owen, but as the road took them along the sides of shallow valleys and across acres of rolling fields, he almost forgot Owen's arrogance. Instead he felt mildly sorry for him.

'So he's been sacked? And you feel responsible? Sounds like Owen had it coming.'

'Yeah, I suppose so.'

Nick concentrated on driving while Jake drummed his fingers to a rousing chorus filling the car. Soon they were on the so called straight Roman Road into Otley Bottom and then the Grundisburgh Road.

'Not far now,' Nick said as they passed the village green and slowed to negotiate a narrow lane leading to the south of the village. 'We've made good time. It's somewhere along here.'

Bungalows, built in the late 1960s were huddled close to each other, but set back from the road and screened by mature shrubs and hedges.

'He rents it with his girlfriend, Prosecco. She's a make-up artist,' he explained.

'Cool. They must be doing OK for themselves.'

'This'll be the one.'

They parked at the side of the road and got out of the Fiesta, Jake humming the piano riff behind Say My Name, while Nick breathed in the faint scent of hedge rose and honeysuckle. He led the way, his footsteps crunching on gravel as they brushed past an untidy beech hedge. Ahead the drive swept in front of the bungalow, completely hidden from the road and with square plate glass windows staring from pale brickwork, vacant and unwelcoming. A metal pole supported the large concrete slab that passed for a sixties-styled porch. A small white Citroen van was parked to one side.

'Looks as if he must've finished working on the van,' Jake said and then fell silent.

Everything seemed so still. 'Owen? Hi Owen, are you around here somewhere?' Nick called, but in a muted way, reluctant to break the peace.

'I thought you said he was expecting us.'

'I did, or rather, he's expecting me. I hadn't said you'd be coming too.'

Something struck Nick as he took in the scene. It reminded him of a stage set, uninhabited, waiting to come alive with the players.

While Jake stood under the porch and rang the doorbell, Nick gazed at the van. It had been reversed into position and now the windscreen caught the sun. He wandered past a climbing rose and wooden trellis screening the bins by the side of the bungalow and looked more closely. The van didn't appear to be jacked-up. But he could see it had been because a couple of blocks of wood, chocks to stop the van rolling forwards, had been kicked free of the front tyres.

'Untidy, sloppy bugger,' he muttered. But he wasn't surprised, not after his experience with Owen's false wall.

He took his time, circuiting the van. An axle stand rested on its side, just visible on the ground under the sill. A trolley jack, collapsed flat, poked out from under the rear of the van. Nick ambled around to the far side.

He stared at a pair of legs. Nothing moved.

'Owen?'

The back of his neck tingled.

'Hey mate, are you OK?' Nick bent nearer, trying to peer under the van to see the rest of him.

'Hey Owen mate, say something. Don't mess around.' This time Nick thumped the side of the van to get his attention.

And then he saw the pool of dark liquid. His guts twisted. Was it blood? His eyes tried to make it engine oil, but deep inside he knew. The stillness told him.

'Jake. Quick, there's been an accident,' he yelled, as if his lungs would burst.

While Jake came running, Nick steeled himself to touch the legs, shove at them gently and see if he could get a reaction. Nothing.

'What the shit's happened?' Jake whispered, breathless next to Nick.

'I don't know. The van must've fallen on him.'

'Shit, is he OK? Let's try and get him out.'

'We could try and jack it up, but... he's not moving Jake. Take a look under for yourself. It landed on his back and his head. There's blood. I don't think he's breathing.'

'Oh God.'

'I'll call an ambulance.'

Nick moved as if in a dream, disconnected from reality, frozen inside. He held his mobile to his ear and stood by the trellis with its climbing rose. It helped to distance him from Owen's body. An old long-handled broom and a broken wicker cat carrier, discarded near the bins, momentarily distracted him, and then a bee flew into focus and the emergency services answered.

'Yes, an ambulance, and maybe the fire service.... No the van isn't on fire but I reckon they might need heavy lifting gear…. The police? I guess so.' Later, that's all he could remember of the call.

•

'So where's this… Prosecco? You said Owen lives here with his girlfriend, right?' The question was directed at Nick.

Jake leaned against the metal pole while the uniformed policeman sat down next to Nick on the porch step. The paramedics had already confirmed Owen was dead and the policeman seemed friendly enough as he watched Nick's face.

'That's what he told me, yeah. But I don't know where she is.'

'And he sent a text saying he was going to change the oil on his van.'

'Yeah, it's still on my phone if you want to see.'

'So why's he lying on his front? Don't you think that's a bit odd?'

An image of the back of Owen's legs, encased in jeans and lying on the ground, flashed into Nick's mind - one leg stretched out straight; the other rotated, with the knee slightly bent. And his grubby trainers - one sole upwards, exposed to the sky; the other resting sideways on the ground.

'Yeah, it's weird. I suppose you'd expect him to be on his back,' Nick breathed.

'And you're sure neither of you touched any of the jacks or moved the chocks?'

'I haven't touched anything, except Owen – to see if he was alive.' Nick shivered as he remembered the cold denim.

'And you, Jake. You're sure you didn't catch your foot on the jacks or chocks when you came running?'

'Shit no.'

'Everything's as we found it,' Nick added.

'Hmm… so you haven't taken anything, or moved anything. I think I need to make a call,' the policeman said slowly and stood up. They watched him walk down the gravel drive.

Jake looked puzzled. 'What the hell is he getting at? It's perfectly obvious what's happened isn't it? There's been a horrible accident.'

'I think he's wondering why the chocks and the jacks… well, for everything to fail like that? And another thing – if Owen was draining the oil from the sump, which he'd have to before changing the oil or filter, well I didn't notice a bowl or socket-set or….'

'There was a spanner on the ground near the axle jack on its side. I noticed it while you were calling 999.'

'Hmm, well maybe Prosecco knows what he was doing. Where the hell she is?'

'Prosecco? God, she's going to be upset. Do you think we should hang around for her, Nick?'

'I've only ever spoken to her briefly, and I got the feeling she didn't like me much. I don't think she'd want me… us around. I can't see how we'd be any help.'

'So what shall we do? I can't stay here while they remove his body.' Jake's voice caught on the word.

'Yeah, it kinda sick. I noticed a pub as we came through the village. We could drink ourselves legless, or… we could go canoeing?'

'Or both?'

'Shit, this is awful,' Nick groaned. 'Let's see if the police still need us. They've got our names and contact details now.'

CHAPTER 11

'So where was Prosecco? Did you find her?' Chrissie asked. She watched Clive as he threw himself down on her sofa and leaned his head back on the cushions. It seemed like they'd both had a tiring Saturday.

Chrissie had spent the day with Sarah, a friend she'd first met years earlier at an Ipswich fencing club, back in the time when she was still an accountant. By a happy coincidence she also lived in Woolpit. Sarah was bubbly and enthusiastic, so who better to ask to come to Cambridge with her that morning to view a yellow, mid-seventies tin top VW Campervan?

She knew it was a crazy idea. A second hand transit van to carry furniture would be a more sensible buy, but while she flirted with the idea of the Campervan, she didn't want to weather disapproval. Both Nick and Clive would have kept reminding her it was underpowered, need constant maintenance, and without a full rear door would be awkward to load.

Sarah, naturally, could see why she'd like the door and windows along the sides, the bright yellow bodywork, and the quirky fun factor. She even enthused over the hatch-like window at the rear. But the rust eating away the front panel, sills and bottom twelve inches of the Campervan, was impossible to ignore. It blistered and flaked away the paint, leaving dirty, ragged-edged holes.

'It's a rust bucket,' Sarah had said, and Chrissie agreed.

Disappointment and being sensible had sapped her energy. By the time she got home without buying the Campervan, Chrissie felt tired.

It was Clive's turn to cover the weekend and he'd been over in Ipswich most of the day. When he returned hours later, she didn't mention the failed Cambridge trip. Anxious to distract him from the inevitable *I told you it wasn't a good idea* scenario, she'd asked about his day instead.

'You'll never guess what I was called out for?' he'd said, and of course she didn't.

While she made fresh coffee, Clive had explained.

'What?' she'd breathed, incredulous when he casually dropped the names. 'Owen is dead? And Nick and Jake found him this morning? You're kidding me?'

While Clive talked, Chrissie had followed him into her living room. She set the coffee down and watched him, expecting to catch a curve of his lip, some sort of clue he was spinning a yarn. But she could see he was serious, deadly serious.

'You're saying you don't think it was an accident. So where was Prosecco? Did you find her?'

She looked at him on her sofa, now with his head back on the cushions, his eyes closing.

'Hey, don't stop now. You can't fall asleep. Here, drink your coffee.' Impatient to hear more, she sat down beside him and rubbed his shoulder.

Clive half opened his eyes. 'Prosecco was doing the make-up for the bride and bridesmaids at a wedding in Woodbridge. She'd cycled over there with a backpack, and then left her mobile in it.'

'Sounds like hard work.'

'It's only a couple of miles. And it's been a nice sunny day, good for cycling.'

'And good for weddings. Is she fizzy like her name?' Chrissie asked, momentarily distracted.

'I'd say hysterical with grief, more than fizzy. In fact we couldn't get much sense out of her. I'll talk to her again tomorrow, of course. Hopefully she'll have settled a bit by then.'

Chrissie tried to take it all in. While her mind spun, next to her Clive's breathing deepened and within seconds a long gentle snore rippled through the air. She could see he was tired, but she felt irritated. Was he pretending to be asleep just to avoid telling her more? She prodded his shoulder. No, he was definitely out for the count. If her suspicions were unkind, she blamed the nutmeg grater.

'So the run of quiet weekend duties is finally broken,' she murmured. Tomorrow he would be interviewing Prosecco.

While she struggled to make sense of an accident that might not be an accident, she leaned forwards and let her eyes rest on the colourful rug at her feet. Its traditional ethnic design, with the mix of burgundies, midnight blues and pale beige, looked warm against the old boards. Her thoughts churned around while the repeating geometric patterns spelled order. She worried if Nick was OK and focussed on each colour in the design. Every section made part of the whole. She had felt shocked and drained, but now slowly, her exhaustion lifted.

Should she call Nick and offer sympathy? What about supper? She decided to let Clive sleep on - she hadn't even thought about what to cook. And the nutmeg grater? It was still in its opened packaging, waiting for her to trace the post office or depot it had been sent from.

She dug her mobile out of her bag and tapped the automatic dial for Nick. It seemed to ring for ever but eventually he answered, 'Hi?'

'Nick? Is that you?' She didn't recognise the voice.

'No, it's Jake.' The words slurred, 'Nick's driving.'

She made sense of the engine noise. 'Are you both OK? I've just heard about Owen.'

'Yeah, we were the ones who found him. Look, I can't really talk about it. At least Nick wasn't there on his own.'

'A nightmare. So what are you doing?'

'Well…,' there was a long silence, 'we went canoeing in the end, and then we've had a bit of a skinful, at least I have. Not really thinking straight. Look we're OK thanks.'

Road and car noise fuzzed into her ear. Then Jake's voice broke in again, 'Nick says he's OK. Don't worry, Chrissie. Just need to get it out of our system, that's all. Bye.'

While Clive's breathing sounded like waves lapping on a sea shore, Chrissie went through to the kitchen. At least Nick and Jake were OK, if OK meant getting rat-arsed in each other's company. With frustrated energy, she whisked up a marinade for some pieces of chicken and slipped red peppers under the grill. Minutes later she left the charred peppers to cool while she searched out a stock cube and couscous. 'Right, that's supper almost sorted.'

Next she turned her attention to the nutmeg grater. She'd put it up on the shelf with the printer, but now she lifted it down with its packaging and set it on her small kitchen table. First she looked at the box, turning it around, scrutinising every surface, inside and out. She'd originally thought it was a shoebox, and now as she examined it, she realised it was indeed a shoebox but cut down, foreshortened. The logo on the side was the give-away. The label had been torn off, but a bar code and article identifier were still decipherable.

'So what have we got?' she murmured as she flipped open her laptop and keyed in the make of shoe. In seconds she was on the manufacturer's selling site. She keyed the eleven digit identifier into the search box and waited.

'So this is what they wear in Warwickshire, is it?' A black leather sandal filled her screen. No heel to speak of, but with thin straps, delicate and stylish. The amount in the price box made her eyes water.

'Wow,' she breathed. But of course just because the shoebox had once held a woman's sandal didn't mean the rogue seller was female or that he or she had ever bought the sandal.

She turned her attention to the layers of newspaper and bubble wrap filling the box. She knew it was a long shot. Only in a film would the newspaper be some regional freebie, local advertiser, or something associated with a specific town or place. So what had she got? She smoothed the pieces of paper on her table. 'Scraps of a daily national.' It was just her luck.

Finally she checked the outer wrapping with its postage label. It was the only thing left to give her a clue. At least in the payment process on the website, the postage included item tracking, but now she wasn't sure if she could believe anything. A closer look and she'd located the tracking number, but no *sender* or *return to* address.

A quick netsurf and she read *contact the carrier. Make sure you have the tracking number and ask for additional information about the parcel's location.* The advice was for the customer who hadn't received their parcel.

'What if I phoned the carrier and pretended the package hadn't arrived?' But would she be able to charm them into giving the name of the post office or depot where it started its journey? And how would that help?

'Needle in a haystack,' she murmured as she looked up the carrier's contact details.

Charm, in her experience, usually worked better over the phone than with email. But it was early Saturday evening and not necessarily the best time to coax information out of a skeleton weekend workforce, if indeed they took enquiry calls after five o'clock.

She rang the number and listened to the automated message instructing calls to be made Monday to Saturday during normal working hours. 'Great,' she muttered.

Now she was left with the last clue. The nutmeg grater itself. An idea slowly took shape, something she'd been thinking about but not seriously considered before. If her grater looked as if it had been made by the same hand as made the Brighton Pavilion-styled grater, should she buy it as well? Would she be able to track the Brighton Pavilion one back to the seller? Would it lead to the same seller? She keyed in the memorabilia site to check if it was still for sale. It wasn't an auction site, so she knew the price. 'And what a surprise, it's pretty much the same as my Rotunda one.'

It was time to email Matt with her plan and then all she could do was wait.

'Not bad,' she murmured, 'not bad. Less than an hour and supper's almost sorted, Nick's almost OK, the Rotunda grater's almost tracked to where it was posted, and I've almost decided to buy the Brighton Pavilion. God, what an almost Saturday.'

She sighed as she pictured the almost Campervan. Even Owen's death had been almost an accident.

Brrring brrring! Matt? She snatched up her mobile and checked the caller ID.

'Hi Sarah.'

'Hey Chrissie. I've just seen the most wonderful thing. You've got to buy it, honestly you've got to.'

'Buy what? What've you seen?'

'It's yellow, actually very yellow, and it's a van. A Morris Minor 1972 AA breakdown recovery van.' It was obvious she was reading from something. 'It'd be brilliant. What do you think, Chrissie?'

'Are you serious? An old AA van?'

'If you've got your laptop, I'll send you the link.'

'Yes OK, go on then.'

Seconds later and Chrissie clicked on the link. A page in the *Old and Classic* section of a *Vans for Sale* site opened in front of her. The picture of a yellow Morris Minor van filled her screen, glowing like a huge buttercup.

'It's even got a yellow metal sunshield across the top of the windscreen, like a beak,' she squealed.

'And Chrissie, there's an orange flashing light on the roof. Hey don't you think it's fantastic?'

'But Sarah, I can't drive around in a recovery van,' Chrissie yelped.

'What's all the excitement?' Clive asked though a yawn as he wandered into the kitchen. He stared at the yellow image blazing from her computer. 'Hell, Chrissie, you're not serious are you?'

'But what's wrong with it, Clive? It's got rear doors for loading.'

Saturday evening had unexpectedly come alive.

CHAPTER 12

'You're not sayin' much, Matt. You OK?' Maisie had drawn a few steps ahead, and turned to face him as she spoke.

'I was busy thinkin'. Anyroads, how'd I talk to you while you're stridin' away like that?'

'But I don't want to miss the bargains. Early bird an' all that, right?'

'Yeah, yeah Mais.'

'Look, there're a couple of clothes stalls that way. I'll meet you there in ten minutes, OK?'

'Sure.'

Matt was pleased to be left to walk at his own pace between cars and tables roughly aligned in untidy rows. It had been Maisie's idea to visit the Sunday morning car boot sale laid out in a field at Stonham Barns. In a couple of hours she'd be working the Sunday shift on a supermarket till back in Stowmarket, so the early bird start had been ideal. At least it had been for Maisie, who seemed to juggle a series of part-time jobs with varying shifts.

'Go on, take me car bootin' early Sunday mornin', p-l-e-a-se,' she'd wheedled.

'But Mais, it'll hardly be light.'

'Go on, it'll be romantic. We'll have breakfast there.'

So, hungry and sleepy, but with the promise of breakfast, he'd made the short journey on his scooter to pick her up at a quarter to eight. They'd ridden the three and a half miles due east from Stowupland to the car boot sale. It had been, in Maisie's words, 'Awesome.' The Piaggio popped and whined as they'd zipped along the empty road, disturbing three Roe deer, spooking a cat returning from its night on the prowl, and setting hares chasing across fields of wheat stubble. With her arms around his waist, she'd leaned with the scooter, hugged him as they'd waited at a road junction, and then finally whooped and hollered as they passed through Stonham Aspal and turned into the entrance to Stonham Barns.

'See, it's great, yeah?'

'Mega,' he'd grunted. And now he wondered what the hell he was doing ambling over well-trodden grass while brushing shoulders with early bird bargain hunters on a Sunday morning.

He hovered in front of a stall selling DVDs and computer games, his mind still wrestling with the Priddy question. Damon had told him to leave another message for the girl, hoping she'd call back so they'd capture her number. But he hadn't, at least not yet; just as he hadn't told Damon he'd already as good as interviewed her for a spoof student magazine and amassed more than enough information for the debt collectors. So what to do?

And just when he'd thought he'd tucked the Priddy question into a backwater in his brain, Chrissie's Saturday email brought it back. She wanted to buy another grater. He supposed that's when his subconscious must have got to work.

Last night he had tossed and turned in his sleep, twisting his duvet and jettisoning his pillow. When he awoke blurry eyed and exhausted, the shadowy kernel of an idea was already forming. But he needed time to think it through, nurture it and grow it into a plan. Collecting Maisie and the car boot sale wasn't helping.

'Coincidences,' he murmured.

'Coincidences? Don't know that one. If we've got it, it'll be under C,' the stallholder barked.

With unseeing eyes Matt gazed at a stack of DVDs. But in his mind he saw links to the nutmeg grater on the memorabilia site, Chrissie's link to the grater in *The Waldringfield Wives* review, and the Facebook shot of a girl in front of a billboard. Were they really all a coincidence? He heard his own words, *before you go, Priddy – one last question. The prop you're proudest of?* The answer rang clear in his memory. *A nutmeg grater.*

'Phishin' hell. It aint a coincidence.'

He turned and hurried away before the stallholder could speak to him again. That's when his plan dawned in one mind-boggling flash.

'I'll call an' ask her if she made it. I'll say I'm askin' cos if she did then I'll feature it in me article.'

'Who you talkin' to, Matt? What you witterin' on about?'

He spun around, almost knocking the coffee out of Maisie's hand as a mouth-watering aroma of fresh doughnut played into his nose.

'Hey watch out, Matt. I was gettin' us somethin' and now you've nearly sent it flyin'. What's up with you this mornin'?' she screeched.

All he could do was gape and stare.

'Look,' she spoke slowly, 'I said, "see you at the clothes stalls" cos I was gettin' us a coffee. I thought a doughnut might cheer you up.' She sounded cross.

'Thanks, Mais. I was just… it's work. I was thinkin' up a tracin' scam, that's all.'

'Yeah well. So who you tracin'?'

'Priddy.' He took the doughnut and kissed her cheek.

'Awe thanks. Do you really think so?'

'Yeah,' he said, baffled by her smile and reply.

He bit through the sugar icing and into the soft dough. He knew the sugar rush would soon clear his mind and fell into step beside her as they headed for the clothes stalls. *Yeah* was a winner. Good for *yeah*, he thought. It covered most situations when he couldn't follow what she was talking about.

Later that day, when Maisie was back in Stowmarket working her shift, Matt lay propped up on his bed and flipped open his laptop. Within seconds he had the memorabilia site on his screen and then a picture of a wooden nutmeg grater, turned and painted to look like the Brighton Pavilion. He clicked on it.

'Forty quid for that?' he muttered as he read its provenance and looked at photos of The Waldringfield Wives stage production. The grater was shown with the actors mid scene and in pole position.

'Right, here goes.' He pressed *call* on Priddy's number, still captured on his mobile.

The conversation went much as he'd expected. He, supposedly Felix Lighter, an undercover CIA agent with a Suffolk accent, pretended to be an investigative journalist for the Student Chronicle, while she, flattered and surprised, came clean.

'Yes, I'm amazed,' she said. 'You found a picture of my nutmeg grater? Part of me will be sorry to see it sold, but hey, your article might even help to sell it and then someone else can enjoy it. So yes, you can say I made it and of course you can put a picture of it in your article.'

And that was that. Not for the first time, it crossed Matt's mind that he rather liked the sound of Priddy Jones.

He made a decision. He'd email Chrissie with an update but Damon could stay in the dark about Priddy Jones. On a need to know basis, he reckoned Damon didn't need to know about this latest development. Let him find her contact details for the debt collecting clients himself, if he must, but Felix Lighter was going to keep her secret. At least for the moment.

Hi Chrissie. Don't buy the Brighton Pavilion grater yet. I'll be in Bury with Damon 2morrow evening. We may be able to hide a key logger bug on your email for seller to open. Also – think I've found out who made it. No news on Rotunda grater yet.

'That should do it,' he mumbled and clicked send.

He closed his eyes, his stomach now churning. Was the shock of an early morning start for the car boot sale still twisting his guts? Or was it disappointment the summer break was nearly over? Excitement and angst mixed in equal measure as realisation took hold. Tomorrow morning, come nine o'clock, he was due to begin his final year of the Computing & IT course at Utterly Academy. Over the summer he'd missed the computer lab, the canteen, the library, and Rosie the young library assistant, but once he was back at Utterly he knew he'd long for his daily immersion in the Balcon & Mora office. More accurately, he knew he'd got used to the extra cash.

Matt made a mental note to check his new timetable, but he guessed he was back to riding to Bury on Mondays, for the three-till-late session, and Fridays for the occasional half day.

'And Chrissie and Nick?' he murmured.

They wouldn't be coming to the Monday apprentice release days anymore. 'They aint apprentices now.' He'd never see them at Utterly again.

Was that why his stomach churned? For a moment he slipped back to the security of his childhood comic-strip world with its superheroes and super villains. In his mind he flew over the Brighton Pavilion, fired a net at a giant pepper grinder, and put his body between a nutmeg meteor and Ickworth House. Crashing to Earth, he landed on his bed in his mum's semidetached bungalow on Tumble Weed Drive. 'Trojan,' he breathed.

He might not be too good at putting his emotions into words, but he knew what to do. He pressed Nick's automatic dial number.

Nick picked up immediately. 'Hi Matt. I guess you've heard. Thanks for calling, mate.'

'Yeah hi.' And then for good measure, 'Yeah.'

Confused, he had no idea what he was supposed to have heard, but while *yeah* was working for him, he'd stick with it.

'Jake said it was a help seeing his legs first. It kinda gave an idea of what to expect.'

'Yeah?'

'Turned out the poor bloke had been crushed. Can you imagine?'

Matt couldn't imagine and bit back the yeah on the tip of his tongue. Mystified, he waited.

'Shit, Owen used to be on our course. I know he wasn't really a friend but you don't expect people our age to die. Old people yes, but not….'

'Yeah, our age,' he parroted.

'I went up to Ipswich earlier today. Gave my statement to the police. Thought I might as well get it out of the way while it was still fresh in my mind. So that's me done till the inquest. I expect Jake'll have to leave it a day or two. Still hung over, I bet.'

'Yeah,' Matt said, finally absorbing the words crushed, statement and inquest. Was Nick saying Owen was dead? But how? Did he mean crushed to death?

'I suppose now it won't matter Owen's lost his job. So what are you doing?'

'Nothin' much. Back at Utterly tomorrow.' There he'd said what was foremost on his mind while he struggled to take in Nick's oblique meaning. Owen must be dead.

'Tell you what, Matt. I could do with a blast of air. Are you up for a ride around on the Piaggio?'

'Yeah. I'll just check what they're sayin' on the news sites about Owen, then I'll ride straight over.'

'Thanks, mate.'

Matt typed Owen's name along with, crushed and death in his laptop's search box.

CHAPTER 13

Nick threw himself down on the grass at Barking Tye. He stretched out on the expanse of green, soaking up the sunshine while Matt pushed the Piaggio onto its parking stand. They'd ridden a ten mile circuit around the Wattisham Airfield, skirting close to the perimeter and then following the lanes taking them east and south down into Bildeston, before crawling back up to Nedging Tye and Great Bricett. They'd scootered through a vista of hedges and rolling fields with earthy shades of ploughed-in wheat stubble broken by occasional clumps of trees.

'Funny how you can feel on the top of the world, when really you're barely two hundred and eighty feet above sea level,' Nick said, relaxed and feeling almost weightless now the constant buffeting from the wind on the back of the scooter had ceased.

'Yeah. But the airfield's pretty much the highest point round here, so I reckon we are on the top of this bit of the world.'

'Awesome. You don't half get blown away perched on the back of the scooter. God knows what it'd be like if you could get more speed on it.'

By unspoken agreement, they hadn't stopped off at a pub. Matt was driving and Nick knew from Saturday night it wasn't going to help. The uplift from being blown around on the back of the Piaggio and feasting his eyes on nature's quilt would last longer than the best pint of hoppy amber liquid. His mood had lifted, but he wasn't ready to go home yet.

He watched Matt fuss over the scooter. He seemed subdued. Was it due to an unaccustomed sensitivity to his feelings or because Matt didn't know what to say?

'You can talk about the Owen thing if you want, Matt. I've sort of had time to come to terms with it.'

'Yeah, well since you ask, I was wonderin' if you'd managed to warn him about that miracle mineral stuff. I mean, it wasn't what did for him, was it?'

'I texted him as soon as you texted me. But from where I was standing, it looked like he'd been crushed by a Citroen van. I suppose if the van was loaded with hundreds of bottles of the stuff, then maybe it added a few hundredweight. But no, it was a van that did for him, Matt.'

'Yeah, I got that. What I mean is, could it've made him so ill he were careless when he jacked up the van?'

'I don't know. Maybe. But he was well enough to want to go canoeing.'

'See, I feel kinda bad cos I could've told you sooner. I read up about the stuff after we'd been drinkin' last week, but I didn't think to say anythin'. It were only when I was tellin' Damon and… that's when I texted.'

'Well, I keep wondering if it would've made any difference if Jake and I got there earlier. Seems we're all wondering.'

'There weren't much about the accident when I looked it up before I rode over, but I guess if it weren't for the jacks you'd assume he was run over.'

'I reckon the post mortem will be able to tell the difference, Matt.'

They lapsed into a companionable silence. Nick let his mind drift. Funny, he thought, how they all reacted differently. Take Jake. By Saturday evening he'd sunk into alcohol soaked creativity and penned two verses and a chorus on the back of a couple of beer mats. Oil Sump Blues was the working title, and so far, the riff sounded pretty catchy. And how had he distracted himself? Yvonne, the canoeing instructor, had been really sweet, singling him out for special attention during the afternoon. So he'd spent his time between pints of beer on Saturday evening, and sending her text messages he hoped were both witty and poignant. Now, in the soothing warmth of Sunday afternoon, he realised some of the texts may have been lines from the burgeoning Oil Sump Blues.

'So you won't be comin' to Utterly anymore, right?' Matt's voice broke into his thoughts.

'What?'

'I said, so you won't be comin' to Utterly anymore. No more apprentice release days.'

'S'pose not. I'm meant to be fully trained.' He screwed up his eyes and focussed on Matt. 'Are you OK? Another year and you won't be going to Utterly either. Life moves on, and all that.'

'Yeah, sure. But it'll feel different.'

'We'll still be drinking at the Nags Head. Nothing much changes there.'

'Yeah.'

'Hey, that reminds me. On Saturday we landed a gig for the band out at Orford, through a canoeing club connection. So why don't you ride over with Maisie, make an afternoon and evening out of it? I'll text you the date.'

Nick wasn't really sure why he'd referred to Yvonne as a canoeing club connection, rather than call her by her name. He supposed he wasn't ready to be quizzed by Matt. For a moment he imagined an afternoon canoeing around

Orford Ness with her, followed by the gig. With any luck it might prove a winner. But he could see Matt knew him too well.

'So what's this canoein' club connection, then?'

He watched Matt's eyes light up. Yes, he thought, life moves on. That was the whole point about life, however troubling.

•

By Monday morning Nick had successfully banished the Owen episode from the front of his mind, so much so that he'd momentarily forgotten about it as he drove into Needham Market and the Willows parking area. He was more concerned about which client and job he'd been assigned, and if he'd be working alone or with one of the other carpenters. But the memory of Owen was still there, lurking somewhere in the shadows, ready to leap out and grab him if he let his guard down. And his guard? To remember Owen as he had been in life – someone he hadn't disliked, but also someone he hadn't counted as a friend. It was all about the shock of death, and time was beginning to rub the rough edges smooth.

A distant train rumbled and wheezed as it accelerated out of Needham Market and along the line to Ipswich. For a moment he listened, a reminder of the forces of life, working schedules, timetables. Nick locked his old Fiesta and hurried past the secure parking area for the Willows vans and in through the workshop side entrance. The restroom doubled as an office for the carpenters and already it was filled with mumbled greetings. A kettle whistled and requests for sugar in tea rode the stale air. Nick tossed his packed lunch onto the filing cabinets along one wall, as Dave struggled to force his into the small fridge.

'Morning, Mr Walsh,' Nick said. 'What am I doing this week?'

The other carpenters called the foreman Alfred, but Nick couldn't bring himself to drop the formality of "Mr Walsh". It was how he'd addressed the aging carpenter throughout his apprenticeship, and now it felt uncomfortable to change within the space of a couple of days.

'We've had a late delivery of the European oak for Mr Carson's kitchen, Nick. It's put Kenneth right behind. The units are supposed to be completed and ready to fit by the end of the week, and then it's the Moore's kitchen. So I want you and Kenneth making units. See if we can get back on schedule. Tim will lend a hand when he's back from hanging a fire door over at The Beeches.'

'Right.'

No one seemed to have heard about Owen's death. The fatal accident out towards Ipswich had remained a low profile news item, particularly as the Paralympics were still in play, so Nick was thankful to be spared any comments or questions as he sipped his mug of tea and studied the kitchen plans. Dave ambled across, looked over his shoulder and tapped one of the sketches.

'Say you'll make the butcher's-block trolley. That way, if Kenneth's measurements are more than a few mils out, it won't matter as much as a fitted unit,' Dave murmured under his breath.

Nick glanced round. 'Thanks,' he said as he saw Dave's half smile. 'What are you working on?'

'If you'd got here five minutes earlier, you could've volunteered. But someone had to put up their hand, so it seems it's me helping Lester with a construction mock-up of a crashed biplane.'

'What?'

'Yeah, first I'm going to look up the plane on the computer here - familiarise myself with the propellers and the wooden struts and spines making the framework for the canvas wings. Then I'll drive over to their warehouse outside Ipswich. I'll be working over there.'

'What?'

Priddy's words flew back to Nick. Hadn't she said something about a replica plane if he was interested, and having a word with Lester? Did today's request for help with the film set have a subtext?

And something else bothered him. He was sure old Mr Willows had said that Lester wanted him whenever he could spare the time. So why hadn't Mr Walsh simply assigned the job to him rather than ask for a volunteer? Lester certainly wouldn't be expecting Dave.

Dave must have caught his look. 'Hey, it's just a bit of fun for me. When I've found where it is, I'll text you. Lester will be working deadlines, not eight hour days, so why don't you come after you've finished here? But don't expect to get paid. Not unless Alfred sent you.'

'Yeah, I know. It's not on his work schedule for me today.' He knew Dave was star-struck, but it still felt like a betrayal.

At least Kenneth seemed happy enough when Nick volunteered to make the butcher's-block trolley.

'Yes, a thick block for the top. All wood – so you'll need to glue the pieces together to get the ten centimetre thickness.'

'Modern glue or half a tree trunk? It's a no-brainer. I'll get started on that, and then cut the other pieces while the glue's setting.'

The design was straight forward: a butcher's-block top and a drawer underneath; four legs acting as a frame, the front two on wheels; a towel rail doubling as a handle to use to push the trolley; and two slatted-shelves jointed into the frame. He decided to make a list of the pieces he needed to cut and it turned out to be dozens. Undaunted, he threw himself into his task.

The whining clattering rumble from the table saws and thickness planers in the workshop soon drowned any non-work related thought. The noise seemed to insulate, while the ear defenders cocooned. His head was filled with measurements, as he watched rotating blades and protected his fingers. Time flew, lunch flew, coffee and tea breaks flew.

By four o'clock, when Mr Walsh tapped him on the shoulder, Nick was ready to shrug him off and press on with the mortise and tenon jointer.

'Are you intending to go and give Dave a hand? He said he'd sent you a text? Seems Lester has a deadline.'

'What?' Nick pushed his ear protectors off. He hadn't read Dave's text. He hadn't given him a thought and he certainly hadn't had time to check his phone. All he felt was irritation.

'It's four o'clock, Nick. We're starting to pack up here. No overtime for this job.'

'I want to get the last two mortises cut while it's all set up right, then I'll check my phone.'

'OK, but let me know if you decide to go to Althorne House, and I'll charge Lester for your time.'

A couple of mortise and tenons later, Nick brushed up the wood drillings around the machine and put his cut lengths in a neat pile alongside the layers of wood already glued and clamped for the butcher's-block top. Reluctantly, he fished his mobile out of a back pocket. He couldn't put off reading Dave's text any longer.

Can you get to Althorne House by 5 pm? Need help dismantling fake wall, ready for filming schedule 2morrow.

'But?' He read the text again.

So it wasn't a mistake. Alfred really had meant Althorne House. Dave's obsession with the film stars was almost amusing, but his apparent willingness to edge Nick out of the way when it came to working on the set, really hurt. Still piqued, he'd determined to say, 'No way,' to driving over to Ipswich after work. But now he'd been wrong-footed. He couldn't use the excuse of working overtime at Willows, and dismantling a fake wall was a two-man job. Dave obviously needed help.

'He can sweat a bit. I'll make him wait till five to see if I turn up,' he muttered.

By the time Nick drove over to Moats Tye and on to Althorne House, it was close on five o'clock. He knew Dave would have taken a Willows van to the Ipswich warehouse, and sure enough, a Willows van was now parked on the gravelled area to the side of the house, alongside the refreshments trailer selling coffee, tea and all-day bacon baps.

Nick pulled up in the shade cast by a mature sycamore and got out of his Fiesta, lifted his toolbox from the hatchback and strolled over to the van.

'Hi,' he said, slapping its metal side as he looked through the driver's open window.

'Agh,' Dave choked, mid bacon-bap bite.

'Hey, I thought you'd be inside, watching Gavi or Cooper.' He waited while Dave coughed, retched and then swallowed.

'There's,' he cleared his throat, 'there's more action out here. That Cooper bloke, he and Gavi were definitely an item earlier.' His voice cracked and gravelled as he smothered another cough. 'And the girl frying up the bacon in the trailer here, well don't expect a bacon bap for a while because,' he coughed again, eyes watering, 'she's just nipped out the back of the trailer and headed off with him into the shrubbery.'

'So how long've you been sitting out here? I thought you were making broken biplanes somewhere in Ipswich.'

'I was, but Lester got a call from Merlin. A sudden change in schedule. So I guess I've been here about half an hour.'

'Any messages for me from Lester?'

'Should there be?'

'S'pose not.' He felt silly. 'Look, I'll go on in before they start wondering where we are. And don't choke on the rest of your bap, Dave.'

It was only as he walked through the side entrance and into the cool of the passageway that he wondered if Prosecco would be at work. A week's compassionate leave seemed the minimum scenario after finding your boyfriend crushed to death on your front drive. But of course, she hadn't found him had she. He slowed his pace. He let his eyes run along the floor ahead, and tried to imagine how Prosecco would have taken the news. He no longer saw the old boards, part covered with sisal and jute runners. Instead, an image of a pair of legs in jeans and trainers sticking out from under a white Citroen van flashed into his mind.

He stopped, mid-step, his whole consciousness suspended for a second, and then just as instantly, the image vanished. He expected to feel his chest tighten, but it didn't. In fact all he sensed was a shadow of foreboding, a much lighter touch than the stomach-gripping dread when he'd first spotted Owen's legs.

'Hi.' The word seemed to strike from nowhere.

'What? Oh hi, Prosecco.' He inhaled his surprise. She stood facing him. Had he conjured her up, just by the power of thought?

'You look surprised to see me,' she said, her voice a little sharp against her wan complexion.

'Well yes I am. I mean, I was miles away. How... how are you?'

'How'd you expect me to be?'

'I-I don't know. Feeling awful, I suppose.' He knew he must sound clumsy, but he hadn't expected.... The passageway became claustrophobic.

'You found him, didn't you?'

'Yes. We called 999 and waited around afterwards, you know in case we could be any help to you, or at least so you wouldn't be alone, but—'

'We?'

'Yeah, Jake and me. He's a canoeing mate. Why?'

'I thought it was just you... and O-Owen.'

'Look, Prosecco. I'm really sorry—'

'What? That you didn't get there any sooner?'

'Yes... no, I mean, it's just so tragic. We got there when I said we would. I just feel so sorry for you and Owen and... well the whole thing sucks.'

'Thanks for finding him and calling for help.'

'That's OK. I suppose it's better than you finding him later on. Will you stay there? It looked a nice bungalow.'

'I don't know. Still trying to get my head round everything. All I know is I've got to keep working if I'm to pay the rent.'

'At least while you're working you're with other people.'

'Yes, there is that.' For a moment she looked wistful, then shrugged and walked past him.

'And you've a cat?' he said remembering the broken wicker cat carrier. But he spoke to empty space.

He turned and watched as she moved on in an unhurried fluid way, her hair so right for a Prosecco – short, blonde and curly; so reminiscent of a light sparkling wine. Does it grow like that naturally, or do you style it to match your name, he wondered.

'Poor Prosecco,' he breathed. Life could be such a bitch.

CHAPTER 14

Chrissie hardly registered the sound of the delivery truck's shuddering engine and its distinctive diesel rattle, as it moved slowly out of the courtyard and back along the track to the Wattisham Airfield perimeter lane. Her thoughts were solely on the American black cherry, now lying in a neat stack on the barn workshop floor.

'It was lucky they had it in stock. Pity they couldn't deliver on Saturday, though.'

'Well, first thing Monday morning is the next best thing, and you can hardly say it's held you back more than an hour or so, Mrs Jax.' Ron eased himself off his work stool and walked stiffly over to the pile of wood.

'Come on, let's have a proper look at it on the workbench,' she said, cutting the ties and freeing the lengths of board, seven centimetres thick and thirty wide. The uneven finish didn't do it justice, and she ran her fingers over the fine textured surface, tracing the grain as it flowed along the wood.

'I love these darker areas,' she said.

'I think they were gum pockets. Come on, let's look at all the boards and then you can decide which pieces you'll cut the legs from, and which have the best grain for the plant stand tops.'

This was one of the highlights of her job: handling the raw material, letting the grain patterns themselves decide how to use the wood best, giving it voice, and then picturing the finish on a drawer front, a tabletop or a chair back. Ron stood opposite, helping to turn the boards. She guessed he too would be getting the same buzz from seeing the character and features in the quality wood, and smelling the natural oils and resins. Simply heaven. It never failed to deliver. The whole experience was akin to a state of true happiness, and without the need for humming or meditation.

Within an hour, she had assigned the selected boards and was busy measuring out rough widths and lengths before marking out her first table-saw cut.

'Coffee, tea?' Ron called from one end of the workshop.

'Tea please, Mr Clegg. Goodness, is that the time? I meant to call the carrier at nine o'clock, but the wood arrived and... damn, damn, damn.'

'Which carrier, Mrs Jax? Why?'

'I want to track the nutmeg grater. I need the sender's contact details.'

'Ah.... You make your call now and I'll put the kettle on.'

While Ron fussed with the kettle, Chrissie banished all thoughts of Arts & Craft-styled plant stands. It was time to concentrate on couriers and parcel tracking numbers. She'd scribbled it all down when she was at home, but now as she read her writing, she felt less certain. Should she pour out the truth about how she'd been duped, or summon the angst of a customer whose parcel hadn't arrived? With deliberate slowness, she picked up her phone and keyed in the courier's number.

'Hello, how can I help?' The words were non-confrontational, the voice efficient.

'I'm trying to track a parcel–'

'Tracking number please?'

Chrissie read out the sequence.

'Just a moment… yes the parcel was delivered to a… Clegg Cabinet Making and Furniture Restorers on August the 30th.'

'But–'

'The parcel was delivered to the delivery address last Thursday, four days ago. If you have any issues, then please contact the sender. Anything else, Madam?'

'Can you tell me the sender's details?'

'Were they on the package? An address for returns?'

'No.'

'Then the sender wanted it withheld. We get this with box numbers, free-samples, returns, gifts, and parcelling and wrapping services. It's not unusual.'

'But you've got the details up on the screen in front of you, haven't you?'

'I've got that it was a *tracked delivery within a week* deal. Regular clients have account numbers, but I can't tell anything from looking at my screen, Madam.'

'But can you tell me if the sending depot where it started its journey was in Warwickshire? Pl-e-ase.'

'The depots have serial numbers not addresses.'

'But pl-e-ase.' Chrissie hoped she sounded broken, hollow, desperate - a chord designed to win over the most unreceptive ear.

'It's not in Warwickshire. Now anything else, Madam?'

'Thank you. That's really helpful. You've been incredibly kind.'

'No problem. The depot code is 058. Now have a nice day.' The call ended.

'What? Zero…?' Chrissie wasn't sure if she'd heard correctly. It was as if the information had been slipped in as an afterthought, barely loud enough to hear. She grabbed a pencil and scribbled 058 before she forgot the numbers.

'Any success, Mrs Jax?' Ron asked as he set down a mug of strong tea for her.

'I don't know. The courier's depot code for the parcel is 058 and 058 isn't in Warwickshire.'

'So we know where it didn't come from. But depot codes? Why can't they just use names?'

'Because it would make life too easy, and codes fit neatly onto spreadsheets.' Chrissie sipped her tea. She was deflated by the one step forwards and two steps backwards situation.

She decided she'd pass this latest snippet of information to Matt and concentrate on the American black cherry. There was a limit to how much time she could spend on her search, particularly as internet access at the workshop was frustratingly slow and unreliable. It didn't take her long to send the text message, after all there wasn't a huge amount new to say other than a depot code number.

Several hours later, after frequent mugs of tea, a rushed lunch break, and resurrecting the tapering jig for the table saw, Chrissie stood and admired the wood. It was now transformed into numerous tapering legs, and thickness-planed sections ready to cut into aprons, curving brackets, shelves and tops.

'Thanks for helping me to divide some of the cherry, thickness-wise on the band saw, Mr Clegg.' She felt she was flying.

'No problem, but a little advice from an old hand who's messed up plenty at this stage. You've done a lot today and it's already well after four o'clock. Why don't you stop now and start again when you're fresh tomorrow? Now is when you'll begin to make mistakes. Believe me.'

She knew he was right. 'But Mr Clegg...,' her voice drifted as she remembered something Clive had said, just before leaving for work that morning. She hadn't given it much thought at the time, but now his words came back.

'I should finish on time today,' he'd said, 'so I'll make supper. You're not going to be late are you, Chrissie?' And then he'd left before she'd had a chance to ask what he was going to cook, and if sufficient ingredients were in her fridge. Yes, it would be nice to get home at a reasonable time and spend the evening with Clive.

'OK, Mr Clegg, you're probably right. I'll call it a day.'

She took her time driving cross-country back to Woolpit. The TR7 seemed to come alive in the warmth of the late afternoon, and with the hood down, the air breezed pleasantly across her arms and worried her short blonde hair. Did she really want to drive a transit van, Campervan, or a Morris Minor AA breakdown recovery van? Even with the windows fully open it was going to be a pretty tepid experience by comparison. And how often did she really need to transport furniture around? 'Hmm, but the plant stands won't get to Aldeburgh by themselves,' she reasoned.

Clive's car was nowhere to be seen as she drew up outside her small Suffolk-brick end-of-terrace cottage. She glanced at the stone plaque bearing the date 1876, high on the front wall of the middle cottage. By force of habit she automatically added and subtracted.

'A hundred and thirty-six years. I hope my plant stands survive as long.'

Mildly disappointed but hardly surprised to be home before Clive, she unlocked her front door and dropped her keys on the narrow hall table. She headed to the kitchen and another mug of tea, but before she'd had a chance to fill the kettle, her mobile burst into life. Clive's ID showed on the screen.

'Hi, Clive.'

'Hey, something's come up. I'm really sorry, but I haven't left work yet and I'm going be a little late.'

'Don't worry. Do you want me to start the cooking or…?'

'Oh no, I'd forgotten. I was going to cook wasn't I?'

'Yes, but that's OK. I can rustle something up, or we can walk to the White Hart and eat there. Or if you're going to be really late, you could grab a bite your end.'

'Look, I shouldn't be too long. We've just had the preliminary post-mortem findings through on Owen, and there are some things which need checking. But it's only a question of organising other people.'

'Oh good. Not about Owen, I mean about it not taking too long.'

'OK, then? See you in about an hour or so. Bye.'

Curiosity offset disappointment. Apart from the obvious question of whether she was cooking or waiting for Clive to demonstrate his culinary skills, there was the *would they be too late to eat at the White Hart* factor to consider. There was also a far more interesting question. What was the latest on Owen?

She decided to take a practical approach while she waited for the kettle to boil.

'Hmm, not very promising,' she muttered as she checked the crisper drawer on the lowest shelf in the fridge.

Sad lettuce wilted next to a handful of tomatoes and shrunken dried-out mushrooms. If she threw together some pizza dough it would be ready to make a pizza by the time Clive got home. Mozzarella, parmesan and some basil plucked from the pot on her scrubbed pine counter would soon dress-up the leftover tomato paste, fresh tomatoes and mushrooms. He was much more likely to speak freely about the Owen case if he was eating at home.

'Never let it be said I'm a schemer,' she mumbled as she measured out flour and stirred in yeast, warm water, olive oil and a pinch of salt. By the time she'd used up the last of her energy kneading the dough, she was ready for her mug of tea.

'Right – dough to rise in bowl under tea towel, pizza stone ready in oven to heat when oven set to come on in… forty minutes, wine & beer in fridge, mug of tea in hand – yes, time to sit down.' She headed for the living room.

A wave of exhaustion washed over her, pulling her down to the sofa and channelling her thoughts towards oblivion. Leaden arms sank onto cushions while her sluggish head lolled back. She couldn't fight it. Unresisting, she drifted into sleep. A dreamless, bottomless sleep.

'Chrissie, Chrissie.' The voice sounded thready, distant. For a moment the word had no meaning. It didn't connect. 'Chrissie?' There it came again, but it wasn't relevant to her.

'Chrissie!' She tried to ignore it, but the voice seemed closer, louder, insistent. And then she was awake. Dragged back to consciousness from somewhere so still and dense, it had no memory, no texture.

'Hey, Clive,' she murmured, focussing on his face as she took in her surroundings. 'I must have dropped off. How long have you been back?'

'Long enough to save us from the pizza dough. It was about to escape from its bowl and take over the kitchen. Are you OK?'

'Yes, I think so. I came over tired, that's all.'

'Do you want me to roll out the dough and pop a pizza in the oven for us?'

'That would be nice,' she said, thinking how it was funny the way situations turned around, and now he was the one helping her with dinner.

She eased herself up from the sofa, picked up her mug of cold tea, and followed him through to the kitchen.

'So tell me about your day,' she said, emptying her mug into the sink.

While Clive knocked the dough back, gave it a quick need and rolled out a portion into the size of a twelve inch pizza, he seemed relaxed. It was as if the activity released his tongue.

'Of all the days to die in suspicious circumstances, Saturday has to be the worst. The labs are virtually closed the whole weekend, and as for a post mortem, you're lucky to be squeezed in for Monday.'

'Is this about Owen?' she asked, getting a beer for Clive and retrieving the ingredients for the pizza topping out of the fridge.

'Hmm.'

'So how did he die?'

'Crushed. Definitely crushed. The underside of the van fractured the back of his skull, and his nose and chin were smashed on the concrete and gravel. And if that hadn't been enough to do for him, his chest was crushed, so his ribs were also smashed along with a couple of vertebrae. There was nowhere for his heart and lungs to go, so the sudden squashing force tore his diaphragm, and drove his guts out.'

'Drove his guts out?'

'Well if he hadn't been lying on his front, it might have been enough to rupture his abdomen. As it was, it gave him traumatic femoral and inguinal hernias. At least that's what the pathologist called them.'

'So he hadn't been bashed around the head and then placed under the car?' Chrissie felt mildly light-headed as she watched Clive skin and coarsely chop the tomatoes.

'The van has been taken away to be checked over, but there was certainly blood on its under surface at the time. As I said, the SOC team took specimens, but everything waited for Monday before even beginning to be analysed. So we didn't have anything much to go on till late this afternoon.'

'But what other things were you asking people to do? At least that's what you said when you called.'

'Ah yes, Owen had pieces of wicker impaled in one hand. An oil sump spanner might have made sense. But why bits of wickerwork? I sent the team back to scour the area for anything to explain it. Luckily for us, the rubbish isn't collected till tomorrow, so some poor bugger in the team's got a load of bin bags to sort through as well as sweepings from all around the area.'

'And that's your case? All you've got?'

'Well no, the toxicology results and the full post-mortem results – stomach contents, microscopy of kidneys, liver, etcetera are still to come through. And the jacks and chocks are being dusted for fingerprints and checked for any faults or signs of interference. And also I thought I'd get Owen's mobile dusted for prints as well.'

'Why his mobile? What can that possible tell you?'

Clive paused for a moment and looked more closely at the mushrooms. 'I don't know. For completeness I suppose. Anyway it didn't take them long because there weren't any prints. It had been wiped clean. Do you think these mushrooms are OK?'

'Yes, they'll be fine. Just slice them up. So what's the relevance of no prints?'

'Owen wasn't wearing gloves, so how did his phone get into his pocket without his prints on it? Odd, don't you think?'

'I guess....' She let her voice fade as she thought it through.

'It was a touch screen mobile. If you look at the screen with the light catching it just right, you can sometimes even work out the key code from greasy fingertip marks. There are always finger and palm prints on mobiles. It was wiped. But why? That's the question, Chrissie.'

'Because someone other than Owen was looking at it or using it? Someone who didn't want anyone to know? I'd say it's intriguing.'

'Of course we've asked for his call record now, and someone is working on unlocking his phone, but....'

'I expect my phone probably tells you what I've been doing half the day.'

'Traces of flour, wood dust and whatever was lurking at the bottom of your bag?'

'Exactly,' she said, and lunged out and tweaked his ribs.

'Aghh!' He choked on a laugh.

'Got you! Here, some fresh basil to go on before you put it on the brick. Eight to ten minutes top shelf, 220C.'

'Shall I make a second one?'

'I only fancy a small slice, so don't make another on my account. I've kinda lost my appetite after hearing about squashed hearts and lungs.'

'Yes, it's a bit sick isn't it? Enough of work. So what's the latest van, yellow or otherwise, you're thinking of buying?'

CHAPTER 15

Matt gazed around the library. He hadn't set foot across its threshold for almost four weeks, and now he drank in the bookshelves, computers, and large windows with the views across the Academy gardens. It felt better than he had expected to be back and starting the second and final year of the computing and IT course. His eyes darted involuntarily to the library assistant's station. Where was Rosie? It was Monday, the first day of the autumn term, and he'd assumed she'd be there.

A twinge of anxiety threatened to engulf his exhilaration. He already knew Chrissie and Nick wouldn't be around on Mondays, and now it seemed Rosie had gone as well. His comfort blanket was worse than threadbare. It had developed gaping great holes.

The old floorboards stretched the length of the library. Downcast, he avoided the other students and ambled along the lines, heading for his favourite computer station, out of the way near the wall.

'Hi, Matt. You look as if you've had a good summer.'

'What? Hey Rosie!' He looked up from his study of the tramlines to see a girl with a smiling face and auburn hair scooped into a careless ponytail.

'Hey, I thought you... you aint left have you, Rosie?' Concern tinged his sudden relief.

'Why d'you say that, Matt?'

'I dunno.' His face flamed. 'Yeah, I had a good summer. Got me tan at the V festival.'

'Maybe not all you got,' she murmured, eyes on his tee shirt.

'Oh this?' He smoothed the cotton fabric encasing his chest.

'Yes, *The A Team*,' she said, reading out the writing on his tee. 'That's an Ed Sheeran song, isn't it? I probably sound a bit sad knowing that, but I'm a fan. He was at the V this year, wasn't he? I wish I'd been able to go.'

'Yeah well,' he stroked his beard and hoped Rosie would see his uncanny resemblance to Ed. 'He were great live.'

She smiled. 'You'll have to tell me about it another time. It's a bit hectic today. We've lots of new students needing to be shown how to use the library system.' And with a last glance at his tee, she hurried away.

He knew Maisie had picked a winner when she'd given him the tee shirt as a *something new to wear* for his first day back at Utterly. He liked the sound wave represented in black across the front of the sand-coloured cotton. It was suitably techie. If you knew about these things, he figured you probably wouldn't need the title written in words. It would be obvious from the sound wave pattern. But at least it was in small lettering and people had to get close to read it. Rosie's reaction had been amazing.

By contrast, he had taken a less subtle approach when he'd chosen a tee for Maisie. A full face shot of Ed on peach-coloured cotton. He reckoned the memorabilia site had done him proud.

It didn't take him a moment to log onto the computer and into the Academy site, his mood buoyed up by the knowledge that Rosie, his favourite library assistant, would still be around. He scrolled through the module titles for the second year of the computing and IT course, rolling his tongue around the familiar words in a mix of Suffolk and occasional Estuary, as he read out, '*Programmin' II, Computer Architecture, Mathematics for Computer Science II, Advanced User Interface Design, Computer Game Technologies, Software Engineerin' II, Website Design & Construction, Computer Security & Forensics*, and… there's flamin' loads.'

He wasn't complaining, he'd read the list before. The first year had been largely a foundation and many of the topics were being visited again, but at greater depth.

'Trojan,' he murmured.

Next he clicked on the timetable and the allocated tutors' names. He had intended to check through it days ago, even up until late the evening before, but his courage had failed. He hadn't wanted to face any trouble with Damon if he couldn't make it to Bury on Monday afternoons.

Mr Smith's name popped up. It seemed the head of the department, would be featuring more in the second year.

'Spammin' hell, I'm meant to be at his tutorial.' Matt looked again, angst gripping his stomach. 'Frag. It started at nine o'clock… but it's been cancelled.' He took a deep breath, the sudden seismic shift in his world settling. 'Old Smith must've reckoned no one'd turn up so early first day. Seems he's set some readin' instead. Yeah, I'm cool with that. Hey, and that's mega – Monday afternoons are still free.'

He leaned back in his chair, the whole morning stretching ahead, begging to be filled with uninterrupted computing and reading. Life in the second year was going to be OK after all.

When Matt's phone pinged a text message alert an hour later, he distractedly pulled it from his pocket. 'Hey

Chrissie,' he murmured, surprised but pleased, and opened the message.

I phoned the carrier just now and the depot code is 058. They said 058 isn't in Warwickshire. The parcel was delivered to the correct address on time & undamaged, so they wouldn't give sender details. Chrissie.

058? I'm on it, he texted back. It would be a break from brushing up on programming languages. 'OK,' he whispered as he checked Chrissie's earlier texts and emails for her parcel carrier details. He keyed the carrier into Google search and quickly found a webpage for the carrier titled *Find your nearest depot by entering your postcode.*

'Yeah well, that's the whole point, I aint got the sender's postcode.' He pulled at his beard. Now what to do, he wondered, and on the spur of the moment entered Chrissie's postcode.

'*058 / Ipswich Industrial Estate, Ipswich,*' he read aloud, surprised and confused by the result. He checked again. 'Blog Almighty, it is Ipswich!' But was Ipswich the sending depot or receiving depot?

'Or both?' he breathed, picking up a girlish scent of roses and peonies.

'I've always thought of this as a quiet area in the library, except when you're sitting here.'

'What? Oh hi, Rosie.'

He looked up to see Rosie standing next to him, a pile of books in her hands and her eyes on his computer screen.

'I can't think what you're finding so exciting on that computer, but do me a favour, don't burst into song.'

'What?'

'Only joking, Matt. Just remember you're no Ed. Some of those new students think they're a bit special.' She moved away as she spoke, tossing the words back to him.

He watched her drift across the library and drop the pile of books onto a table near the photocopier. He guessed they were for the group of students hanging around close by. Her action seemed theatrically deliberate from where he was sitting. Was it some kind of message, he wondered. So did she think he looked like Ed or not? He turned his mind back to the thorny issue of depot 058. It felt like safer ground.

By midday Matt's internal clock was crying out for food. It was time to grab a quick sausage and chips from the canteen before riding his scooter out to Bury and Damon's internet people tracing agency. There wasn't anyone from his course amongst the crush of students at the canteen door, so with his backpack slung over one shoulder he quietly wormed his way into the queue and waited to be served the Utterly Academy's version of a take-out meal.

Hugging the warm polystyrene package, he trudged down the main staircase, followed the trail of students through the Utterly Mansion entrance hall, and sauntered out into the mild September air.

The ride over to Bury cleared his head, the wind chasing away his niggling insecurities. By the time he stood waiting for Damon to open the Balcon & Mora office door, he was happily licking ketchup from the corner of his lips and his world was back in regular orbit.

'Hi Matt,' Damon said opening the door, his hazel eyes widening as he stared.

'Hiya.' Matt pulled off his helmet.

'Is that blood?'

'Nah, ketchup. I ate me last sausage on the way. 'Fraid me tongue aint long enough to get the bits on me visor. Least not while I'm ridin'. Thought I'd bring it up here an' wipe it down instead. OK?'

'Sure.'

'I've still got some chips if you want any?'

'No thanks, Matt. But thanks for the offer.'

Matt moved around the cramped office, shedding his denim jacket onto the back of his chair, tipping water onto a paper towel and rubbing lunch from the inside of his visor. It seemed like a good moment to ask Damon how he'd got on with his search for Chrissie's rogue seller.

'Your friend, Chrissie Jax?' Damon said. 'I'm still trying to get into the managing setup of the selling site. I'm using a password breaker for the login, but it's proving a bit tricky. The programme's still running, so no results yet.'

Matt settled into his plastic stacker chair, faced his blank computer screen and swigged down a mouthful of bottled water.

'What I don't get,' Damon continued, 'is why she sent those two other links with a different nutmeg grater on them. What's the relevance?'

'Cos with Chrissie, she sees wood like say… I see numbers. It's about patterns, similarities. It's a carpentry thing. She thinks the Rotunda an' Brighton Pavilion graters were made by the same person.'

'She is alright is she, this Chrissie Jax?' Damon tapped his head.

'Yeah, course she is. She wants to buy the Brighton Pavilion grater to see if it's the same seller.'

'And how's that going to help? I thought you said she wasn't crazy.'

'She reckons we could do a bit of phishin', install a key logger, a Trojan, somethin' to trace the Brighton Pavilion seller–'

'And use the information to see if it matches the Rotunda seller?'

'Yeah, somethin' like that. I mean she don't need to actually pay for it. She could make some email enquiries, then pull out.' Matt already knew the Brighton Pavilion trail would lead back to Priddy, but he wasn't going to say anything. His face burned.

'Neat.'

'Yeah, Chrissie's sharp. She managed to get the depot code from the parcel carrier. The one deliverin' the Rotunda grater. 058. I looked it up. It's the Ipswich depot.'

'Now that's interesting. I seem to remember Warwickshire being mentioned. So what was the receiving code, you know, where it started its journey?'

'058 is all they told her.'

'Only one depot? Sounds like the sender is closer than Warwickshire.'

'Yeah, Suffolk.' And then Matt made the connection. If Chrissie was right, and she usually was, then Priddy could be behind both nutmeg graters. He'd already traced her to Ipswich. She'd told him she lived in a flat somewhere off the Norwich Road. And now he'd discovered the carrier depot was in Ipswich. It seemed like too much of a coincidence.

'I could hide a key logger bug on an attachment,' Damon said as if he was thinking out loud. 'Yes, Chrissie could send an email asking the Brighton Pavilion seller if it's similar to a nutmeg grater she's already bought, and attach a file with a picture of the Rotunda grater and the hidden key logger. If the seller opens the file to look at the picture, then–'

'The bug is planted.'

'Exactly.'

Matt stared at his blank computer screen. Would Damon ever be able to find out from the key logger that he, a.k.a. Felix Lighter, had already made contact with Priddy, knew her phone number, email address and virtually where she lived? And also that he already knew she'd made the Brighton Pavilion nutmeg grater? He felt his guts twist.

'Are you OK, Matt?'

'Yeah.'

'Good. I've just remembered. Did you leave another message for Priddy Jones?'

'Flamin' malware,' Matt breathed. 'Yeah,' he said, turning in his chair to look Damon straight in the face.

'Good. And by the way, you've a blob of... ketchup on your tee. It's kind of changed the sound wave profile for *The A Team* into... *Drunk*.'

CHAPTER 16

'Hi Nick. It's Clive. I hope I haven't called at too inconvenient a time but I need to have a word with you, ask you a few questions.'

Nick held his mobile close to his ear. He knew Clive as Chrissie's boyfriend, but he didn't always feel entirely at ease with him. Perhaps it was the policeman thing. 'But I've already given a statement. What more...?' His mouth felt dry.

'Yes I know, and that's fine. But the situation has moved on from when we thought Owen's death was a tragic accident, something to do with the way he'd set up the jacks. Now it seems there are one or two inconsistencies.'

'Inconsistencies?'

'Yes. You may be able to shed some light on a few things. But there's no immediate urgency.'

'Oh good, because I'm at work at the moment. Well, I'm on my lunch break, but I'm in the Willows workshop today.'

'Needham Market? That's OK,' his voice soothed, 'Perhaps I can call in and see you?'

'What here? Now? I'm not sure that's....' The words died on Nick's tongue.

'I can call in on my way home after work, if that's easier. Or if you'd prefer, I can drop in to see you at home. Barking Tye isn't it? Not that far out of my way. Otherwise I'm afraid it means a trip to Ipswich for you.' Nick caught the edge in his voice.

'No, that'll be fine, Clive. Home will be fine. What time?'

They settled on five thirty, and Nick slipped his mobile back into his pocket, an ear burning and a fissure tearing through his stomach. He tossed the half-eaten sandwich back into its cling film wrap, his appetite gone. What inconsistencies, he wondered. What light could he possibly shed on anything? And now Clive had him thinking about Owen's death again and he didn't want to.

Most of the staff didn't know, and that's how he wanted it to stay. But a visit from Clive would change everything. He guessed Dave would have heard from Lester, but Dave knew when to ask questions and when to stay quiet, and at the moment he was over in Lester's Ipswich warehouse working on the replica biplane. Just picturing Dave working with Lester merely added more salt to the wound.

There was nothing else for it but to throw himself into his work. He tried to focus as he headed back to his workbench. The butcher's-block trolley was almost ready to be fitted together, but initially without glue.

Nick lost all sense of time as he put tenons into mortises, and sanded and planed the European oak to make fine adjustments and snug joints. He knew to leave the legs the same length at this stage. Shortening the front ones for the wheels could wait until the end.

'It looks good. Nice job, Nick,' Kenneth said.

'Can you give me a hand with these bar cramps when I'm glued up?'

'Sure.'

Nick didn't want to admit it out loud, but the butcher's-block trolley was turning out well.

By the time he drew up in Barking Tye and parked outside his parents' house, dominated by steel and glass panels, he'd almost managed to forget about Owen. 'Five o'clock,' he sighed as he checked his watch. There was still time for a quick shower and change from his work clothes. He let the smoked-glass front door swing closed behind him before taking the open-tread stairs two at a time.

'Hey, Mum, I'm home,' he called from the upstairs landing, his voice sounding through the house. 'I'm going to take a quick shower. A friend's dropping round in about half an hour. OK?' He didn't wait to listen for her reply. What could she say? It's inconvenient? And on a need to know level, he reckoned he could spare her the detail that a detective inspector was calling round to interview her only child about a dead body.

'One day,' he murmured, imagining having enough money for his own place.

When the doorbell chimed on the dot of five thirty, Nick ignored the sudden tightening in his guts.

'I'll get it, Mum. It'll be Clive,' he called as he hurried to open the front door before she came out of the kitchen.

'Hi,' he said, now conscious he must look scrubbed and clean, as if he'd made an effort. Would his appearance infer guilt? But guilt for what?

'Hello, Nick. I'm sorry to trouble you like this, but it won't take long.' Clive seemed relaxed, his smiling eyes giving no hint of threat and the sharp edge to his voice on the earlier phone call a false memory.

'Come on in. Tea, coffee, a beer?'

'No thanks, but don't let me stop you having something.'

Nick watched Clive glance around the downstairs open plan living area.

'It's OK. Mum's in the kitchen. We're kind of open plan, but the kitchen's got a door. She won't come in.'

'Right,' Clive said, sitting down on the sofa. 'I'll come straight to the point. We've been looking at Owen's phone. You know the kind of thing, his last calls and texts.'

'Yeah… but why?'

'What time did he ask you to pick him up on Saturday?'

'Ten thirty. But I thought I'd already said. You can take a look for yourself if you don't believe me.' Nick sat down next to Clive and opened his message log. 'Here… his texts will be under *Owen*,' he said handing his phone to Clive.

'Thanks Nick.'

'I'm only showing you because….'

But why was he showing Clive, he wondered. Was he mad? He imagined a solicitor saying, 'Don't give the police anything you don't have to.' Except he had nothing to hide, at least he didn't think he had. And then he recalled some of his texts to Yvonne. His cheeks flamed. So while Clive scrolled back through Owen's messages, Nick felt anxious in case Clive took a look under *Yvonne*.

'This is interesting,' Clive murmured.

'What? What's interesting?' Nick asked too quickly.

'You sent Owen a text warning him off some miracle mineral solution. What was that about?'

'Owen told us about it when we met in the Nags Head. You can ask Chrissie, she'll remember. I guess it's some kind of cure all. Matt wondered if it'd help his sunburn, but when he looked it up he realised it was basically bleach. Reckoned it wouldn't help with his tanning routine.'

'But why text Owen about it?'

'Because…,' Nick thought for a moment. 'Matt reckoned from his reading it could have made Owen ill. He didn't have his number so he asked me to pass on the warning. Funny thing is, Owen made no comment and came straight back asking me to take him canoeing.'

'You don't seem to have mentioned Jake in these texts. Did Owen know Jake was coming along as well?'

'No, I suppose not. It was a last minute thing. Why?'

'It's just that… and you didn't ring Owen and tell him? We'll know if you rang from the call log. We've already requested it from the service provider.'

'No I didn't ring him. Anyway, what's so important about whether he knew if Jake was coming? I don't understand, Clive.'

'Well, your text about the miracle mineral stuff wasn't on Owen's phone. Seems he never received it, or if he did it was deleted.' Clive sounded as if he was thinking aloud.

'So?'

'I'm sorry, Nick, but I'm going to have to ask. Did you look at Owen's phone when you found him? Did you delete any messages, wipe his phone down to remove your prints, and then slip it back into his pocket?'

'What?' Nick's world spun. He thought he was going to be sick.

'Because I think someone did. And if it wasn't you, who was it?'

'I don't know. What are you talking about, Clive?'

'Hmm, because I get the feeling someone wants us to think it was you.'

'What? But why?' Nick tried to control his rising panic.

'Look, from what the pathologist found, he thinks it is highly unlikely Owen would have been well enough to want to go canoeing. And as for changing the oil....'

Nick spun deeper into a pit of confusion, his stomach churning.

'You see, I'm trying to figure out why he was under the van in the first place.' Clive spoke softly, the smile long gone from his eyes. 'Did you notice anything? Anything strike you as odd?'

'I... I've been trying not to think about it, Clive. But if you want me to....'

'And of course there was all that business with the scenery wall toppling over. Are your photos still on this phone, Nick? The ones of the extra drillings? The holes with missing bolts?'

'The photos? I... I'd forgotten about those. Yes, they're still on my phone. Do you think it's all connected?'

'I don't know. But I'll need to keep your phone for the moment. I'll give you a receipt for it, and you will get it back eventually. I'm afraid it's evidence. Also it would speed things up if you'd authorise the release of your calls and texts to us, from your service provider.'

'But if you take my phone, what will I use? I need a phone. And Yvonne? I don't really want you looking....' He caught Clive's raised eyebrow.

'I think, Nick, I may have an answer. I'll have a word with our cyber tech experts. If your photos, messages and emails are stored on your phone, we'll keep the phone, but... maybe you can carry on with what's in essence a clone of it, or rather your current SIM card in a new phone.

You'll be starting afresh but at least you'll have your old directory and your current number. We'll see if we can dig something out for you.'

'What?'

'Oh yes, and I need to know where you were earlier on Saturday morning, from around eight thirty onwards.'

'Oh God… is that when Owen…?'

'Yes.'

Nick swallowed. 'Well I picked Jake up from the station, Needham Market at about nine forty-five. Earlier – I was here. Got up, had a shower, got my canoeing kit together, yes, and Mum cooked Dad and me a full English breakfast. You can ask her if you like.'

'Hmm, I think I will. She's in the kitchen, you said?'

He watched Clive get up, noticing how his height made him a force to take seriously. At least he seemed relaxed as he walked across the pale laminate floor and knocked on the kitchen door.

'Mrs Cowley? Can I have a quick word?' Again, the reassuring tones.

Oh shit, Nick thought. How did I get into this mess?

CHAPTER 17

'You never told me about this miracle mineral solution, Chrissie,' Clive said as he studied his mobile, a hint of grievance in his voice.

'Miracle mineral…?' She glanced across at his phone's screen and caught a glimpse of webpages and his internet browsing.

'I didn't know you'd be interested in something like that, otherwise I'd have said,' she murmured as she sat down on a battered captain's chair. 'I'm not quite sure what it's supposed to do, but I think Owen was taking it. Of course that might not be the best recommendation, but he seemed to think it was helping. At least that's what I remember him saying when we all met in the Nags Head.'

She edged her chair closer to the scrubbed pine table and picked up the glass of ginger beer. 'Thanks, this is just what I needed,' she said and downed a couple of mouthfuls.

He didn't say anything. He seemed to be in a world of his own, so she left him to netsurf a moment longer while she relaxed and soaked in the atmosphere of the small pub. It was only Tuesday, warm, and still early evening but already she felt drained by the week.

'When's Dan arriving?' She knew Clive had an old friend calling on some whistle-stop visit from Canada. It was a last minute arrangement, somewhere to break his journey on his way up to Newcastle. She could guess the format; an evening of reminiscing, drinking, a few hours of sleep, and then back on the road. 'Pity my spare room isn't larger,' she murmured, not really sure if she meant it. She assumed Clive would be spending the rest of the evening making up the bed in his guest room and nipping around with a vacuum cleaner in preparation for Dan.

'At least your house in Lavenham is getting used,' she said, more to herself than Clive. Apart from when his two stepchildren occasionally stayed over with him, he hardly seemed to spend much time there anymore.

She drank her ginger beer, but this time slowly while she banished any thoughts of his ex-wife, now on her third marriage. Yes, this was a good spot to meet up with Clive, a mile out of Lavenham on the Brent Eleigh road.

'So why are you interested in the miracle mineral stuff, Clive?' she asked, giving up on the Dan question.

He looked up when she said his name, the familiar word seemingly cutting through wherever his thoughts had drifted.

'What? Sorry, Chrissie.'

'I said, why are you interested in the miracle mineral stuff?' She tried to keep the irritation out of her voice.

'It seems it's pretty corrosive stuff. Here,' he tapped his phone's screen, 'it says it contains 28% sodium hypochlorite and if you mix it with citrus juice as suggested, it produces chlorine dioxide, which at this concentration is a powerful bleach – strong enough to use for industrial water treatment and stripping textiles. And apparently Owen was drinking the stuff! Nick told me, and now you've just said the same. I was thinking it might explain why Owen had gastric erosions. I'll have to ask the pathologist if it fits.'

'Did you just say gastric erosions? That sounds painful.'

'Yes, I guess they'd be damned unpleasant. More post mortem results came through today. Seems his kidneys showed signs of damage as well.'

'I'm not surprised. You said a van landed on them didn't you?'

'Yes, but the pathologist said he hadn't expected to find nephritis, along with the blunt trauma.'

'Nephritis? What's that?'

'Some kind of kidney disease. Apparently it stops the kidneys working properly.'

'So how do you get nephritis?'

'I don't know. I didn't even know it existed until I spoke to the pathologist today. He said eating or drinking something toxic, or an infection, or just bad luck. I was wondering if it could be related to the sodium hypochlorite.'

'Or maybe something else he was taking.'

'Something else he was taking? Why do you say that?'

'I don't know. If he was crazy enough to drink this sodium hypochlorite stuff then God knows what else he was doing or taking.'

'Yes, you've got a point. It's worth asking his doctor. I'll get my DS to check with his GP.'

Clive fell silent. Chrissie knew the faraway look on his face. 'Have you still got Stickley with you?'

He gazed across at her, an unspoken question lifting his brows.

'Stickley,' she repeated. 'Is he still your detective sergeant, Clive? Honestly, you really are miles away. Have you even thought to look at the menu yet? There's a lamb tagine on the specials board.'

'Sorry, Chrissie, but, I was talking to Nick a little earlier. I'm convinced there's something about Owen's death that isn't all it seems. It's staring me right in the face but I can't quite see it yet.'

'You were wondering about the pieces of wicker impaled in his hand, weren't you?'

'Hmm... that's another strange thing. I'd sent the team back to collect everything from the vicinity outside. Amongst lots of other stuff, we found a broken wicker cat carrier, a long handled broom and a dead cat.'

'A dead cat?'

'Yes, unfortunately our pathologist baulked at PM'ing it so we're waiting on a veterinary pathologist.'

'But you don't think Nick...?'

'Of course not. But I think he's the key to it.'

'What?'

'Nothing, just forget I said that, Chrissie. And don't go talking to Nick about it. I'm being serious.' He cast a stern look.

She felt confused and itched to ask more. But she'd known him for long enough to understand how he worked, and this wasn't the moment to press him. So, she thought, the subject of Dan's visit had failed to draw him, and now he'd clammed up about the investigation into Owen's death. It probably also wasn't the moment to bring up the subject of planting a key logging programme in an email.

'Phishing,' she murmured, starting to wonder if she should have stayed at home and settled for an early night.

'Fish? Is there fish on the specials board?'

'No, Clive. I was just thinking out loud. You know I can't decide which van to buy?' She decided she'd be safe on the subject of classic vans. 'I should have finished the

144

plant stands by Friday. I want to drive them down to the customer in Aldeburgh. What do you think of a series II or III Land Rover?'

'Please don't tell me you've seen a yellow one somewhere. Come on, Chrissie, you need a small modern reliable van that's easy to drive and you can leave outside without it turning into a heap of rust.'

'So you don't think the advert Matt saw for a Land Rover hybrid with a Land Rover body on a Range Rover chassis and a Mazda diesel engine might be the one for me? I gather the bodywork is a bit rough, but you can still tell it's yellow. Some part of it dates it 1966. Matt emailed the link. You should have a look.'

'Now I know you're winding me up.'

'But it's going cheap.' She caught his smile. She wasn't going to tell Clive it wasn't the only thing Matt had emailed her. The file with the picture and imbedded key logger was currently safely parked unopened in her inbox. She was still plucking up courage to follow through with her plan and attach it to an email to the seller on the memorabilia site.

'If you must have Sarah and Matt looking out for suitable vans for you, I suppose this is only to be expected,' Clive said mildly, obviously unaware of her darker plotting.

'I know, but it's fun isn't it. Did you catch any of the Paralympics today? Oscar Pistorius seems to be the one to watch.'

'Catch any of the Paralympics? I wish. I heard on the commentary that our own Jonnie Peacock may be a match for him in the hundred metres.'

Hmm… and to think it'll all be over by Sunday. I'm hungry. Come on, what are you going to have?'

They ordered the lamb tagine.

By the time they finished eating, Chrissie felt mellow and Clive seemed less distracted. She'd made up her mind to use the key logger spyware as a Trojan. It was time to do a spot of spear phishing.

CHAPTER 18

The Nags Head was busy for a Thursday night. Matt swigged back his lager, eyes glued to the large TV monitor.

'So, Mais, you think those running blades are sexy?'

'Yeah, but don't go gettin' any ideas. You break your leg trying one and you won't look sexy on crutches.' She sipped her rum and Coke and snuggled closer, while on the large screen the runners crouched into their starting positions.

The drinkers in the bar momentarily stilled as the TV camera panned over the T44 one hundred metres finalists. There'd already been one faulty start. Anticipation dampened conversation and glasses hovered mid-way to mouths. *Pop*! The starting pistol fired and excitement erupted in the Paralympic Games stadium.

'Go... go!' Matt croaked. He had no idea why he was so fascinated, but to him it was the merging of his fictional superheroes and the reality of eighty layers of carbon fibre fused into the shape of a J or a C and imbued with the ability to store enough kinetic energy to–

'Jonnie Peacock's going to win!' Maisie squealed.

'Yeah go. Go! Pea cock. Pea cock. Look, he's flamin' won,' Matt shouted as around him drinkers clapped and cheered. 'Them running blades are awesome. Did you see his blade? A hundred metres in less than eleven seconds,' he bellowed to anyone who'd listen.

'I bet he got up more speed than your scooter.'

'What, Mais?'

'I said I reckon his blade is faster than your scooter.'

'Nah, but I reckon I'd be wicked on a pair. What you say, Mais?'

'Wouldn't you have to have some of your leg off first?'

'Nah – they make jumpin' stilts for people like me. It's the same kinda idea but cheaper, and with a fibreglass leaf spring instead of–'

'Metal?'

'Nah, there's eighty layers of carbon fibre on them runnin' blades. With stilts, your foot is kinda on a platform partway down the fibreglass J.'

'Cool. I think I've seen models in fashion shoots on things like that.'

'Fashion shoots? It's an extreme sport, Mais.'

'Yeah well, you're an extreme kinda person, Matt.'

'Mega,' Matt breathed and pictured himself doing inverse twist turns in the air on a pair of jumping stilts. For a moment he was transported to the tattered pages of his comic-strip books. He was Sonic Strider, a leaping superhero.

'Course you might pick up somethin' like them in Diss. There's a vintage stage & entertainments sale this Saturday.'

'Diss? At the auction rooms?' Just the mention of a stage & entertainments sale brought Priddy hurtling back into his consciousness. He stared into his glass and hoped Maisie couldn't read his thoughts.

'Yeah, me uncle collects old film posters and he's on their emailin' list. He was sayin' there's some interestin' stuff in this Saturday's catalogue.'

'Jumpin' stilts? Have they got jumpin' stilts? They aint vintage, you know. They're now, Mais.'

'I don't know 'bout stilts, but there's them monocycles – you know, one wheel bikes with no handlebars. There's vintage comics, posters and… vintage fashion.'

'I don't fancy a monocycle. What'd I do with one of them? But vintage comics, now you're talkin'.'

'Hmm, I kinda fancy some vintage fashion.'

'I reckon another pint. Rum an' Coke for you?' he asked, his mind bounding on, as he stood up with his empty glass and tried to read Maisie's face.

Later that evening, while Maisie slept curled at his side, he propped himself against his pillow and balanced his laptop on his knee. Somewhere beyond his bedroom walls, muffled TV drama drifted from the living room. He guessed his mum would be asleep in front of it by now, jaw lax and a dead cigarette butt teetering between her fingers. He let the thought go, and seconds later he was logged on and reading the Diss Saturday auction catalogue.

Maisie was right. Lot 43 was a monocycle. He studied the photo – a single ten inch wheel with small pedals at the hub. Not much of a saddle on the top, more something to grip between your thighs. It was like buffer tech. By comparison, curved fibreglass jumping stilts grabbed the imagination. They shouted infinite possibilities. They were the killer app of the auction lots, and as such there weren't any in the sale. And vintage comics? He already had a stash of comic-strip books under his bed. Maisie was always on at him to ditch them.

'Scammin' hell. Is that the reserve price? I'm sittin' on a bleedin' fortune,' he murmured. He glowed. The comic-strip books weren't just his childish security blanket, the emoticons of his earlier life; they'd morphed into a flaming silk quilt. Just knowing their monetary value justified his attachment. 'Wait till I tell Maisie.'

Vintage clothes and fabrics were the obvious thought progression from a comfort blanket. 'She'll like these,' he murmured, as he scrolled over some wigs and hair pieces, the shaggy dog, permed look and the Mary Quant straight bob. Platinum blonde or sleek black? How could he choose?

Some of the items reminded him of the sorts of things he'd seen on the memorabilia sites – clothes and props from past stage tours and TV series, but for the most part it was pretty much anything from the sixties, seventies and nudging into the eighties. He wouldn't have been surprised to see another nutmeg grater alongside posters for punk and acid house music, autograph collections and boxes of vinyl. Spammin' hell, he was thinking of Priddy again.

He closed his eyes, but still she was there in his thoughts. He'd discovered too much about her and it was going to get him into trouble with the people he liked. That was if they ever found out how much he'd known all along. So why didn't he just split on her? Tell Damon and Chrissie all he knew or had guessed? He didn't owe Priddy anything. Or did, he? She'd been nice to him when he'd pretended to be a reporter for the Student Chronicle. That had to be worth something.

But the key logger had been activated and he figured Damon would already be analysing the keystrokes. Soon Chrissie would know as much about her as he did, and Damon would send Priddy's details to the debt collecting agency.

'Felix Lighter,' he murmured. To Priddy he was Felix the journalist; certainly not a CIA operative, nor Matt Finch the computing & IT student. The journalist might want a scoop and to smash a memorabilia scam, but what did Matt want? He felt a kernel of anxiety.

Maisie stirred. 'Will you drop me off at work in the mornin', Matt?'

'Yeah sure, Mais.' He didn't want to do anything to upset her.

•

Nick examined the replacement phone: black glass screen, slim yellowy-orange casing. He hesitated to call it gold and of course it wasn't new. That hadn't been part of the deal. The fine scratches across the glass bore testament to that. He imagined someone jettisoning it in a police waiting room, or tossing it into a bin. Or perhaps it was just boring – lost, found, handed in and never claimed.

'What secrets are you hiding?' he murmured.

He supposed he should have sounded more grateful when Clive rang him earlier that morning.

'We've got a substitute phone for you. Sorry it's taken a few days, but we've put your old SIM card in it,' Clive had said. 'It'll be waiting for you to collect. Just drop in at the Stowmarket station, give your name, and sign for it. OK?'

'Thanks, Clive.' Nick had wondered what cast-off he'd be given.

'Oh, and just a quick question, Nick. Do you remember seeing a cat when you found Owen under the van on Saturday?'

'A cat? No... but I saw a broken cat carrier by the bins. Why?'

'Nothing. Thanks, Nick. Bye,' and he was gone.

And so Nick had called in at the Violet Hill Road police station to collect the phone during his Friday lunch break. He'd barely had time to turn it on before it burst into life, ringing in his hand with such urgency and gusto, he nearly dropped it in alarm.

'Hello?' he said, trying to keep the surprise out of his voice.

'Hey, Nick? I've been trying to ring you. Why haven't you been answering your phone?' Dave's irritation was almost palpable.

'It's a long story. Phone troubles – but it's sorted now.'

'Good. Can you help out tomorrow? Over at Althorne house.'

'Saturday?'

'Yes, and maybe into Sunday, if you want. The weather forecast says it's going to be sunny, so they're filming outside over the weekend. Lester pulled me off working on the biplane and we've been on site making the old cart house look like a dairy, and the stables into a milking shed. We've just about got it ready for shooting scenes with Cooper and Gavi.'

'But....' Nick remembered he wanted to go canoeing again on Saturday. Except he also recalled he hadn't heard from Yvonne. Lack of a phone could have been the reason.

'There'll probably be nothing much for you to do, other than hang around and get sunburnt. I really wish I could be there,' Dave continued, 'but I've promised the wife I'll take her to Norwich for the day. I'll be free to help if the shoot runs into Sunday.'

'Oh, alright then, Dave,' Nick said, mentally changing his canoeing plans to Sunday.

'Thanks, Nick. And... are you OK? I heard about Owen. It must've been dreadful finding him like that over in Grundisburgh last Saturday.'

'Yeah.'

'Thing is, to keep busy.'

'Yeah, I know. That's what I've been doing. If you remember, I've been helping Kenneth make kitchen units.'

'So it'll be a good thing to be working on the Althorne House shoot tomorrow. It'll make a bit of a change. Bye.'

'But I was going to go canoeing,' he said, as the line died.

·

They'd escaped the busy road to Thetford, already teeming with Saturday traffic near the large food stores to the south of the old market town. The scooter's engine whined and buzzed under Matt and Maisie's combined weight as it soldiered up the hill. Timber-framed houses nudged close to Victorian brick buildings as the centre of Diss gave way to a more recent suburbia.

'Nearly at the Auction Rooms,' he shouted through his visor.

Maisie squeezed his waist by way of reply.

He rode past trees casting dappled light behind a slatted fence. They partially hid a large car park. 'Here,' he said and tooted his horn, as he swung the Piaggio through the entrance.

Matt hadn't been to the Auction Rooms before, but he recognised the long, low barn-like buildings from his Google Earth search. He let the engine idle as he took in the scene. Morning sunshine bathed rough grass and gravelled areas where some outside lots were displayed. A smattering of buyers ambled from the parking area, pausing near the grass and pointing at an old wooden shepherd's hut on a cart base.

'Come on, Matt. Aint we goin' to park?'

He didn't remember seeing the shepherd's hut in the catalogue. 'It is the right day, aint it?'

'Course it is. Now hurry up, it'll be starting soon.'

He manoeuvred the Piaggio into a shady spot close to a hornbeam tree, brushing his arm against its silvery-grey bark as he pulled the scooter onto its parking stand.

'Ouch! Hey you go in ahead, Mais. Then you'll get a chance to see them wigs and kaftans.'

She didn't pause to say anything, just pulled off her helmet and tossed it to him to stow, then hurried away between the parked cars. He didn't mind. He was too exhausted to care. His regular journey to Bury was easy, but it was a few extra miles from Stowmarket to Diss and the route was unfamiliar. He reckoned the early start had nearly killed him. And to add to the pressure, Maisie was due back in Stowmarket to work an afternoon and evening shift.

He slumped down and rested his back against the hornbeam.

'Come on, Prosecco.' A girl's voice carried through the still air. 'The auction starts in ten minutes. I've marked the lots I think we should bid for.'

Prosecco? Where had he heard–?

'Good idea printing out the catalogue. I want to have a closer look at the hair pieces.' A second girl spoke.

'Yes, as long as they're of the era, you can cut them to the style you want.'

Prosecco? Not many girls were called Prosecco. Wasn't Owen's girlfriend…?

Without thinking he craned his neck to look around the tree trunk. Two girls were walking away from him. One with short curly blonde hair and the other with–

'I thought those knitted jumpers could be made to look like the ones in the Bridget Jones film.' The voice sounded fainter, more distant. He had to strain to catch the words.

'You mean the Christmas ones her mum knitted?' The girl turned her head as she spoke.

'Spammin' hell,' he breathed as he took in the face framed by shoulder-length wavy brown hair. He'd seen her before. The photo on Facebook. The one where she'd been standing outside the Wolsey Theatre with the billboard for The Waldringfield Wives production. His stomach lurched.

'Priddy Jones,' he whispered.

Like a fibreglass leaf spring, he jerked back behind the tree. If she saw him he was done for. Or was he? There were no photos of Felix Lighter out there because Felix didn't really exist, so she couldn't know what he looked like. But if he opened his mouth, even uttered a sound, would she recognise the voice? He hadn't immediately placed hers because it sounded richer and more resonant than over the phone. But would she identify his? He reckoned he wasn't going take the risk.

Matt realised he was stuck behind the tree, his stomach churning. He sank onto the cool earth near the base of the trunk and toyed with the idea of putting his helmet back on and keeping the visor down. It was either that or passing himself off as Ed Sheeran.

Ping! A text alert sounded somewhere deep in his pocket. He read the message. *Where are you?* He pictured Maisie with a speech bubble, as in a comic strip. Capitals or bold dark print would mean a shout, anger - so he reckoned lower case meant she was OK. But he daren't go into the auction rooms to join her, not if he sounded like Felix Lighter. Would she understand if he tried to explain? He made a decision.

Feeling sick. Staying with scooter. Come back when you're ready. No hurry – taking a kip. He read it through a couple of times and then pressed send.

OK, came the reply.

He placed his helmet like a pillow under his head and stretched out on the ground. Everything was going to finish up all right, he decided. Hadn't Maisie just texted and said *OK*? Gentle sunshine played over his face. His anxieties melted away, as he sank slowly into a dreamless sleep.

'Hey, Matt.'

Something nudged his leg.

'Hey wake up, Matt.' The voice was insistent. 'Matt!'

'Maisie?'

'Come on, wake up. We need to get goin'. Me shift starts in just over an hour. Are you feelin' any better?'

'What? Any better? Yeah, 'ave I been asleep?'

'Yeah. Hey what d'you think of me kaftan? Cool, aint it?' She held up something bright and busy with tie-dye patterns.

'Mega. But is that all you got, Mais? We come all this way and–'

'Nah, I got a poncho, and a silk kimono-style wrap, but the wig I wanted – some stuck-up bitch got it. Yeah, she got loads of stuff. Wouldn't 've hurt her to let the wigs go.'

'So were you OK at the biddin'?'

'Yeah, just kept stum and pretended I weren't interested, then came in with a bid at the end.' She seemed her usual chirpy self.

'Cool. Come on then,' and he rammed his helmet on and jolted the Piaggio off its parking stand. It was time to get back to Stowmarket.

CHAPTER 19

Saturday was proving to be as sunny as the weather forecast had predicted. Nick sat outside in shorts and tee shirt, feeling surprisingly comfortable on a canvas foldaway camping chair. It was one of several positioned so as to be out of the way of the cameras, but still close enough to watch and be part of the shoot. The walls of a derelict potting shed were conveniently placed to cast shade across the chairs, but it would be another hour or so before the sun really warmed the crumbling bricks. Ahead he had a good view of the modest coach house and stable block, dressed to look like a dairy and milking shed. At his side, his toolbox was ready for action.

He had arrived at eight that morning, only to learn that Gavi and Cooper had been in make-up and costume since six thirty, and although he wasn't needed for anything, the activity and buzz made him feel excluded and late. The food trailer was doing a brisk trade, so he'd waited in line to pick up a paper cup of tea, while around him crew ate bacon baps, and bit-part actors ran through their lines and drank bottled water.

'Hi, Kay,' he'd said, recognising her from working on earlier set repairs. 'Today must be important if you're here.'

'Until Merlin can control the weather we've just got to get as much on camera as we can in the time allowed. Let's pray the sun keeps shining. And... well I'm also filling in for Priddy. She's got to disappear for a few hours. She volunteered to take Prosecco to see some kind of therapist this morning.'

'Poor Prosecco. So she's not here for the big powder and paint session?'

'Yes she's here all right. She couldn't miss this. But she'll be leaving shortly with Priddy. You know, Prosecco's a real trooper. She promised to be back in time to do the make-up repairs after lunch. Luckily, Caroline is helping out for a few hours.'

Nick was surprised by how disappointed he felt, not about Prosecco, but about Priddy. She was always good for a cynical remark and a knowing nod, and he was going to have to take a quick look at the dairy and milking shed transformation without her.

By the time he threw himself down into the camping chair to watch the first take, he'd had enough of make-believe. The dairy was reasonably convincing. The props department had seen to that. The milking shed, however was far from realistic. Dave and Lester had removed the stable doors and opened up the stalls. They'd also knocked together some rough wooden milking stools. The cobblestone floor had been hosed clean, and tall milk churns and pails were arranged along one wall. But it didn't smell of cow. It lacked the cloven-hoofed presence, the puddles of yellow pee and green dungy cowpats outside.

'So where are the cows?' he asked anyone who'd listen.

A girl in skinny shorts and holding a clipboard turned and put a finger to her lips.

'Shush. They'll add cow noises to the sound track later.'

'Right,' Nick murmured. He should have guessed.

'Gavi must be sweltering in those boots and leggings,' a technical assistant said as he hurried past.

'There wasn't such a thing as summer breeches or cool smocks provided as uniform for land girls in those days,' the voice with the clipboard explained to the warm air, 'Just scrubby, hardwearing material and sensible thick cotton. Gavi'll be roasting, for sure.' She didn't sound sympathetic.

'It'll be cool in the dairy, though. That was the whole idea, wasn't it? To stop the milk turning sour. Keep it fresh.'

'Sure. Except you're forgetting we're looking at a cart house pretending to be a dairy. Not quite the same thick stone walls. Merlin told her the heat would bring a sexy flush to her cheeks. Trouble is, if she starts sweating it'll mess up her make-up. Where the hell is Prosecco?'

'I heard, counselling,' Nick said under his breath, but the girl wasn't listening. She was reading a message on her phone.

'They want bottled water already,' she muttered and hurried away.

The sunshine was proving a mixed blessing. Nick thought Gavi looked rather attractive with her smock catching a light breeze. And then he spotted one of the film crew with a large electric fan positioned out of the camera's frame. Nick rested back while the lesson in make-believe continued.

It wasn't long before Merlin called for him. 'This milking stool is all wrong,' he said distractedly.

'Why? What's wrong with it?' Nick stared at the circular seat, stained and fatigued to look old. Three broom handle-like legs were wedged through holes drilled into the seat. It was a simple but effective tripod design.

'When Gavi is sitting, she's too low while she's talking to Cooper. It makes it impossible to get both their heads in the same frame.'

'OK, so how much do you want it raised?'

'About this much,' Merlin said, one hand held about eight inches above the other.

'But won't it be too tall then? I mean she'll be sitting too high when she milks the cow.'

'Yes, Nick. But that's why we need more than one milking stool - a low one for scenes with the cow, a slightly taller one when Cooper's in the frame.'

'Right.' He was starting to get used to the craziness of it all. 'How soon do you need it?'

'Five minutes ago.'

Nick carried his toolbox and the offending milking stool back to his car. It didn't take him long to set up his portable workbench and run a lead from a socket just inside the back corridor. He drilled out the wedges and knocked the broom handle legs out of the seat. Armed with a discarded leg, he hurried through the garden to the derelict potting shed.

'I knew it,' he muttered triumphantly as he retrieved an abandoned rake and hoe. Their wooden handles were suitably weathered and pretty much the same diameter as the discarded leg in his hand. He made a mental note to ask Lester to put them on the reimbursement list for the owners.

Cutting the hoe and rake handles into the requested leg lengths was the work of a moment. Planed and sanded, he cut a slit into the top of each leg, fitted the legs into the drilled seat holes, made wedges to fit into the slits, and then hammered them home. A few cuts with a gauge and the top of the legs were flush with the seat. He hadn't used glue but he reckoned the wedges would hold, and anyway he couldn't rely on the glue drying it time.

'That's good,' Merlin said a few minutes later, as Gavi sat on the stool.

'Don't worry.' She flashed Nick a smile. 'If it's only a matter of an inch or so, I can sit up straighter.'

It should have been Dave, Nick thought. The smile was to die for.

The takes ran on and Nick was relieved there were no further milking stool issues before they finally broke for lunch. By early afternoon he was back on the foldaway camping chair, ready to enjoy the afternoon shoot. A bottle of effervescent spring water stood on the armrest casting blue and grey light over his golden-cased phone, ready in his hand. He reckoned it was time to text Yvonne.

'Hiya, Nick. You look comfortable.'

He recognised Priddy's voice immediately.

'Poser,' she muttered, not unkindly. 'Like the phone, by the way. I think I've seen one like that on–'

'Hey, how was the counselling?'

'Counselling? How did you hear about that? And it was Prosecco. I'd call it more like therapy.'

'It was nice of you to take her. So where did you have to go?'

'Diss.'

'Diss? That's a long way for therapy. Isn't there somewhere closer?'

'Hmm, I think next time she can drive herself. Look, I need to take this to Cooper.' She held up a hip flask. It was typical of the period, with leather case and carrying strap. The kind of thing a gentleman might take on a walk, or when watching cricket or even hunting, rather than something discrete to slip into a dinner jacket pocket.

'So what have you filled it with?' Nick asked, intrigued.

'Water. It's a hot day. Not a good idea to feed him gin or vodka during a shoot.'

He watched her hurry across the grass to Cooper who was wearing some kind of lightweight Burberry material flying suit. He could see why water was the responsible choice on a sunny day. Merlin had both of his stars roasting.

'Why's Cooper all trussed up like that?' he asked Priddy as she returned from her water mission.

'He's supposed to be testing the Sidcot Flying Suit. It's all part of his role in the Royal Flying Corps' Experimental Flight. He's meant to have landed in the field here on his way back to Orford Ness... for a romantic tryst with Gavi in the dairy.' She threw herself down onto the grass.

'He doesn't look very racy. He'd look sexier in his leather coat,' Nick said to Priddy, and catching sight of Prosecco, only a couple of paces away.

'I don't know if I'd agree. And keep your voice down, Nick. The sound bounces off this wall,' Prosecco said, tilting her head at the potting shed as she carried a large make-up box and moved gracefully towards him.

'Hey, Prosecco? Good to see you. How are you?'

'Keeping occupied, Nick. Do you mind if I join you?' She sat down next to him on one of the foldaway camping chairs and stretched out her suntanned legs in a lithe sinuous movement.

He couldn't help noticing how strong her muscles looked.

'You have to see the actors as the camera sees them, Nick,' she continued. 'Mostly head and upper torso shots. Cooper will look good climbing out of his plane and jumping down onto the grass wearing the flying suit. A bit like a modern-day racing driver, and those shots will probably be full body. A leather coat flapping around would be difficult in the continuity cuts.'

'Right.'

'Also, for the milking shed and dairy shots, there'll be close ups of eyes, mouths, necks. You get the drift. A smear of engine oil on Cooper's glistening skin will look better above the pale material of the–'

'Sidcot Flying Suit,' Priddy butted in. Nick hadn't thought she was listening.

'Yes, the partly unbuttoned neck of the Sidcot Flying Suit. And I need to be on hand to either spray a fine mist on their faces to make them look as if they're sweating, or – use a fan drier or apply powder to remove unsightly beading.'

'Beading?' Nick queried.

'That's the point before the sweat breaks free and runs in a rivulet down the face.' Prosecco spoke softly, not turning to look at Nick, but all the time seeming to watch Gavi and Cooper, twenty yards away. He sensed her tension when Cooper leaned in close to Gavi.

'Could be approaching a make-up smearing moment,' Nick murmured.

Prosecco tucked her feet under the chair and stood up with one graceful, fast flowing move. It reminded Nick of a dancer.

'I don't think you should have said that,' Priddy muttered under her breath, as Prosecco almost sprinted to Camera One and Merlin.

'Why, what did I say wrong?'

'Nothing, except I believe she's got a bit of a thing going for Cooper.'

'But I thought she was devastated by Owen's....'

'She is.'

Nick didn't understand. 'So how does that work?'

'Don't ask me. This is the world of film. It's filled with gorgeous people, fragile egos and rampant hormones. Image is all. And like most everything else in this business, a lot is not what it seems. It's probably make-believe.'

'So you mean having a bit of a thing going for Cooper isn't real, it's–'

'Only skin deep. Yes, something like that. Uh Oh! She's coming back.'

Prosecco strode towards them.

'Message from Cooper. Why only f-ing water in the hip flask?' she said, firing her words like bullets as she thrust the flask at Priddy.

'Thanks,' Priddy said calmly. 'Just because he's taken it out on you doesn't mean I'm going to slip him some alcohol. It's more than my job's worth. He'll have to make do with cold lemon tea.'

'At least it'll look like brandy,' Nick murmured. He sensed the undercurrents of emotion in Prosecco, and felt awkward.

While Priddy hurried away to fill the hip flask, Prosecco sat down beside him again.

'Will you be watching the Paralympic highlights later? Or don't you follow the games?' he asked, trying to find a neutral change of subject.

She didn't answer. Her generous mouth appeared to be locked in a tight line.

'Did I hear somewhere that you liked cats?' he tried.

Without a word she turned to stare at him, her mouth still unreadable, her cheekbones sphinx-like.

'Lovely day, though,' he said, and gave up.

CHAPTER 20

'So what's the relevance of a dead cat?' Chrissie asked as she settled back in the passenger seat. For once Clive was off duty.

'Dead cat? Whatever made you ask about that?' Clive said as he drove along the gently rolling B roads towards Wickham Market and then Aldeburgh.

'I would have asked sooner, but what with Dan's visit and Owen's murder, I've hardly seen you all week.'

'Now come on, that's hardly accurate. I cooked pizza on Monday and we had lamb tagine out on Tuesday. It's only Saturday today. And anyway, Dan's stopover was just the one night. Hey, did I tell you I discovered a great pub with him - live jazz? We must go, sometime. You'll love it. Long Melford.'

'Hmm, well it seems longer than Tuesday.'

Even their leisurely breakfast of thick-cut marmalade on end-of-loaf toast seemed ages ago. Since then they'd driven to the Clegg workshop and picked up the two Arts & Crafts-style plant stands. Chrissie had wrapped each stand in old blankets. She wasn't going to risk scratches and bruises to the warm coloured wood after all her work polishing the American black cherry. Now the stands stretched along the back seat like sinister bundles.

'The dead cat? You still haven't said.'

'Ah yes, the cat. But you still haven't said what made you suddenly ask? You haven't been talking to Nick have you?'

'No? Should I? You'd asked me not to say anything to him about the murder investigation.'

Irritation vied with curiosity as they powered smoothly through a vista of harvested fields, the views restricted from time to time by hedgerows and leafy trees. Hadn't Clive just batted her questions straight back, as if she was a suspect in an interrogation? Why was he being contrary? She knew it wasn't in his character. There had to be a nugget of evidence he'd discovered. She decided she needed to act as if she was happily relaxed if she was going to wheedle anything out of him. Subtly was the name of the game. After all, Clive was doing her a favour by helping her transport the plant stands; she should feel appreciative. The irritation built.

'So why are we delivering today? On a Saturday?' he asked.

'Because Mr Fortson was out all day yesterday and then he's away in Amsterdam next week. It was either today or... weeks away. And in any case, you were the one who suggested it this morning, remember?'

She bit back *we've already been through all this over breakfast. You thought it would be nice to combine the drive over with a day at the coast. And it was you who said I should phone Mr Fortson to see if it was OK*. Instead she said, 'It's really nice of you to help out. Really it is.'

'Saturday at the seaside. It makes it feel like a proper day off. And the fish and chips – they're famous in Aldeburgh,' he murmured.

'Hmm. But getting back to the cat. You obviously thought it was odd at the time. I'm curious. And you know me, I can't let things go. I won't tell anyone.'

'OK then, have you heard of monkshood or wolf's bane or devil's helmet?'

'They're plants aren't they? I thought we were talking about the cat.'

'We are... indirectly.'

'So what have monkshood, wolf's bane and devil's helmet got to do with anything?'

'Well firstly they're all names for the same plant. The Aconitum plant.'

'I didn't know you were into Latin plant names.'

'I'm not. But I've had a tutorial from the pathologist and the toxicology expert, and it seems the Aconitum plant contains aconitine. And aconitine is a deadly poison.'

'That's probably why I've heard of monkshood. So I'm hearing deadly poison and thinking dead cat. Is that what killed the cat?'

'There – now you know and I haven't had to tell you. The aconitine acts on the muscles, heart and nerves. Apparently if you swallow it you get burning, tingling then numbness in the mouth, stomach and your guts. In the meantime your muscles get weak and you have trouble breathing. Your heart beats irregularly, then less strongly and eventually stops.'

'And you die?'

'Exactly. And if you don't swallow it, you can absorb the poisonous sap from the stalk and leaves through your skin. Then you get the heart problems before your gut has a chance to react.'

'It sounds horrible.'

'It is. By mouth it's an agonising death. Apparently it tastes very bitter, so the unpleasantness warns off most potential eaters. And all parts of the plant can kill – root, stem, leaves and flowers.'

'And you think the cat ate it despite it being bitter? I thought cats were pretty choosy about what they ate.'

'They are. So the question is how did the aconitine get into the cat? Apart from tasting bitter, it's not very soluble in water, and I can't imagine anyone mixing it in alcohol for a cat.'

'You hear of dogs drinking beer.'

'But we're talking cats, and besides, the alcohol needs to be pretty concentrated. There's too much water content in beer.'

They fell into silence as Clive drove past a wilderness of gorse bushes, their yellow flowers vibrant in the sunshine. The scenery had taken on a more coastal feel with occasional tall Scots pines standing straight against the huge sky. Within a mile fields had given way to houses, set well back from the road and with neat shrubby front gardens, hedges and ornamental grasses. Soon they passed smaller mid and post-World War houses, brick built or with painted pebbledash and with names like Oyster Cottage, Gull House and Sandy Ridge. The words conjured up a promise of the seaside, as each squeezed closer to its neighbour. Chrissie gazed up at occasional white fluffy clouds, high and seemingly motionless.

'You can sense the sea, can't you,' she said.

'Hmm, we're almost near enough to see it now.'

She craned her neck searching for the first glimpse of indistinct ocean as the road took them down a short hill past a flint church and into Aldeburgh High Street.

'I still can't make out the sea. It's almost as if the road's been set back in order to hide from the seagulls and salty winds. You know, to let the houses right on the front take the worst of it while these ones shelter.'

'I expect it's more likely most of these houses were built later in Victorian and Edwardian times when the town grew, and they simply made a parallel road.'

'I guess so. Come on, let's have a look at the sea.'

Clive eased the Mondeo down a narrow alleyway between old brick and timber-framed buildings and slowed to a stop.

'There – look, the sea!'

Chrissie saw the sweep of water as far as the horizon ahead. She heard more than saw the waves, as they broke on the shore. Banks of shingle hid the surf as it whisked and dragged at the small stones, swishing and whooshing – wearing them smooth.

A sleek cat jumped onto a low wall close to the car. The sunlight caught its fur, luxuriant in its blackness.

'Hey, that's meant to bring good luck,' Clive said.

'What, the black cat? I don't reckon jumping onto a wall next to your car counts as crossing our path. I bet it's on its rounds of the houses.'

A sudden thought struck her, 'You know, I'd assumed the poisoned cat belonged to Owen and Prosecco, but I suppose it doesn't automatically follow, does it? The cat might have been doing its rounds. It could have eaten the poison anywhere on route and, well it might have belonged to someone else. It would explain why if it wasn't your cat you might chuck it away in a bin bag, I suppose.'

'That's a good point. Prosecco said it adopted her a couple of months ago. She told us she thought the cat was either lost, or its owners had moved away and the cat somehow got left behind, abandoned. Apparently it looked thin and hungry, so she gave it some food and it never left.'

Chrissie watched the black cat sit, twist and stretch out a back leg before giving its tummy a considered lick. 'Do you think if the cat brushed past some broken monkshood and the sap got onto its fur...?'

'It would lick its fur clean? I can believe a first lick, but more than one? It's bitter remember, and tingles and burns. And would one lick be enough to kill? I don't know, Chrissie.'

'It was just a thought. Come on, let's get the stands delivered and then we can come back and have a stroll along the beach.'

They drove at little more than a walking pace along the narrow seafront. On one side the low wall edged back the shingle beach, while on the other side they were hemmed in by old fishermen's cottages, now gentrified and turned into colourful holiday lets. Visitors and bathers inched past the car or hopped out of their path onto the wall to make way for them. Cyclists dismounted and wheeled their bikes past, the space was so tight. Another fifty yards and they turned back up another alleyway and onto the High Street again.

'We have to take this road,' Chrissie said, studying the directions she'd hastily scribbled on a scrap of paper. 'Mr Fortson said to turn off the High Street, up here. It takes us behind the High Street and away from the sea. He said to keep following the road. It slopes up hill a little, then along a partly tarmacked track. His house looks out across the Aldeburgh Marshes.'

'It sounds nice. I hope you're charging plenty for the stands.'

Despite Chrissie's misgivings, Clive found Mr Fortson's house easily enough. They drew up in front of a modern build - part wood, part flint, but designed to look like a cross between an observation hide and the control deck of a boat, with long horizontal glass windows and weathered copper roofing. While Clive unloaded the stands, Chrissie rang the front door bell.

'Hi, good morning,' she said as a middle aged man with thinning hair opened the door.

'Hello, Mrs Jax. Thank you so much for driving over, and on a Saturday as well. I'm really looking forward to seeing the American black cherry. It's going to look fantastic. I just know it will.'

She smiled at his optimism, and quietly crossed her fingers. 'I hope you won't be disappointed,' she murmured, 'and it's Clive who we have to thank for driving here, not me. I'm afraid my TR7 just wasn't designed to take plant stands.'

'You need a van, Mrs Jax.' He stepped back and frowned, as if considering her requirements more fully. 'And not just any van. You should have something with style. Something individual.'

'And not something yellow,' Clive said under his breath at her shoulder.

'I think I know just the van for you. If I said Forestry Commission, what would you say?'

'How do you mean, Forestry Commission, Mr Fortson?'

'The van, it's ex-Forestry Commission. I've a friend who lives across the other side of the River Alde, Tunstall Forest. He bought the van a year or so back. Thought he'd use it but, you know how things don't always turn out as you imagine.'

'Yes.' Chrissie pictured the plant stands and kept her fingers crossed, hoping they'd turned out as Mr Fortson had imagined.

'He's been meaning to sell it. If you're interested, I can give him a call, and directions how to get there. It's not very far.'

'That sounds like an excellent idea,' Clive butted in.

Chrissie stepped back onto Clive's foot. 'I was hoping for something individual, special.'

'Well, it's almost a one-off, despite looking like a pretty ordinary small green Citroen panel van. There's a yellow stripe along the side, it's got a sump guard, good ground clearance and decent traction for a bit of off-road. Quite subtle really.'

'Yellow stripe?'

'Oh no,' Clive breathed.

'Yes, I'm pretty sure it was yellow, but the overwhelming impression is forest. I'm sure you could get rid of the stripe it you wanted. What do you say? Should I phone him?'

She hadn't intended to look at vans. It was meant to be a day at the coast with Clive. But then again, she didn't want to risk offending a customer, particularly a customer standing in front of her and gushing about her Arts & Crafts-style plant stands.

'They are simply wonderful, Mrs Jax. Stylish but understated,' he said, running his hand over the wood. 'I love them.' He had the look of someone who might commission future pieces.

'OK, then. Thank you for the suggestion. We'll take a look at the van, if you think your friend won't mind.'

It didn't take him long to phone his friend, and minutes later, Clive was retracing the route back to Aldeburgh's high street, and Chrissie had a name, phone number, a time and directions written in small neat handwriting.

'Hey, is that the queue for the fish and chip shop?'

'It must be,' Clive answered.

'Are you thinking what I'm thinking?'

'Yes, let's give it a miss. There's a great pub in Snape, and it's on the way to the van. It can't be as busy as this.'

'I was thinking – wasn't Owen's van a Citroen?'

'Yes, but what's that got to do with this ex-Forestry Commission one? You're not planning on crawling around underneath it are you?'

'Of course not.' She felt a little silly.

•

When Chrissie saw the van, she knew she had to have it.

'So this Citroen Berlingo came off the factory line in 2006, part of a special order for the Forestry Commission, you say?'

Nigel Grabham shifted his weight and pointed at the logo on the side of the van. 'Well, the Forestry Commission in Scotland, if we're being pedantic.'

'And this one was specifically developed for off-road capability with higher ground clearance and....'

'That's right. It's got a sophisticated limited slip differential. So you get good traction without the costs of running a 4x4.'

'It's diesel and got manual gears, right?' Chrissie said, getting back to basics.

'Yes, and this one never got the rear passenger seat conversion. So it's basically a panel van with attitude. I understand only a hundred were custom-built like this for use in the Scottish forests, so it's got a rarity value. And you've got the slightly-before-its-time feature, for its year of manufacture, of having a sliding side door as well as the rear doors. So it would be great for loading furniture.'

'And it's got a stripe.' She felt the need to keep Nigel grounded. He was dressed like a ranger in a loose cotton jacket and lightweight walking trousers. A blur of forest colours. She guessed in his late forties.

'So do you want to take a drive in it?'

'You bet,' Chrissie said as she caught Clive's eye and tapped the yellow stripe along the passenger door before opening it to get in. She knew he'd check the registration and chassis number to make sure they weren't on the police records. He was already getting his mobile out of his pocket as Nigel started the engine.

'So why are you selling it?' she asked as Nigel drove smoothly off the partly shingled drive and onto the quiet lane.

As they swept past conifers, broadleaved trees and heathland, she learnt he was a wildlife enthusiast but his interest was more of a weekend leisure pursuit than a source of income. He might dress like a ranger on a Saturday, but weekdays were spent working near Ipswich in a telecommunications research and development centre.

'The kids are ten and twelve. I suppose you could say it's down to family demands.'

He reminded her of Matt with computing and electronics filling one compartment of his life. But flip the coin and he was virtually dressing and living out his dreams in his spare time. Thank God Matt didn't deck himself out like a ranger; thinking he was Ed Sheeran was bad enough.

She swopped into the driving seat and took her turn at the wheel. It was a hundred times easier to handle than the thirty year old VW Campervan, and she guessed it would also be a damned sight easier to drive than the forty year old Morris Minor AA van, or an indeterminately aged but old hybrid Land Rover. By comparison, the little Citroen van had modern brakes, suspension and economic fuel consumption. The decision was a no brainer, and besides, she knew the yellow stripe was a sign it was meant for her.

'Price?' she said. 'We need to talk about a price.'

The discussion was conducted after the test drive and as soon as she'd had a chance to check with Clive that his search hadn't turned up any surprises.

'I can't believe I've just agreed to buy a modern van,' she said, more to herself than Clive, as they drove home late in the afternoon. It was going to take her a week to sort out the payment and insurance, and anyway, for good form's sake, she needed to run it past Ron first.

CHAPTER 21

It had been a long, airless Monday afternoon, and Matt stretched his arms to ease his muscles before gulping down a mouthful of spring water straight from the bottle. The little knot of anxiety tightened in his stomach. They were taking a break and he knew from past experience this was the time Damon liked to talk about general computing topics, Damon's equivalent of an arm stretch, but in his case, a brain re-boot.

'Did you watch the Paralympics' closin' ceremony yesterday?' he asked, hoping to divert Damon. Priddy hadn't been mentioned all afternoon and Matt wanted to make sure it stayed that way. There seemed little point in stirring up a hornet's nest.

'No.'

'But you did catch some of the games, right? Those runnin' blades – they're just awesome.'

'Sure, if you're into that kind of thing.'

'I thought I'd try a pair of jumpin' stilts. They've got blade springs.' An image of Sonic Strider flashed through his mind.

'What? You're crazy.'

'I know, but I reckon if a bloke's got half a leg missin' and can run on them blades, then it'll be a breeze for me on ones with a foot rest.'

'You mean the jumping stilts?'

'Yeah.'

'So how does the running and jumping part work? I didn't have you down as an athlete.'

'Well I reckon the spring does all the work. As I see it, me weight bends the fiberglass blade, then when I make to move, the energy's released and boing....'

'You're flat on your face.'

The knot in his stomach eased. He'd got Damon's attention and he was on safe ground talking blades.

'Well I could wear me scooter helmet,' he suggested happily.

'I think you need to approach this with a bit more thought and planning,' Damon murmured as he keyed something into his computer. 'Have you seen the price of jumping stilts? Hey, but look - this might be an idea.'

'What? What might be an idea?'

'I'm sending you the link now.'

'*Olympic Fever Taster Sessions created in response to unprecedented public interest in running blades,*' Matt read out from his screen.

'Yes, it seems there's an indoor skateboarding warehouse on the Ipswich Industrial Estate. It says there's taster and teaching sessions on jumping stilts. There's even an option to buy a pair at a discount. It could be a good deal for you.'

Matt clicked on the locater map. 'Scammin' hell,' he breathed. It was virtually next door to the depot with the code number 058, the carrier service delivering Chrissie's nutmeg grater.

He turned and glanced over his shoulder at Damon, but Damon seemed unaware of him, engrossed in whatever was on his screen.

'Hey, click on the video. It's amazing,' Damon said.

'Wicked!' Matt watched someone on jumping stilts vault over a bar and make somersaults and twist-turns in the air. 'Cool dude!'

He reckoned it was only a matter of time before the mention of the skateboarding warehouse being on the Ipswich Industrial Estate would jog something in Damon's memory and he'd be reminded of depot 058. It was bound to bring the talk back to Chrissie, the key logger bug and then the discovery of Priddy behind it all. His edginess grew as he waited for Damon to say something.

'Are you OK? You've gone all serious. Having second thoughts about the jumping stilts?'

'Second thoughts? Course I aint. Well maybe about the price but not about anythin' else.'

'Hmm, perhaps you could pick up a pair of used ones? OK, well I guess we've wasted enough time on this for the moment. I'll send you the next batch of names, if you're ready.'

'Yeah, I'm ready,' Matt muttered.

'And before I forget, your friend Chrissie Jax - it seems she's sent the key logger. And the seller of the Brighton Pavilion nutmeg grater fell for it and clicked on the attachment.'

'What? Flamin' malware,' he breathed. Could Damon read his mind? His worried thoughts must have somehow conveyed themselves to Damon and made him see the link between the industrial estate and Chrissie. Now it was only a matter of time before....

'It's early days but I'm starting to get something back,' Damon continued. 'It appears the seller uses the name Tony Mopar, but there's also another name using the computer.'

'Another name?'

'Yes. It's not that uncommon, you know; families, couples... people sharing access to the same computer. And you'll never guess. The name's Priddy! Now I know there may be loads of Priddys out there, but wouldn't it be nice if when I get a surname from the key logger, it turns out to be Jones? The same Priddy Jones as on our list?'

'Yeah, that would be neat.'

'Of course, it could be an alias. People do that for dating sites or pennames.'

'So... are you tellin' Chrissie all this, or are you waitin' till you find out more?'

Damon didn't seem to be listening; his mind was obviously running along a different track, judging by the matter-of-fact, 'I've got the computer entry passwords from the key logger. If your friend Chrissie forwards me the emails from the seller, I'll find the computer IP address from the email header.'

'And with the IP address and password, you can hack into the seller's computer remotely, right?'

'Yes, but even without the password I can get a rough idea of the whereabouts of the seller's computer - if I use a geolocation database of IP addresses.'

'Mega cool.' Matt relaxed a little. While the talk was on general computing principles, he was engrossed. This was more like a normal break.

'Of course we're sailing close to the wind. It's a fine line between harmless spyware and actually hacking into a computer – the ability to take control of it.'

'Yeah, but I've read IP addresses can change. Or you can hide 'em. You know, usin' Virtual Private Networks, like the Onion Router.'

'Hmm, well let's hope the seller isn't that smart.'

'So are you tellin' Chrissie what you've found so far?'

'Not yet. I'll give her a call when I've got the information she wanted.'

The end of the afternoon merged into early evening as Matt worked through the names on his list. By the time he was ready to ride back to Stowmarket he'd made up his mind. Trying the jumping stilts wasn't just an empty dream; it made it possible to shift from comic-strip illusion to reality. All he had to do was contact the skateboarding warehouse and book an Olympic Taster session. But he knew well enough he might bottle out at the last moment if he turned up by himself.

As he closed the office door and trudged down the flight of stairs, he toyed with the idea of asking Maisie to join him, and then changed his mind. By the time he stood next to the Piaggio in the backstreet below Balcon & Mora, he'd pulled his mobile from his pocket and called Nick.

'Yeah, that could work quite well. I'm with Lester at their warehouse tomorrow. I reckon it can't be too far from the skateboarding place. We could check it out after work, if you like.'

'Cool.'

'You do know what jumping stilts are, don't you?'

'Course I do,' Matt muttered.

And so the following afternoon Matt rammed his helmet on and rode the Piaggio out of the Academy car park and along the back roads to Ipswich. The overcast day chilled his soul as the wind buffeted his chest and pulled at the sleeves of his denim jacket. He'd only ever imagined himself on jumping stilts in sunshine – the warmth of the brightest day like a spotlight, while he, Matt Finch acted out the stuff of comic strips. But as his temperature dropped his enthusiasm waned, and then reality took a hold. By the time he scootered into the industrial estate the grid of galvanised metal-clad warehouses sent stark messages against the cloudy sky.

He'd arranged to meet Nick after work, although Nick had warned him about Lester's rather fluid view of when the working day ended. 'Aim for about five,' he'd said. They'd reckoned it would give them a two hour window to make it to the jumping stilts retailer and sign up for lessons.

He dropped his speed and idled past each unit's frontage, small deserts of concrete laid before massive sliding and roller-panel doors. They yawned open on shadowy interiors, exposing delivery vans and crates of stock. Signs and logos were everywhere. He knew what he was looking for but it took a moment to unravel the anagrams and acronyms serving as business names.

'Holy codec,' he muttered as the letters on a large blue notice announced *IS & FSD & C Ltd*. The words *Ipswich Stage & Film Set Design & Construction Ltd* were written below and in smaller print, but Matt had made the connection twenty yards before he was close enough to read them clearly.

Nick had only ever talked about the film set in terms of people's names and locations: Althorne House, Owen and his girlfriend Prosecco, Lester, the stars Cooper Brice and Gavi Monterey, and the director Merlin Leob. Matt had never thought to ask the name of the set design company. It hadn't seemed important. But now as he sat on his scooter, a deeper chill gripped his stomach. This was the business he'd rung trying to trace Priddy Jones, and somewhere inside the building was a receptionist who had taken his call. Why hadn't he made the link when Nick gave him directions? 'A blue notice,' was all he'd caught at the time, his head bursting with images of jumping stilts. He felt stupid.

'Frag,' he wailed. This wasn't at all what he wanted. Without thinking, he twisted the handle grip accelerator and the Piaggio responded with a peppery two-stroke outburst. No wheel-spin, that was out of the question, but within seconds he was up to twenty miles per hour and zipping along the estate grid-road. He took a sharp left and then another. Before he knew it he was whirring around the block. A final left and he was approaching the blue notice again. 'Frag!'

He was forced to slow as a car pulled out of a forecourt. More vehicles began to appear. Of course, he thought, it was just after five o'clock and for many businesses it was the end of the working day. He hadn't even noticed if a Willows van was parked anywhere near the blue notice when he'd ridden by the first time. But on this approach his brain was totally operational and focussed. He needed a plan.

'Yeah, he's still here,' he said and swung over a rough pavement and through a wide entrance onto the concrete.

A low crumbling wall, barely a foot high, served as a symbolic boundary between pavement and forecourt. The Willows van was lined up against it, nose to the brickwork and flanked by a 4x4 and sporty Mini. There were plenty of gaps between the next few cars. It definitely had the look of an emptying parking lot.

Reassured, Matt pulled up in one of the spaces and rocked the Piaggio onto its stand. *I'm outside waiting for U,* he texted.

Grt. I'll be 10 mins. Come in, tk a look at the biplane while U wait, came the speedy reply.

No I'll B outside.

OK?

Why the question mark, Matt wondered. Was it or wasn't it OK with Nick?

He hated subtle meanings, half-smiles and emoticons; now he added punctuation to the list as he sat on the Piaggio and waited, his face hidden behind his visor.

Time dragged as cars passed within spitting distance along the estate road. A delivery van trundled onto the forecourt of a neighbouring unit and briefly distracted him. By the time a couple of blokes straggled out of the Stage & Film Set Design & Construction warehouse, his boredom was killing him.

'Lightin' crew,' he muttered as one carried spotlights while the other pushed a trunk on castor wheels in its base. They loaded the equipment into a van.

'Where are you, Nick?' he groaned.

He was on the point of barging into the warehouse, receptionist or no receptionist when he spotted a familiar figure. 'Hey, over here,' he shouted, and then thought to take off his helmet.

'Hiya,' Nick called. 'Why didn't you come in? You're daft sitting out here when there's loads to see inside.' His words sounded peevish, but the smile on his face seemed happy enough.

'I didn't want to meet the receptionist,' Matt said, thankful he'd appeared at last.

'The receptionist?'

'Yeah, well whoever answers the calls. See, I phoned – spoke to her a few weeks back, but I was pretendin' to be someone else.'

'Someone else?'

'Yeah, I was tryin' to trick her into givin' me a number for a girl I was tracin' for work. It's the kinda stuff we do for debt collectin' agencies, remember?' Matt had said more than he'd intended. The waiting had got to him.

'Hey come on, you're pulling a fast one on me. Taghrid's bloody attractive. We've all made a play for her. I bet you just said that because you tried to chat her up and she wasn't interested. So what's this girl's name?'

'What's her name got to do with anythin'?'

'Because otherwise I won't believe you. I'll think you made the whole thing up because you're so embarrassed by your terrible chat-up lines.'

'But I aint s'posed to tell.'

'C'mon. You can give a first name, can't you?'

'Priddy – but don't say I told you, right?'

'Priddy? Hey I know Priddy. She does props and stuff. She's nice.'

'See, I knew I shouldn't have said.'

'So did you get her number?'

'Yeah. But she sounded nice so I didn't pass it on. She thinks I'm Felix Lighter, a journalist.'

'What?' Nick squeaked, his voice breaking. 'You're kidding me.'

'It's all true. Stop laughin'.'

Matt watched him snort and cough.

'I've told you her name, so now do you believe me? And it aint funny. It wouldn't matter but - the thing is I think she's behind sellin' Chrissie the nutmeg grater, the one supposed to be an antique, but it weren't.'

'Well who'd have bloody thought? Priddy behind a con like that? I knew she was sharp, but....'

'Yeah, but she's kinda crossed a line. Right?'

'Hey lighten up. There's no real damage done. Chrissie'll get over it. She's angry because she's been conned. It's her pride that's been hurt. Somebody got one past her, and now she's trying to find out who it is. And when she's exposed them, it'll be like getting one back at the seller. Can you see that?'

'No.'

He thought back to the Diss auction. 'But Chrissie aint the only one bein' had, and there's more than one doin' the connin'.'

'You're probably right. But it isn't anything to do with us, so I'd stay out of it if I were you. Don't go poking around.'

'Yeah, but Chrissie's to do with us. And now Damon's working on it.'

'Look, for Chrissie it's about not being played like a fool. Leave it to Damon and her to get to the bottom of it. Now let's go and find this jumping stilts place. OK?'

They decided Nick would drive the Willows van while Matt rode the scooter. That way Matt could legitimately keep his helmet on after he arrived.

'Don't want you looking like a nervous pedestrian,' Nick said. 'And we don't want you killing yourself on the stilts either,' he added quietly.

'So you're sayin' Lester'll ask you to work longer if you leave the van parked out here? Scammin' hell. Yeah, take the van as well.'

It wasn't difficult to find the skateboarding warehouse. Brash banners gave fair warning of an outdoor skateboarding area complete with ramps, jumps and half-pipes. The warehouse stood close by. Large sliding panels had been pulled open to give direct access from it to the outside.

Youth seemed to predominate. Wide baggy shorts, baseball caps, vest-like tees, tattoos, elbow pads, and wrist protectors – it was a sea of swirling activity. And instead of gull calls and breaking waves, voices shouted and yelled across bangs and clunks as wheels rolled and boards flipped.

They parked on waste ground, a temporary area set aside on the edge of the estate behind the warehouse.

'Come on,' Nick said as he led the way towards the entrance doors.

Inside it had the feel and smell of a gym, something far removed from Matt's natural habitat. When he stood in front of the admission desk he saw a huge open area with a wooden sprung floor. It stretched away from him, intimidating him from the other side of a scratched Perspex screen.

'You're here for the Olympic jumping stilts taster?' the girl asked from behind the counter. Her voice pulled his attention back. He focussed on her nose stud.

'You bet we are,' Nick said cheerfully.

'Will that be the beginners or intermediate level?'

'What?' Matt hugged his helmet.

'I'd say begin–'

'Intermediates! Book them into the intermediates,' a voice from behind interrupted smoothly.

Matt spun around to see a girl with short curly blonde hair. She stood observing them, as if faintly amused. 'Frag,' he murmured, recognising her immediately.

'Hey, Prosecco! What are you doing here? I'll be with you in a moment, Matt,' Nick said and drifted to one side to talk to her.

'So, is that two for the intermediate level?'

The impatient voice pulled Matt's attention from Prosecco.

'No, don't take no notice of her. She was just kiddin'. Two beginner tasters, please,' he said firmly.

'OK, if you're sure.' She typed something into her keyboard, eyes on her screen display. 'OK, that's two beginner tasters. The session starts on the half hour, so you've got ten minutes to fill in the forms and get fitted up. You'll be with Brandon.'

'So what was that about?' Matt asked a few moments later while they filled in their injury disclaimer forms and waited for Brandon.

'What was what about?'

'Prosecco? Weren't she Owen's girlfriend? You seemed surprised to see her.'

He'd been trying to figure out what her game was. Skateboarding? Running on jumping stilts? Matt reckoned it was more likely she'd be after some old stilts and selling them on the memorabilia website as belonging to....

'Prosecco? Yes, I didn't expect to see her here. I hadn't got her down as a skateboarder or someone into jumping stilts.'

'So why's she here?'

'She said she was returning Owen's jumping stilts. No use for them now. I wish I hadn't asked. It just brought everything back and… well, it affected her.'

'I didn't know Owen had jumpin' stilts. That's cool.'

'Yeah, I was surprised.'

'You should've asked how much they were goin' for.'

'What? No way. I don't want a dead man's stilts. That's sick. Now fill in your injury disclaimer.'

CHAPTER 22

Nick limped from the Willows van to the Stage & Film Set Design & Construction warehouse. He'd always thought of himself as being pretty fit but with each step, pain burst through his quads and calves. Muscles he didn't know existed stabbed and twisted as he pushed the door. At least Matt would be feeling a hundred times worse, he thought. It was little comfort.

Taghrid hadn't arrived and the reception desk looked deserted. It would be another half hour before the switchboard was manned, and secretly he was relieved. He didn't want to be seen limping, his body wiped out by an hour on jumping stilts.

Moving stiffly, he headed down a corridor. He paused at a set of double doors and tapped in a code to open the lock. The workshop would be his therapy. He hoped the discomfort would melt a little as he slowly worked his body. It was just a question of getting on with it.

'Hi, Lester,' he called as he leaned on a table where plans and sketches were laid out.

'What happened to you? You look as if you've been in a fight,' Lester said.

'No, not quite a fight. Just an hour in the gym with jumping stilts.' Nick grimaced, and then regretted the movement as the graze on his cheek stung.

'Ah – so you saw all the banners around the estate. I guess you tried the taster session at the skateboarding place.'

'Yeah, it was awesome. And this wasn't a fall, at least not my fall.' He pointed at his face. 'Some joker tried to run before he'd learnt to walk.'

The vision of Matt surging towards him loomed large, the slow hesitant walk accelerating into an uncontrolled sprint. 'Yeah, you could say I broke his fall.'

'So are you hooked? Are you going to buy a pair?'

'I don't know. I think I'll give it another go first. It's a lot of money.'

'I'd heard the props department have a pair. No, on second thoughts, I think they're going to trade them in. That's right... they reckoned they'll hire some if they're needed. That way the liability for any accidents shifts to the hire company.'

The mention of the props department brought Matt's words rushing back. Had it really only been the previous afternoon? At the time he hadn't wanted to think too deeply about what Matt had told him, and now he wasn't in the right frame of mind to chew it over. 'So what are we working on today?' he asked, changing the subject.

'We need to get these Royal Flying Corps wooden huts finished. We've six more panels to make.'

Nick gazed at the plans. 'I still don't get it, Lester. Why are we making enough panels for one and a half huts? And some are identical but four fifth scale?'

'Because we've got to pretend the airfield is still on Orford Ness. Remember I told you they had to drain the ground before the airfield was originally made there. Now it's no longer in use, it's all lagoons and flooded ditches again. It's a bloody wildlife reserve.'

'Yes I understand that bit. So...?'

'To create the illusion we need one of the huts to appear as if it's still there. The view from the old airfield looked across the River Ore. In the background you could see Orford with the outline of Orford castle and the church against the skyline. We have to keep that deception.'

'But haven't they got the same view from the field they're going to be using instead on the mainland, next to Orford? It's only a slightly different angle, but virtually the same.'

'Yes, but Merlin wants shots over the water, and then there's a scene with Cooper being rowed across the River Ore and landing on Orford Ness in order to get to the airfield.'

'Right.'

'There's a tiny scrap of ground near the old airfield which is OK for us to use. We've got permission to drive in four short poles to hold the two mock-up hut panels. It's got to look as if it's further away than it is, hence the smaller size. Hell we've had to wait till September and the end of the breeding season as it is.'

'Right, now I've got it. Do you want me start measuring wood for the scaled-down frames?'

'Yes, good idea.'

The workshop had been designed for a purpose, and two long workbenches spanned one end while the rest of the space was mostly clear, leaving a large area where panels could be constructed and sets part-assembled. It gave a sense of space and theatre.

Long pre-cut lengths of four-by-two pine were stacked on a rack along one wall. It was the basic timber used to make the scenery frames, the starting point for many of the projects. He knew it was important to get the measurements precise and he suspected Lester might have left those particular panels to him for that very reason. Dave would never have done that, but then Dave was over in Haughley for a couple of weeks, working on a loft conversion. At least it gave Nick a foothold on the film set construction. He reckoned it had to be a damn sight better than sitting around all day at Althorne House, just in case he was needed. Although the way his quads and calves were hurting, he wondered if it might not have been such a bad thing today.

'I'll get my calculator,' he said as he walked stiffly to his toolbox. 'Better check the four fifth sizes.'

His toolbox was on the workbench where he'd left it the previous day. With all the excitement of the jumping stilts trial, he'd forgotten to load it away in the van. He found his pencil and calculator lying where he'd left them on the lift-out tray, but the small notepad had worked its way deeper into the box and was caught beneath a rubber headed mallet. The top sheet rucked and crumpled as he pulled the pad free. 'Damn,' he muttered as he smoothed out the paper and tried to brush off the rubber marks.

Bang! Bang! Bang! Behind him, Lester fired nails into strips of weatherboard as he attached them to a frame. Sections of the full sized Royal Flying Corps hut were beginning to take form inside the workshop.

The rhythmic shots triggered Nick's memory. The muted bangs seemed to fly. They were like the sounds he'd heard for an hour at the taster session - jumping stilts banging and resounding with each bounding impact on the sprung wooden floor.

But it wasn't the only thing he'd remembered. The sound sparked an association, and now it was staring him in the face. 'Rubber marks,' he breathed. An imprint streaked his notepad. Traces of black, rubber from the mallet head.

'Of course the pads,' he murmured.

The pads on the bottom of the jumping stilts were black, like the rubber soles of a shoe, but oblong in shape and small compared to the size of a human foot. They were fixed at the end of the spring-blades, a bit like undersized rubber hooves. Nick had been too preoccupied with the techniques he was learning to register all he'd seen. But now it made sense. The black marks peppering the sprung wooden floor were prints – small oblong marks left by the rubber pads. But there was a problem. He'd seen marks like that somewhere else.

'Oh God. The marble floor.'

At the time he'd assumed they were scuff marks from ladders, but now he wasn't so sure. He'd noticed them behind the mock wall when he'd gone to check it out, just before it toppled over. There should be a picture on his phone. An uncomfortable creepy feeling gripped him as he pulled his mobile from his pocket, the slim yellowy-orange casing almost but not quite gold. He'd know in a moment. But when he tapped on photos – an empty file, nothing.

'Shit, they're on my old phone's memory, not the bloody SIM card.'

'Everything OK?' Lester asked between weatherboard strips.

'Yeah, yeah. Did Owen really have a pair of jumping stilts?'

'Not that I know.' Lester shrugged and picked up the nail gun again.

CHAPTER 23

'Guess what the call was about,' Chrissie said, as she slipped her phone back into her bag.

'I couldn't help hearing you say Lester, so I imagine it's something to do with the console table. The one you repaired after the accident at Althorne House.' Ron sat at his workbench, a mug of tea close by. He was working on a piece of boxwood veneer, cutting it into the shape he needed to repair the inlay on the back of an Edwardian corner chair.

'Is everything all right?' he asked, looking up from his work.

'I don't know.' She guessed she must sound vague and evasive, but she was still collecting her thoughts. The call coming out of the blue had thrown her a little. 'And you're right. It was about the console table.'

'Solid walnut legs, burr walnut veneer on the curved rail... and Lester. He haggled the price down, didn't he?'

'Yes he did, Mr Clegg,' she said tightly.

Ron's words, the ones about haggling down the price, focussed her thoughts. Flattery was all very well, but she was running a business. What was her accountant's nose telling her?

'The thing is,' she explained, 'he wants to commission me to make a matching console table.' Just saying the phrase *commission me* triggered another buzz of excitement in her.

'What? They haven't broken it again, have they, Mrs Jax?'

'No, nothing like that. He wants me to make another one so there'll be a matching pair.'

'But that's wonderful. Well done, Mrs Jax. I must say that's how they were originally intended to be used, as a pair in a room. They have more decorative impact that way.'

'Yes, but don't you think it's strange he's asking me, rather than the owners calling? And making one from scratch is going to cost a lot more than the repair did. As you said, he haggled me down last time.'

'Hmm, but I'm guessing the owners must have asked him to act as the middle man. Otherwise they'd have come straight to you, and they haven't.'

'No, you're right. They haven't. But I assume they're in on the request. I mean I'll need to borrow the original table if they really want an exact match.'

Ron gazed at the piece of boxwood veneer he'd cut.

'Are you sure you're not being asked to make a fake antique, Mrs Jax?'

'But that's the thing, Mr Clegg. I think that's exactly what he wants me to do.'

'Really? I hope he wasn't asking you to take the repaired table apart and then use the pieces to make two antique tables out of the original? That would be... well that would definitely be dishonest.'

'No, but he wanted it to look like the original, with the same repairs. "An exact copy." Those were his words. And for the record, Mr Clegg, I'm not a crook, nor a faker. And I'm not like the Camms, the ones who stole that set of four antique Chippendale dining chairs and then made a set of six out of them to cover their tracks and double the value.' She drew herself up.

'Of course you're not, Mrs Jax. So what are you going to do?'

'I don't know.' But it was a question that needed to be answered.

She cast around, glancing up at the old wooden beams, laced with cobwebs and spanning the barn workshop. She ran her hand over one of the Regency mahogany quartetto tables she'd begun to repair. Her mouth felt dry.

'I'm going to make a mug of tea. Do you want a refill, Mr Clegg?'

'Excellent suggestion.'

While she fussed over the mugs and kettle, her mind worked double time. Lester had the potential to be a good source of work, but only if he passed on legitimate projects. She certainly didn't want to get drawn into his shady deals and dishonest practices, if that's what they were. It didn't have the makings of a good business plan. Not with a DI as a boyfriend and a rural catchment area where long memories were the norm. She was bound to get caught. But saying no to Lester might not be such a good business plan either.

'I suppose I could cost it out, then whack on an extra ten to fifteen percent. Get him to turn me down because I'm too expensive. What do you think, Mr Clegg?'

'But what exactly are you costing? A copy to trick a film camera lens? A fake to mislead even the experts? Or an honest replica?'

'I could come up with three different prices and make the cost of the fake astronomical.' But she knew the lines were getting blurred.

'Don't even suggest the fake, Mrs Jax. Only give two estimates; one for a copy for the film set, and the second for an honest replica, and both to be made from new wood.'

She sipped her tea and let his words mill around. He was right; she could set out an itemised estimate listing new walnut, new veneers and modern glues for the honest replica. Pine, plywood, brushes, and paints to give the appearance of walnut and inlays, would be on the list for the table for the film set. That way there'd be no doubt about where she stood. But how would Lester respond?

'Do you know, Mr Clegg, I feel I'm at a fork in the road. There may not be an easy way back if I choose the wrong one.'

'There's nothing wrong with your decision making, Mrs Jax. Besides, didn't you tell me you've settled on buying a modern van? That's another good choice. Aren't you picking it up this weekend?'

A picture of the little green van flashed into her mind. She loved the yellow stripe down its side, understated and stylish. Not everyone would notice, and few people would realise it also had off-road capability. Only those in the know would understand the full significance of the raised ground clearance, unusual in that particular model. The fact that she knew bolstered her confidence. She didn't need other people to know.

And that was the point. She had most of the skills to make a fake antique console table; she didn't need to advertise the fact. But, she reminded herself, it would be easier with the benefit of Ron's knowledge and experience, particularly if she was going to make something completely convincing.

Another truth struck home. If she ever decided to make a serious fake, then Ron would have to be on board. But she'd be bloody careful who else she let into her secret, and Lester wouldn't be one of those people.

'The van? Yes, yes... I'm picking it up this weekend.' She dragged her thoughts back to the workshop and the business. 'You're happy with the yellow stripe, aren't you? I'm going to get a sticker printed with our business name. It'll cover the Forestry Commission one. What do you think?'

'I think it's going to be splendid.' He stood up and limped over to look at the quartetto tables – a nest of four small tables, graduating in size, one slotting beneath the next so that they stored away neatly when not being used.

'They're nice, these Regency ones,' he said, picking up the smallest table.'

'I know. And they may look elegant, but the long slender legs didn't do too well when Mrs Pendle's dog ran through them and tried to kill their African parrot.'

'The damage to this stretcher looks old,' he said quietly.

'Yes, there are a couple more like that. And there's a longstanding split in one of the tops. I can't find a piece of old rosewood long enough to turn more legs from.' She watched him bend to inspect the highly figured dark wood.

'You've had a good look through the wood store, haven't you?'

'Yes, that's where I got the piece I'm going to cut the curved stretchers from, and I can use the rest of it to repair the sliders and the edges of the low-galleried tops... but do you think I should order some new in for the legs?'

'These tables aren't top quality. They've been well used, Mrs Jax. They've even saved the life of a parrot, and I bet you they'll have to stand up to a whole lot more. And the legs? I guess the largest table is thirty inches high.'

'I'll call the wood store and see if they've got some rosewood in stock.'

The barn workshop didn't have an office; Ron had never seen the need. But it hadn't stopped Chrissie commandeering a corner for paperwork and catalogues. A section of wooden counter spanned across two filing cabinets with space between for an office chair. It doubled as a desk and one day, when the internet connection improved, she hoped a computer would take pride of place on it. For the moment the workshop landline phone provided the focus and a stool, the office chair.

'And while I'm about it, I might as well work out the cost of new walnut for Lester,' she murmured as she looked for his file under L. 'L for Loxton.'

She'd started to keep the old work drawings and measurements along with photos of the before-and-after furniture restorations, and sure enough, it was all in his file along with a copy of the bill and an itemised estimate for the repair. It didn't give her enough detail to construct a replica, but at least she'd have a starting point to cost out an order for the wood.

'Oh God,' she breathed, as her thoughts collided. What was Lester's game?

By the time she drove home at the end of the afternoon, she felt tired but more decided. The rollercoaster of excitement and anxiety had been replaced by a more pragmatic mood. The kind that came when she'd worked out a plan. For a while Lester's call had brought back flashes of anger and embarrassment over being duped by the replica nutmeg grater scam. But now it was a reminder there'd always be a loser in the business of fakes.

When Clive rang from Ipswich to say he'd be getting back late, she was sitting in her kitchen, her laptop open on the narrow pine table and a mug of tea close at hand. She'd finished preparing estimates for Lester and had just sent an email to Damon requesting an update on the nutmeg grater inquiry.

'Clive, can I ask you something?' she said.

'Yes, but–'

'I'll be quick. It's about fakes. If someone makes a copy of something and it's a convincing copy, would you call it a fake?'

'What?'

'What I'm trying to say is if it's obvious something's a copy, you wouldn't call it a fake, would you?'

'No, but it doesn't mean a copy is OK. It's illegal if it's breaking copyright law. Hey, I don't understand where you're going with this.'

'And a fake?'

'A fake? Well if there's intent to deceive, to pass something off as the original or as the genuine article when it isn't, I'd call it a fake. False representation. Look, I only rang to say I'm running late. Are you OK? Has something happened?'

'Yes. Well no, not really.'

'This isn't because you don't believe me when I said I'm running late, is it?'

'What? Of course not. What a funny thing to say.'

'Look, there really have been developments in the Owen case, and I really am very busy still. But we'll talk when I get home. OK? See you later. Bye.' He ended the call.

Normally she'd have felt as if she'd been left hanging in the air by Clive's hurried goodbye, but instead she was struck by something he'd said. Copyright. There was no design copyright or patent on the antique console table. There wasn't even a maker's name. 'Muddy waters,' she murmured, 'muddy waters.'

Clive seemed reasonably cheerful when a little over two hours later he walked through the front door and tossed his keys onto the hall table.

'Hey, you're back, that's nice. There's some vegetable lasagne left if you want to pop it in the microwave. I'm afraid I've already eaten. I thought you'd be hours yet.' She caught the faint smell of stale smoke on his jacket as she kissed him. 'Ugh, cigarettes,' she said, drawing back and wrinkling her nose.

'I know.' He sniffed his sleeve. 'The smell gets into everything. It was much worse earlier but it's starting to wear off a bit now. It's a hazard of interviewing people when you're not at the station.'

'I hope it was worth it all, ending up reeking of cigarettes.'

'Well, sort of. It gave me another angle to follow.'

'Now that sounds intriguing.'

She sensed he was in a talkative mood, ready to share, no doubt to prove he really had been working late. Her naturally nosey instincts told her she'd get more out of him if she kept playing the *I don't know whether to believe you were working late* card. 'So why are you late? What kept you?'

'I was out asking questions. Early evening can be quite fruitful. It's surprising what you discover talking to people when they're at home. Particularly if they've just got back from work and haven't had time to go out again. It's a kind of winding down time. They're off their guard.'

'So did it work this time?'

'Well kind of. I wanted to check something with Prosecco. She's staying with an aunt in Ipswich, at least that's the address she gave us. She'd said she wanted a week or two to get herself back together, get her head straight before going back to the bungalow without Owen.'

'An aunt?' Chrissie hoped she looked as if she needed convincing.

'Yes. In fact I ended up talking to the aunt while I waited for Prosecco.'

'And?'

'The aunt was the smoker.'

'Then she must have had something interesting to say, otherwise why breathe in a lungful of someone else's cigarettes?'

'Yes, you're right. There was a photo of Prosecco on her sideboard. I guess she'd have been about fourteen or fifteen, and she had a medal hanging around her neck.'

'And…?'

'She'd won a national competition. But the point is, it seems Prosecco had the makings of a talented athlete or gymnast. Her aunt was very proud.'

'A name to watch. So did she make the Olympic selection?'

'No. Apparently she had some health issues.'

'So an injury?'

'I don't know. The aunt was a bit vague on details.'

'But Prosecco filled you in when she got home?'

'She didn't turn up, at least not while I was there.'

'But if her aunt was so proud she must have talked about the club, the other athletes or gymnasts Prosecco outclassed, other wins, maybe what her trainers said about her?'

'Like I said, the aunt clammed up. When I asked more, she told me she didn't want me waiting any longer and asked me to leave. Hey what is this, an interrogation?'

'Of course not. I'm interested, that's all. We have just had the Olympics, remember?'

'Yes, I was forgetting that. You know, I was probably touching on a raw chord. Maybe that's what upset her. Right, I think I'll heat up some of that lasagne.'

'If you're getting a beer from the fridge, can you get me one too?' she called after him, as he disappeared into the kitchen.

She waited, reluctant to get up from the sofa, comfortable hearing the sounds as he moved between the counter and fridge, setting the timer on the microwave and rummaging in a drawer for a bottle opener. It was all reassuringly domestic. By the time he poked his head back into the living room she was relaxed, mellow.

'Hey, I've remembered now. In the photo, Norwich was written on a banner in the sports hall. I'll get Stickley onto it.'

'So the subtle approach. You still haven't said why you wanted to speak to Prosecco?'

'Ah, that was about Owen. You remember I told you about the post mortem and the nephritis – the kidney damage? Well we've got his medical records now. I don't know why it took so long; I suppose the NHS has other priorities. Anyway, it seems he may have been into eating magic mushrooms.'

'Magic mushrooms? Isn't that rather old fashioned - hippies and the sixties? Are you sure it isn't code for something else?'

'Perhaps.'

'But you think that's the cause of the kidney thing, do you? I didn't know they were dangerous like that.'

'I'm not sure they are, but his GP... and he was another person I spoke to today, said if Owen was picking them himself, or buying them off the internet, well some poisonous ones could have got mixed in by mistake. It's the poisonous ones that can cause kidney damage, he said.'

'So you were going to ask Prosecco about the magic mushrooms?'

'Well yes, but I also thought she might draw the obvious conclusions about her own kidneys if she'd eaten some too, and it seemed kinder to tell her to her face, rather than over the phone.'

'I wonder? Poor Owen. His stomach caused such a lot of problems, didn't it?'

'Yes, but according to the GP, only for about a month before he died. But there were one or two other things I wanted to ask Prosecco. A few gaps in her past not accounted for.'

'Probably when she dropped out of competition, like her aunt said. Do you think it's relevant then?'

Ping!

'Ah good, my lasagne's ready.'

Clive disappeared back into the kitchen only to return a few minutes later carrying a tray with a plate of lasagne and two small bottles of beer. 'Are you picking up your van tomorrow?' he asked, handing her one of the opened bottles.

'Friday? No, I'm busy in the workshop. It's going to have to be Saturday morning. But don't worry, I know you're on duty so I've asked Nick to drive me over there. All the paperwork is organised. I just have to hand over a wodge of cash. It's exciting.'

'Well here's to the little green van,' he said as he picked up his bottle and drank.

'And its yellow stripe.' She sipped her beer, the first mouthful nothing but frothy bubbles.

CHAPTER 24

Matt shifted his weight carefully as he half-pushed, half-leaned on the heavy door into the Nags Head. He'd assumed three days would be long enough to recover, avoiding unnecessary movement as different parts of his body ached and complained.

Had it been worth it, he wondered.

The Tuesday taster session had been, as he'd told Maisie, 'Ace, awesome, a DOS-ing hell.' He'd wheezed and sweated through an hour on jumping stilts, while angry welts developed under straps and bands securing the stilts. By Wednesday, bruises and stiffness took hold of his legs. He'd looked it up on the net, now lactic acid was a new word in his arsenal of pain. All through Thursday, he'd wondered if he'd caught a dose of flu, but by Friday, his legs were easing, only his ribs and tummy muscles hurt.

'Hey Matt, over here,' a voice called out.

He made to raise an arm but his ribs twinged and the Sonic Stridor victory salute turned into a damp squib of a wave.

'Hi, Nick,' he yelled, his words swallowed by the Friday night wall of sound filling the bar.

If he'd been able to make his muscles do all he wanted, he'd have elbowed his way between the drinkers to reach the barman. Instead he waited his turn, leaning towards the counter, pressing against the back of the person in front.

'A pint of lager, mate,' he shouted.

The jukebox burst into life and launched the Rolling Stones' Jumpin' Jack Flash at triple-figure decibels.

'Hi,' Chrissie mouthed, as he made his way over, slopping lager and collapsing onto the bench seat next to her.

'You're still here.' He thrust his legs under the small beer-ringed table, realised he'd just said the obvious, and added, 'Yeah, I know you're here. I meant – you've usually left by now.'

'I know what you meant. Clive's working this weekend so he'll be home late. I think he's hoping to catch up with Prosecco.' Her voice was almost lost behind Mick Jagger's raw vocal.

'Prosecco?' Nick looked up from his glass. 'Now there's a coincidence. We bumped into her on Tuesday.'

'Yeah, at the jumpin' stilts taster.'

'Really? Don't tell me she's into this craze as well?'

'No, no. She said she was returning the stilts. Apparently Owen was the one who was into them.'

'Yeah, see we're not the only ones, Chrissie.' Matt nodded in time with Jumpin' Jack Flash's last chords. As the notes died, drinkers' voices began to reclaim the bar.

'Thank God for that. Why'd you put it on so loud, Nick?'

'More impact. You know, for Matt... all that spring in his step.'

'Wild,' Matt murmured. Mick Jagger's words still pounded in his head. 'What? Why you lookin' at me like that, Chrissie?'

'Damon got back to me. He emailed me an update.'

'Oh yeah?' For once the likely mention of Priddy didn't trigger a reaction. He hadn't the strength. And besides, he reckoned if Damon knew he'd lied about not being able to trace her, then he'd have said something a couple of hours ago, while he was still working the shortened Friday evening session. Matt figured his deception was a safe secret for the moment.

'Well he aint said much to me about it yet. Mind you, I aint asked, just got on with me list of names, this evening.'

He shot Nick a warning. *Whatever you do, don't scammin' mention Felix Lighter*, he thought and hoped Nick got it.

'Come on, Chrissie. Tell us. What's he found out?' Nick asked.

'Well, he's found user names and passwords to the selling site and to several email addresses. And there's an actual address in Ipswich.'

'Shit. All that from a log bugger thing?' Nick stared at his glass.

'I guess so, except he called it a key logger bug,' Chrissie said.

For a moment Matt let the beery atmosphere in the bar wash over him. Damon had told him on Monday that the seller used the name Tony Mopar and there was a second person using the same computer, Priddy Jones. It was all about to come out. Truth will out, he'd heard people say and nodded. He looked at Chrissie.

'That's right isn't it, Matt?' she said.

He nodded again.

'So, has he given you the names? The addresses?' Nick sounded impatient, exasperated.

'Well, there's a Tony Mopar and a Priddy Jones.'

Matt closed his eyes. It was the moment he wished he could spring away on jumping stilts, absent himself for a few minutes while he saved the world in comic-strip mode, and then return when it was over. But of course he couldn't. He had the bruises to prove it.

'Tony Mopar?'

'Yes, Nick. And a Priddy Jones.' Chrissie's voice sounded tight to Matt. He'd heard it like that before when she was cross.

'Mopar?' Nick repeated.

Something happened inside Matt's head. The place, the letters, the image – memories collided into a photographic collage, fragmented and then reassembled. Was it a coincidence?

'Mopar – I've seen it somewhere. Recently. Yeah, on a black tee. In here... more or less where you're sitting now, mate. Owen. It were written on his black tee. Grey letterin', not very obvious. But it was definitely,' he spelled out the letters, 'M O P A R, in capitals.'

'I can't even remember what Owen was wearing... but I've seen the name,' Chrissie screwed up her eyes, 'yes, my TR7. On a packet alongside my spare tyre and jack. Isn't it a trade name? Doesn't it stand for motor parts. MOtor PARts?' She wrote the letters with her finger, tracing it through the puddle of beer on the table.

'Mostly Old Paint and Rust.'

'Thanks Nick. But the name the key logger came up with was a Tony Mopar, not MOPAR, a classic car parts supplier. Surely it's just a coincidence? You can't be saying Owen was connected in some way with Tony Mopar on the basis of... his tee shirt?'

'Course I aint. I was just sayin' I'd seen the name before, on Owen's tee.'

'And Owen is dead.' Nick added.

'Poor Owen,' Chrissie murmured.

While Chrissie talked about Tony Mopar, she wasn't talking about Priddy. It made sense to Matt. 'Did Damon say if this bloke's still sellin' on the memorabilia website?' he muttered.

'I don't know but I'm guessing so.'

'Well it kinda rules Owen out, don't it? Unless he's come back from the dead.'

The swell of Friday night drinkers talking and laughing filled the bar around them. Matt felt uncomfortable. He didn't want Owen jamming up his thoughts, and the sudden hollow sadness surprised him. A glance at Chrissie and Nick told him their mood had also turned grey. No smiles.

'So Chrissie, where are you going with this?' Nick asked.

'Well, I've got two names and an address. I suppose I'll write a carefully worded letter to Mr Mopar saying the nutmeg grater delivered wasn't the one represented on the site. I'll request either a replacement with the genuine grater, or a refund and I'll throw around words like mis-selling, the Trading Standards Regulator, and was this an honest mistake or fraud?'

'What if he doesn't reply? Just blanks you?'

'Then, Nick, I guess I'll ask Clive what to do next. I suppose it could end up in the small claims court and with the debt collectors.'

'Flamin' hell,' Matt groaned, 'not the debt collectors again.'

'What, Matt? What are you moaning into your lager about?'

Matt felt the intensity of Chrissie's gaze turn on him. Why hadn't he kept his big mouth shut? 'I... I've just realised - I've seen a Priddy Jones on the tracin' lists we get from the debt collectors. It were on Damon's list, so I don't know the details.'

'Are you saying this Jones character already owes money?'

'Yeah, Chrissie. If it's the same Jones.' Matt couldn't help glancing at Nick, but he seemed to be preoccupied with swilling the last of his beer around in the bottom of his glass.

'So can you check if it's the same address? Because if it is, then it must be the same Jones,' Chrissie said.

'Another round, anyone?' Nick stood up.

While Nick disappeared into the crowd thronging in front of the barman, Matt tried to explain how Damon wouldn't allow him to look into the firm's database of previous tracings. 'Sorry, Chrissie, but it aint allowed. It's more than me job's worth.'

By the time Nick returned with brimming glasses, Matt had lightened up. Names, except of course Felix Lighter's, were out in the open at last, and nobody seemed to suspect his own duplicity. Perversely, he felt slightly cheated. All that angst about Priddy? Damon hadn't even questioned his broken run of success in tracing the names.

'So what you doing this weekend?' he asked, relaxed but disgruntled.

'I'm collecting my new, well... new to me, van on Saturday morning.'

'And I'm giving Chrissie a lift to Tunstall Forest to collect the van. Hey, do either of you want to give me a hand erecting some mock-ups of the Orford Ness Airfield huts? We'll be mainly working in a field near Orford, on this side of the river. It's only a few miles from Tunstall Forest, Chrissie.'

'Aint you got a gig out at Orford?' Matt asked. He was sure he remembered Nick talking about it.

'Not for a couple of weeks. No, this weekend Lester needs me. The set has to be up by Monday - so that's me bloody spoken for. I'd hoped to get some canoeing in tomorrow, you know, grab a chance to see if Yvonne's still around.'

'Will Lester be there tomorrow?'

'He'd better be, Chrissie.'

'You could always ask Dave to give you a hand.'

'On a Saturday? I'm afraid he'd need the promise of Gavi Monterey being on set. What are you doing tomorrow, Matt?'

'I don't think Matt has quite the same pull as Gavi,' Chrissie said and sipped her ginger beer.

'What? Nah I was goin' to look for a wig, mate. Hey, no. Why you laughin'?'

'A wig?'

'Yeah, for Maisie. She's seen one she wants, but someone else bought it. It aint new, more kinda retro, so I thought it'd be a surprise if….' He watched his friends nod.

'So where are you looking for a wig?' Chrissie asked.

'I dunno, yet.'

'Prosecco. Why don't you ask her? She's a make-up artist. She might even have one going cheap.'

'Wicked! I hadn't thought of that. Yeah, I s'pose I could ask her.' He watched Nick for a moment, and wondered if he was being serious.

'She'll remember you from the jumping stilts. I'm sure she won't mind you asking.'

'Great, rock on!' Chrissie laughed, and raised her glass.

'I reckon this calls for Jumpin' Jack Flash. What do you say? One more time?' Nick stood up and made his way to the jukebox.

CHAPTER 25

Nick stood by his Ford Fiesta and watched as Chrissie manoeuvred her TR7 into the narrow space to the side of his parents' house. Barking Tye seemed sleepy at just after seven o'clock on a Saturday morning. 'Please don't wake Mum and Dad,' he breathed, as Chrissie's tyres scrunched the gravel and a sudden grating yowl signalled her attempt to slip into reverse while the engine over-revved.

But of course he knew there'd be little chance of waking his mother. She'd already be up, watching eagle-eyed through the chink to the side of her steely-blue kitchen blind. Right from his first days at Utterly Academy he'd sensed she'd never like Chrissie. He supposed she couldn't understand how a forty-two year old woman could be just a friend to her only son, didn't see the big sister he saw in the friendship. He'd read his mother's face often enough, heard her say, 'She'll have designs on you.'

He'd bitten back the *I didn't know she was a tattoo artist* quips, tried to make allowances for her jealous insecurity, and vowed to move out as soon as he had sufficient money. That had been two years ago. But he was a qualified carpenter now, earning for working overtime. If the embarrassment of Clive's official visit twelve days ago hadn't been enough to push him into making the move, this morning's eagle-eyed disapproval had.

'I think it's about time I found my own place, Chrissie,' he said, loud enough to be heard through the steely-blue kitchen blind.

'What? You aren't thinking of leaving Willows are you?' she said, as she locked her car.

'No, of course not. I mean a flat.'

'You're sure my car isn't in the way here? Insurance... money... Mr Grabham's address and phone number....' She looked up as she checked through her bag.

'Did you just say you've found a flat?'

'I'm looking. Hey, I'll tell you on the way. Come on, we better get going.' As always, his mood lightened as he started the car and eased out onto the road. It was often like this with his mother – irritation and then self-reproach for his impatience with her. But now the will to cut loose was stronger than ever.

'You'll probably find your mum less... exasperating when you aren't living at home. So have you found anything yet?'

'Not yet.'

'Say if you need any help looking. I can ask around. My friend Sarah may know of somewhere.'

'Thanks, I may take you up on that.' Sometimes he felt half a continent wouldn't be far enough away. It was nice someone understood. Good old Chrissie.

'So why are we going in your car? Aren't you taking a Willows van? You know, with your tools and portable workbench?'

'Yes well I thought about what you said last night at the pub. So I gave Dave a call and he offered to give a hand. It could have had something to do with me saying Gavi Monterey might be there. Anyway, he's coming and bringing a Willows van.'

'Ah... let's hope he copes with the disappointment when he discovers Gavi's not there. So why aren't we all going across in the van, then?'

'Because I reckoned I might drive back via Yvonne. I texted her after I'd spoken to Dave and suggested we check out the Portcullis Arms. It's where we're having our Orford gig in a couple of weeks' time. I thought maybe a drink…?' He let his voice trail away with his imagination, as he threaded along the B roads towards Wickham Market.

'You're a dark horse.'

'Not really, I reckoned if I was over that way, why not–'

'Be an opportunist? Do you know, I love this road. And to think a week ago Clive and I were driving along here - and in a few hours' time I'll be driving back in my Citroen van.'

'So soon? Aren't you going to help as well? There'll be a truck load of hut sections. Lester's driving them over. It'll be like glorified Lego.'

'You've just said you'll have Dave with you, and besides, I don't know if I want to meet Lester.'

'Oh come on, Chrissie. Please come as well. We'll get it done quicker with more people. And what's this with Lester?'

'He phoned me a couple of days ago. He wants me to make a replica console table.'

'But that's cool. Like the one you repaired?'

While Chrissie talked, Nick concentrated on the road ahead. It was difficult to follow her nuances of right and wrong as they cut across flatly rolling fields, then twisted into sharp bends. Trust Chrissie to get caught up in the niceties of *intent to deceive*, he thought.

'Look, Chrissie, life isn't so polarised. The film and stage industry well, it's a bit….'

How to find the right words? He'd spent hours sitting around the film shoots at Althorne House, noticing what happened on the sidelines and behind the scenes. Things which at first seemed like a clear matter of honesty had become blurred. As long as he stayed out of it, he'd reckoned it was nothing to do with him.

'I'd say it's a bit like a restaurant. Tips and gratuities for the people who wait on your table. There's a system. It's the same sort of thing in film and theatre. The support staff, the little guys behind the scenes, they don't get the megabucks the stars and directors earn. I guess there's a mind-set, and memorabilia could be considered... a bit like tipping?'

'You're missing my point, Nick. There are real memorabilia, and there are fakes.'

She's right, he thought. But he didn't want to go there. Take Priddy; he liked her, she was a kind of mate, but what the hell was she up to? He reckoned she'd have told him if she'd wanted him to know. And she hadn't mentioned the bloke who shared her computer, either. Using the same computer implied an intimacy almost akin to letting someone into your bed. It had been a surprise.

A thought struck. Had she kept Tony Mopar a secret because she fancied Nick and wanted to appear unattached and available? He usually noticed when a girl was attracted to him, but he hadn't picked up the signals from Priddy. Had he missed something?

'Yeah... fakes. That's murky. You don't want to get mixed up in that,' he muttered, his thoughts racing down a different track while his mouth formed platitudes.

They made good time, meeting little traffic at that hour on a Saturday morning. They crossed east of the A12, the road becoming narrower, meandering between rough hedges and alongside patches of woodland and forest. It shielded them from endless fields of ploughed-in stubble.

'We'll be in Tunstall soon. Where's the place we're going to for your van?' He became aware of her rummaging in her bag, no doubt for the directions. 'But you were here with Clive only a week ago. Surely you can remember the way,' he said, holding back the laughter threatening to creep into his voice.

'Yes, but we came at it from a different direction.'

'OK, well do you want me to stop while you have a think?'

'No hey, this looks familiar. It's Tunstall Common, or is it Blaxhall Common? I remember passing here, or somewhere like here on the test drive. I probably drove through both. Look at all the gorse and heather. Don't you love these sandling heaths?'

'Come on, Chrissie. Right or left? Sandlings? Oh no, my cheese rolls. I left them in the fridge. Shit. How could I be so stupid?'

'OK, OK... let me think. Left. No, turn round and take the left back there... except it'll be a right now.'

Nick bit his tongue and turned the old Fiesta around, irritated with himself for leaving the cheese rolls behind, and not relishing being hungry later in the day. What was it with Chrissie, he wondered. Give her a technical drawing or a spreadsheet, and she was in her element. Expect her to have a sense of north or south and she was hopeless. He reckoned she'd get lost on a roundabout.

'If there isn't a satnav in this van you're buying, for God's sake, do everyone a favour, Chrissie - ask Clive to give you a satnav for Christmas.'

'No way. That'd be admitting defeat. Do you have Google Maps on that fancy phone you were given? The gold one?'

'But you've just said no way, to a satnav.'

'No, just to asking Clive for one.'

He'd forgotten about his replacement phone with the smart features. He'd mostly only used it for texts and calls, hadn't needed its maps or played games on it, hadn't even taken any photos with it yet.

'Yeah, take a look. I don't know what the signal's like round here,' he said and wrestled it from his pocket as he drove. 'The passcode is three, zero, four, eight.'

While Chrissie unlocked his phone and tapped its screen, Nick slowed. The road had petered into a roughly tarmacked lane. 'Are you sure this is the right way, Chrissie?'

He peered through a hedge at a collection of ramshackle wooden barns, lean-tos and long sheds. Neglect and decay had brought down roofs. Rotten slats had fallen from weatherboard cladding and jagged beams and timber lay at angles where they'd dropped. It struck Nick it wouldn't be long before the nettles and brambles had reclaimed the buildings as their own.

'How could anyone let something disintegrate like that? It's spooky,' he breathed.

'The tracker's frozen, but... keep driving... I'm starting to get something now. It's on the other side of Tunstall Forest. So carry on along here, then turn right at the T-junction and we're there,' Chrissie said, looking up from the phone, and seemingly unaware of the weird carcasses of abandoned farm outbuildings they'd passed.

'Are you OK?' she asked. Her excitement was obvious. It made the sudden glimpse of rotting buildings seem unreal, otherworldly.

'Yeah. You should upgrade to a smart phone.' He didn't want to describe what he'd just seen, didn't want to deepen the weird feeling he couldn't explain. 'So why is the bloke selling the van?'

'Mr Grabham? You mustn't laugh when you see him. He'll be all decked out in ranger kit. You know... binoculars, camouflage fatigues, water bottle, and of course the van matches the image. I reckon he thinks Tunstall Forest is the Serengeti. Would you believe his day job is in Ipswich, something to do with telecommunications? He said his kids weren't interested in spending their weekends roaming the forest. I think his wife is making him sell the van, cut down on the outdoor survival stuff and spend more time with the kids.'

'As long as you don't start wearing camouflage bags. Did you say telecommunications? Are you sure the van hasn't got a satnav?'

'Hey, this must be it. Didn't I say a T-junction? Now turn left and....'

God, she could be stubborn. 'What are we looking for?' he sighed and dropped to crawler speed.

'There.' She pointed across him. 'I recognise the scrappy shingled track.'

He drove the Fiesta through an open gateway and followed the drive as it swept in front of what looked to have once been semi-detached flint and brick cottages, but now were knocked into one. An open fronted cart lodge doubled as a garage and Nick guessed the maroon-coloured estate parked there must be the family car. He'd barely pulled up before Chrissie swung her passenger door open and leapt out. She hurried to a Citroen van parked alongside a rough hedge. The leafy colours of overhanging branches blended into its green paintwork. If it wasn't for the hedge holding back the trees, he reckoned the planted forest behind the cottages would swallow them.

No wonder the van needs a yellow stipe. It could get lost amongst all those trees, he thought as he got out of his car.

Before Nick had a chance to ring the front door bell a man, probably in his forties, appeared from around the side of the cottage. He reckoned Mr Grabham must have been listening for the tyres on the shingle.

'Hi again, Chrissie. Hi,' the man said, striding towards him, 'I'm Nigel. Nigel Grabham.'

'Hi, I'm Nick.' He took in the lightweight trekking shirt and Tangier trousers. Probably had field glasses trained on them from inside a hide, Nick decided.

'We can do the paperwork inside, Chrissie. Coffee, either of you?'

Nick brought up the rear as they followed Nigel through the side door into the kitchen. While Chrissie concentrated on the paperwork and payment, Nick sipped rich milky coffee and took in his surroundings. A large-scale map of the area caught his attention. It was fixed to a corkboard, and red and blue markers pinpointed various locations.

'Why the coloured pins?' Nick asked while Chrissie drank her coffee.

'Sightings of nesting birds. The red markers are the ones Gull spotted first, and the blue ones, Ptarmigan spotted first. They're my boys. Of course that was a few years ago.

Now they're more interested in computer games and their friends. But I keep the map and the markers, just in case they ever decide to take an interest in the nesting sites again.'

'So what did Gull spot here,' Nick asked, pointing to where he figured he'd driven past the disintegrating wooden outhouses. Part of him dreaded the answer.

Nigel peered at the map. 'Barn owls. They were nesting there again this year. Two owlets successfully reared. Of course they've all left the nest now. Hopefully the breeding pair will be back again in March. I've got some photos if you want to take a look?'

'Awesome.' Nick didn't know what he'd expected. Not the ordinary, he supposed. Feeling relieved but slightly short-changed, he checked his watch. Lester was expecting him.

'Shit, is that the time? Sorry – I can't stop, Nigel. I'm meant to be in Orford.' He caught Chrissie's eye. 'If you've finished here now, I'll follow you out Chrissie, but you turn to the left. I'll head on to the right, OK? That's unless you've changed your mind about Lester, in which case Orford is to the right.'

He waited in his Fiesta while Chrissie started the van. She looked pretty composed as she waved to Nigel, the tyres scrunching the gravel in low gear. He drew up behind.

A moment of hesitation at the gates, and then she was turning left while the indicator lights flickered briefly right. He watched her draw away smoothly, accelerating along the lane, the indicator now blinking furiously left, as if signalling to pull in. He guessed oncoming cars would see the wipers, windscreen-wash spray and headlights flashing on and off while she tried the controls. But there weren't any cars. The lane was deserted.

He hung back at the gates for a moment longer, then still laughing, turned right. 'Shit,' he muttered, remembering the cheese rolls he'd left at home. He hoped to God there'd be some sandwiches or baps he could buy when he reached Orford.

•

Chrissie checked her rear view and wing mirrors. No Nigel Grabham or Nick in sight watching, no other cars on the lane. It was safe to pull over, stop and collect her thoughts. The position of the indicator and headlight controls had seemed ridiculously obvious when she'd used them on the test drive with Nigel, only a week ago. Even before starting the engine a few minutes earlier, she'd run through the checklist, reminded herself. And yet when she'd peered through the windscreen, her mind on steering and her hands automatically reaching for the indicator, she'd found the wiper controls instead. Then dipped the headlights, then…. It was no good, she had to familiarise herself with the controls again.

Brrring brrring! Brrring brrring!

Now what, she thought as she rummaged in her bag for her phone. Was Nick ringing to check she was OK, not lost already? Or was it Nigel Grabham wanting to say the nearest filling station was twenty miles away and there were high energy multigrain bars and bottled water stowed with the spare tyre?

'Clive!' she said, 'Thank God it's you.'

'Is everything OK? You sound kind of…. Have you picked up the van?'

'Yes, you're talking to the proud but slightly frazzled owner of a Citroen Berlingo ex-Forestry Commission van. I've used half a bottle of washer-fluid on the windscreen and dipped and un-dipped my headlights five times just turning out of the drive.'

'Sorry, I'm not catching everything. The signal… your voice cuts out. So it's going well?'

'Yes, you bet.' She couldn't help grinning. 'Mind you, we had a few hairy moments when I couldn't find the place. Are you hearing me any better?'

'Chrissie–'

'Now your voice is breaking up.'

'Ah, I can hear you again.'

'Good. Nick's new phone has a map-tracker-thingy option. The internet reception over here is pretty patchy, so it was more a case of just one map frozen on the screen, than a tracker. But in the end I recognised the way,' she lied, hoping her voice didn't give her away. 'Still able to hear me?'

'Yes, it's stronger now. Of course, the replacement phone, I'd forgotten he'd have that with him. Great. Well thank Nick for me. Actually you can thank him for something else as well. He phoned a few days ago and we had a very interesting conversation about the accident with the scenery at Althorne House and jumping stilts, or rather the marks they leave.'

'What? Don't say you're into this craze as well?'

'No, no, but it set me wondering.'

'Please tell me you're not as mad as Nick and Matt. You should have seen them yesterday. Matt could still hardly move.'

'Well that's nothing new. Do you know those stilts might turn out to be good for me? I think I'm close to a break through. If it wasn't for the bloody medical records – it's such a rigmarole trying to get access. It's almost as bad as trying to get hold of juvenile offenders' records. God, the number of hoops I'm having to jump through.'

'Nothing like a bit of paperwork to keep you sane.'

'Don't start me on that. OK, I better go now. I'll ring later. Bye.'

Still a little hot and flustered, she dropped her mobile back into her bag, opened her window, and listened to the tractor-like tones of her diesel engine. It was strangely reassuring in an agricultural kind of way. Yes, she thought, as she slipped the gears into first and drew away, this little van is going to be great.

CHAPTER 26

Matt kicked the stand into position, stowed his helmet and ambled across to the Academy's main entrance. It was quiet, but that's why he'd decided to use the library computers on a Saturday morning. What he was planning to look up needed plenty of bandwidth and privacy, neither of which could be guaranteed at home. And he didn't want to risk Maisie ever seeing his browsing history. Here he could be private and anonymous.

He was in luck. There must have been something going on in the Academy because the main entrance was open, it saved him circuiting the buildings and slipping through a rarely used door near the delivery area.

The muscles around his chest and tummy were definitely less sore than the previous evening in the Nags Head. He reckoned it was something to do with the all the lager giving him a good night's sleep. Thank DOS he hadn't said yes to helping out with the airfield huts. At least here he could keep his upper body stiff and try a rolling swagger by somehow swing-rotating his legs. It saved him flexing his quads. He hoped it looked sexy, but guessed Nick and Chrissie might not agree if they saw him now.

His thighs complained as he trudged up the main staircase to the first floor. Slowing his pace, he paused at the closed canteen doors. Without the familiar smells of frying and cooked cheese, it felt as if the heart of the building had died and gone cold. For a moment his spirit wavered, but then he noticed the library door was slightly ajar and his mood rallied. He wouldn't have to get past the keypad with a code he'd watched Rosie use.

She might be in, he thought although he couldn't imagine why any of the library staff would be there on a Saturday morning. He pushed the door gently and slid between the gap, catching his paunch against the latch.

'Hi!' Luckily the wooden floorboards and high ceiling absorbed the squeak in his voice as he continued, 'Martine?'

She was a library assistant, more brusque, less chatty with him than Rosie was. He'd never understood why.

'The library isn't open. I'm not here,' she said as she strode towards him.

He pulled at his tee shirt, nervously smoothing it over his stomach.

'I'm only here to get my bag. Left it here yesterday.' Without breaking her stride she brushed past him.

He waited, expecting her to turn and ask why he was in the library, order him to leave, but she kept on walking. And then she was gone, the door latch clicking behind her.

'Scammin' hell,' he whispered as he released his breath. If she was going to alert security, then he only had a few minutes.

It didn't take him a moment to settle at a computer station. Within seconds he was surfing the net, his mission clear - Prosecco and the wig for Maisie.

His previous search for the wig on the memorabilia sites had proved fruitless, but he hadn't considered contacting Prosecco direct. Now, after Nick's suggestion in the Nags Head, she was in his sights. But there was a problem. She didn't appear to have a surname.

Without an address and only half a name, directory sites came up with no viable results despite repeated searches. If he typed her in as a trading name, business or product, he was bombarded with information. The wrong information. It seemed Prosecco was a sparkling wine, best drunk when chilled and young. She had a fresh crisp taste, light and comparatively simple but with an intense primary aroma. 'Killer app,' he muttered.

But there was something he remembered Nick saying. Prosecco had been the make-up specialist for the bride and bridesmaids on the morning Owen died. Matt reckoned he might find something if he looked on wedding sites. It was either that or riding the Piaggio up to Diss and somehow breaking into the auction house system and finding the details of the buyer of the wigs, lot 300.

He was reluctant but it had to be done. 'Best without pryin' eyes around,' he murmured, as he typed in key search words and scrolled through yards of white taffeta, and silk. Make-up, nails and hair seemed to be a subsection on most of the sites.

'Yeah!' He punched the air and then regretted the sudden movement. '*Complete your special day with professional make-up designed to look natural for the camera. Make-up artist to the film industry. Prosecco....*' He read out the words, relieved he wouldn't have to trawl through more wedding sites. Now he needed to try the contact details and use his alter ego, Felix Lighter.

Without really thinking, he pulled his mobile from his jeans and pressed in the number. He listened to the ring tone, his pulse loud in his ear.

'Hello? Prosecco speaking, make-up specialist.' She sounded nice.

'Hi, this is....' He was about to say *Felix Lighter* and then remembered he'd seen Priddy with Prosecco at the auction. His voice died in his throat as panic gripped. It might not be the best name to use. She might have mentioned him to Prosecco.

'Hello, are you still there? I didn't catch a name?'

'I'm...,' he looked down at the words on his tee shirt, 'I'm Cool... arl, yeah Carl Stilts. That's Stiltz with a Z. Me girlfriend, I mean fiancée, she's seen a wig, set her heart on it, she wants to wear it at her....'

'You want me to do the whole look? Make-up? Hair? Wig? Have you set a date?'

'No, I mean not for the weddin'. She don't have to get married to have the wig, do she?' he said, his Suffolk starting to break through with his nerves.

'No of course not. But most people.... What's so special about the wig?'

'She saw it at an auction. Dunno where, but she said someone called Prosecco won the bidding, and well, we've been looking through them weddin' sites and....'

'You saw my name?'

'Yeah. She didn't notice but I recognised it. I reckoned it'd be awesome if she wore it to her hen do. That's if you still got it. I thought it'd be a cool surprise if you did her make-up as well.'

'Possibly. So is there a theme, a special look she had in mind?'

He pictured the wigs he'd seen on the Diss auction website, heard Maisie's voice saying retro. 'Marilyn, yeah,' he said, grabbing at straws.

'Monroe? Shouldn't I be talking to your fiancée about this?'

'Yeah, no... it's a surprise.'

'So how do you envisage I do this?' The niceness disappeared from her voice.

'Well, I s'pose I could just buy the wig, or maybe hire it? That'd be a surprise. She'd be pleased with that, I reckon.'

He listened to the silence on the line.

'Hi, are you still there?'

'I think you've got the wrong Prosecco. What made you think it was me who bought a wig at an auction? Have you been following me? Watching me?'

'N-no. She were sure it were you. She described you.'

'Who the hell are you?'

'Like I said, Carl Stiltz... with a Z,' but the line had gone dead.

So what made her cut the call like that he wondered, as he ran his hand over the words printed on his tee.

JUMPING STILTS

Cool bounce; Awesome spring
Rad product; Leaps with zing

'Yeah, I got it. Should've said I was Rad Zing.'

CHAPTER 27

It was early Monday and the film crew were gearing into readiness. Bit-part actors drank tea and coffee while waiting around in Sidcot flying suits or leather flying coats. In the distance, the early morning light caught the outline of Orford with its church tower and castle keep. If Nick moved slightly to the left, he was able to alter his sightline and the silent expanse of tidal water and grass runway gave the impression he was standing on Orford Ness with his feet firmly planted on the original airfield. In reality he was in a field and the River Ore separated him from the Ness.

'Neat outfit,' he remarked, to one of the actors.

'What? If I was wearing the real thing I'd bloody die of heat. This isn't any old overall, mate,' the actor muttered. 'This is a Sidcot. High tech, cutting edge World War One kit; a Burberry outer layer, a middle windproof silk layer and then a fur liner, at least that's what costume wants the film-goer to believe. I have to pretend, it helps me get into character.'

'Should have made your life easier and asked for one of the leather flying coats,' Nick said and laughed.

He spotted Lester walking across the meadow, now mowed and transformed into a WW1 grassy airstrip. A 4x4 with a closed-in trailer was manoeuvring into position, ready to unload a biplane. Probably the mock-up replica without an engine, he guessed.

'Hi.' Nick waved.

'We need to attach the wing sections,' Lester called, beckoning him over.

Nick nodded and raised a hand in half-salute before hurrying to help. After a weekend working with Lester in the field, respect and irritation had grown in equal measure. He'd seen his organisational skills and level temper put to the test when things had gone wrong. The first example of many was when they discovered a footpath and walkers crossing the spot where they planned to erect the airfield hut. But as a carpenter, he'd use only one nail where two would have been better. Speed seemed to be the overriding priority, and at the expense of quality. It went against Nick's nature. At least with Dave's help he'd been able to ensure the hut was erected properly.

'There's a real biplane flying over and doing some touch & go landings later in the day. It's standing by at Duxford,' Lester said, excitement flushing his face, already pink from the weekend weather. 'And you never told me. Did you get off with that girl? Yvette? Was that the name?'

'Yvonne. She's nice.' Nick turned away blocking any further questions as he watched the driver open the trailer doors.

He didn't want to talk about Yvonne with Lester. To be honest, he didn't want to talk about her with anyone. Not yet. Not until he was sure she fancied him for more than a one night's stand. And there was also the risk of anything he said on the subject getting back to Priddy. Until he was sure about Yvonne, he didn't want to sink his chances with Priddy.

It was a three man job, bolting the biplane wings back into position. Nick and the driver carried them out of the trailer, while Lester placed stands to support the wings and then directed fine adjustments as he slipped the bolts into position on the body of the plane.

'Better tie the plane down,' Nick suggested. 'It's windy out here and there isn't a complete engine and fuel tank to help weigh it down.'

The driver brought rope from the trailer and they screwed pegs into the ground to anchor tie-downs to the wings, before slipping chocks in front and behind the wheels.

'OK, we shouldn't have any problems,' Lester said, as he stood admiring their work.

'Right, if you're happy with it, I'll go and check the hut door again. You did say one of the pilots has to fall against it, didn't you?'

'Yeah, that's what Merlin told me.'

It only took Nick a few moments to stride across to Priddy who was setting folding canvas garden chairs outside the airfield hut and draping them with silk scarves, leather flying hats and roll neck jerseys.

'Hi, final check,' he said, opening the door to the hut and then shutting it again, testing the latch, ensuring it closed snugly into the keep on the doorframe.

'Have you got OCD or something?' she asked, looking up from her work.

'What?'

'OCD – obsessive compulsive disorder?'

'No, of course not.'

'It's not unusual on a film set. You know, actors going through routines to ensure good luck and drive away their demons.'

'Well that isn't me. I don't want half the hut falling down when Cooper, or whoever it is, flings himself against 'the door. Wood alters when it's damp, you know.'

'And it rained a bit last night. OK, I'll let you off.'

'So have you got time for a coffee, or are you still dressing….'

'The set? You cheeky bugger,' she said and tucked a wisp of wavy brown hair back under her baseball cap.

He guessed it was a no from Priddy and headed anyway to the refreshment trailer, leaving her to get on with her work. Was there any chemistry between them, he wondered. He reckoned Prosecco should know about any significant man in her life and made up his mind to ask.

Later, when the shoot was well under way he noticed Prosecco strolling across from the trailers parked in an adjoining field. They'd been transported across from Althorne House the previous day and tucked away with the cars and vans beyond the mock airstrip, out of the view of the cameras' wide angled shots. She moved in her usual elegant way, appearing unhurried but with an air of purpose. She pulled something akin to a two-wheeled shopping trolley; he'd heard her call it her mobile make-up bar. Now, he thought. Now was his opportunity to ask.

'Hi,' he said quietly, when she eventually paused next to him, her eyes on Cooper joking with the other pilots while the cameras rolled.

'He's got the looks, even from here,' Nick murmured, hoping he was echoing Prosecco's thoughts.

'The trouble is he knows it. Did you realise he thinks his left is his best side? Look how he keeps turning his face for the camera.'

'But he's an actor. The male lead. Isn't that what you'd expect him to do? Don't they all do it?'

'But Cooper turns his face when there isn't a camera. It's his default mode. He's always conscious of the effect he's having, as if he's playing a part. Sometimes it's impossible to know when he's acting or when it's for real. He's shallow,' she whispered.

'You like him, though? You think he's sexy? Hey, I bet without all your powder and paint he'd be a mere mortal, like me. You're part of creating the illusion called Cooper, the film star, the sexy celeb.' He caught the wistful look in her eyes, sensed emotions passing far deeper than her clear complexion and subtle make-up. Was it a memory of Owen he'd unleashed? Was it something to do with Cooper? The conversation threatened to turn heavy. Time for a shift in direction.

'So, tell me,' he said under his breath, hoping he'd got his timing right, 'has Priddy got a serious bloke at the moment? I'm sure I caught a name... Tony Mopar? Have I got competition?' He waited for her to smile or laugh. Maybe launch into matchmaking advice or a gentle let-down, but instead her expression hardened.

'Tony Mopar?' she said keeping her voice low, her generous mouth unexpectedly tight.

'Well I could be wrong, but I'm sure it was something like that.'

'Who told you?'

'I heard from.... I wouldn't like to say. Is there a problem, something I'm not supposed to know? I wouldn't want to get anyone into trouble by repeating....'

'Maybe you should be having this conversation with Priddy?' She turned her gaze from Cooper and looked Nick straight in the face. 'You're the second person who's recently asked me something I wouldn't have expected them to ask. Unless...? It's kind of spooky. Have you been following me?'

'No, of course not.' He noticed a muscle flickering on the side of her face as if she was clenching her jaw. 'Are you OK, Prosecco?'

'Are you implying I shouldn't be OK?'

'No, not at all.'

'Then don't pry, or you'll find yourself crossing a line.'

He was confused. Was she talking about herself or Priddy? He opened his mouth to ask, caught the warning in her eyes and changed subject, 'It must be hot wearing wigs in this weather. I mean take Gavi. In her publicity shots she's got long hair, but for this, well she's got her hair in a short bob. So has she had her hair cut for the film or does she wear a wig?'

'A wig? Are we talking about wigs now? Or Gavi? And keep your voice down, you'll disturb the take.' She seemed to have turned her attention back to Cooper.

'Wigs, I guess.'

Before he could whisper more, Merlin waved frantically and beckoned her over. Secretly Nick was relieved. Either she was edgy and oozing tension, or she seemed to be setting out to unnerve him. Either way, today it was easier to admire her from a distance rather than run the gauntlet of her spikiness.

By mid-afternoon Lester had left to cross on the little ferry from Orford to the Ness. 'He wants to check out the posts we're going to use to attach the *in the distance* airfield hut fascia,' Nick explained to Priddy.

'Is it true we're only allowed to film there for a couple of days?' she asked as she settled on a vacant foldaway camping chair next to Nick.

'Something like that. Lester and I will be stealing across in the early hours on a specially hired boat with a couple of fascia hut panels. And while Cooper is rowed across in full Royal Flying Corps-style, we'll be standing behind the panels making sure they stay propped up and secured to the posts while the cameras film him coming ashore.'

'Sounds like something out of a comedy sketch,' Priddy said. 'I may have to take a photo for the record.'

'As long as we haven't sunk into the marshes by then. So is now a good time for a coffee?'

'We should be on the next take in a moment so I'd better hang around here. Cooper will be using the hip flask. Would you believe Merlin OK'd a dash of alcohol? So he's got a vodka lapsang souchong teabag cocktail. That's cold black tea, sugar and alcohol – but if I don't guard it, he'll get hold of it too early and he'll swig the lot, demand more and be falling all over the place within the hour. But a skinny white would be great, if you're offering.'

'OK,' he said and left her with her plastic props-box on wheels. Wispy clouds were forming high in the sky and the excitement of the biplane's rotary engine still echoed in his ears. They'd all taken photos, including Nick with his slim almost gold-coloured phone.

The film cameras had rolled as the Sopwith Camel biplane flew in, touched its wheels on the grassy meadow airstrip and immediately lifted into the air, circuited and repeated the manoeuvre again and again. With some clever work in the editing room, there'd be plenty of minutes of landing and take-off shots. Even now, as he trudged to the refreshment trailer, he repeated the spec. 'A single Clerget

9B 9-cylinder rotary engine. 130 horsepower.' You never know, he thought, it might come in useful in a pub quiz.

While he waited for his coffee order, he turned to talk to one of the lighting crew behind him in the queue.

'Awesome, that Sopwith Camel, don't you think?' Nick murmured.

'A bugger to fly. Those early rotary engines had quite a torque on them. Difficult to fly straight and if they stalled – well the bloody plane'd go into a spin. Made it good for dog fights, easy to turn, but a killer for inexperienced pilots.'

'Wicked. It makes you wonder about the machine guns mounted on the fuselage – you know, how many disasters before someone invented something to coordinate the rate of machine gun fire with the propeller turning?' Nick hoped he sounded knowledgeable, repeating Dave's chatter as if it was his own.

'Yeah right, so they didn't shoot off their own propellers,' the lighting man added.

Nick walked back to Priddy, a paper cup of coffee in each hand. He was starting to get the pace of the film industry. Frenetic activity followed by hours of idleness or just plain boredom.

'Thanks, Nick. I could have gone with you. We haven't begun the hip flask take yet,' she said as he handed her a skinny white coffee.

'No problem. It's surprising what you can learn in queues. Now I'm an expert on the torque of a Sopwith Camel's rotary engine.' He wondered if it was the moment to drop Tony Mopar into the conversation, but Merlin waved his arms and it was obvious the filming was ready to move onto the next scene.

'I think you're needed,' he said and held out his hand to take back her coffee. 'Don't worry, I'll guard it for you.'

While actors and crew busied around, Nick sipped from his paper cup.

Prosecco dashed past muttering something about sweat and moments later he spotted her using a battery powered fan to dry Cooper's face. There was something about the intensity of her gaze and Cooper's rather detached manner. Was he staying in character ready for the next scene or was it some interplay between them? Before Nick could decide, he found he was watching Priddy as she cleared the film set of strewn leather flying hats and scarves. She stood for a moment, tilting her baseball cap and looking at her clipboard before bending in an efficient supple move. The hipflask flashed in the sun as she drew it out of her props-box. Cooper must have been on the lookout because he took a couple of strides and lunged for it.

Prosecco squealed, dropped the fan and sprinted. She reached Priddy first and snatched the flask. 'Hey,' she yelled and held it high, as if inviting an embrace from Cooper.

Nick was riveted by the display, but Merlin clapped his hands and called for order. When he looked again, the play tussle was over and Prosecco was occupied with the fan and her make-up trolley.

'Do you ever stop teasing? Where's the flask?' Cooper said, directing his words at Merlin, as if he was the umpire.

'Over there,' Prosecco said. She strolled across to Priddy and pointed down at the grass.

They all watched as Priddy frowned, picked up the hipflask and handed it to Prosecco, who in her turn solemnly passed it to Cooper. He unscrewed the top and drank.

'Thank you,' Merlin said. 'Now can we concentrate on this scene? Camera One? I want you just here.... And no talking, back there.'

'What was all that about?' Nick whispered, when ten minutes later he handed back Priddy's coffee.

'Beats me. More importantly, will the lapsang souchong cocktail be strong enough for Cooper? Now keep your voice down, we don't want to disturb the shoot.'

They sat watching companionably as the take began. Camera One was only ten inches from Cooper's face while Camera Two tracked him as he staggered to the airfield hut door.

'Now your flask,' Merlin prompted as Cooper thrust his hand into his leather flying coat pocket.

The camera blocked Nick's view but he guessed Cooper was swigging from the flask as Merlin called, 'Cut! Good, Cooper. Run that again and after you take the swig, hold it for longer in your mouth before swallowing. I like the face you pulled. It shows real emotion. Again!'

The takes continued.

'I couldn't... save him. There was nothing I could do.' Cooper sounded agonised.

Merlin appeared excited, flapping his arms and signalling the take to keep rolling. No stopping while Cooper was in full flow and on top form.

'I jutht carn... thave....'

'Slurring's good. Keep rolling,' Merlin said.

Nick felt he was in the presence of cinematic history being made. He pictured the BAFTA award, and this particular film clip being shown at promotional events around the world. He sensed it and he was pretty sure the rest of the cast and crew sensed it too.

Cooper gripped his stomach and crumpled, falling back against the door.

'Camera One,' Merlin called.

'Shit, has the door held?' Nick breathed.

'Keep shooting,' Merlin said.

Cooper's knees folded as he slid to the ground, his back against the closed door.

'Yes, it's held,' Nick murmured.

They watched as Cooper tried to stand up, but he didn't seem to have the strength. 'It'th goin' dark...,' he murmured as his legs gave way again.

'Yes! And... cut,' Merlin said.

Nick looked on, horrified as Cooper, now sweating, curled into a ball and vomited, groaned, whimpered, and then vomited again.

CHAPTER 28

The actor Cooper Brice was taken ill while filming on location near Orford yesterday. He was rushed to Ipswich Hospital but pronounced dead on arrival....

Chrissie slowed, distracted by the news breaking on her car radio. 'Cooper dead?' she murmured, hardly believing her ears and desperate to hear more. 'But he can't be.'

The Ipswich waterfront archaeological dig unearths more Saxon skeletons from the seventh century....

'But what about Cooper? I don't want to hear about dead Saxons,' Chrissie squealed, as if her cry could force the newsreader to stop and return to the Cooper story.

Numbed with disbelief, Chrissie pulled-in to the side of the lane and jabbed at the radio buttons. What about trying another station? If she was quick enough she might catch the news on... and then she was back on Radio Suffolk and the weather. 'Damn, damn, damn!'

She glanced at her dashboard. The factory original 1981 TR7 clock showed twenty minutes past four.

'Why is it always wrong?' she whined, venting her frustration as she knocked on its glass face. She checked her watch. 'Seven minutes past eight. I'll just have to wait until the nine o'clock news.' That's if she wanted to learn more.

'But how can he be dead? Did he have a heart attack?' she muttered as she checked her mirrors and pulled into the lane. The last time she'd seen him she was collecting the smashed console table. He'd been in a dark corner in the rear corridor of Althorne House. And if she remembered correctly, there'd been a mystery blonde in his arms. He'd seemed full of life back then. So what happens to a film when the star dies before it's completed, she wondered.

Her thoughts moved faster than her car as she drove the familiar route. She turned off the Wattisham Airfield perimeter lane, barely noticing the red campion and purple toadflax still flowering in the grassy verge near the hedge. The rough track with its potholes and ruts led her to the Clegg workshop where she drew up at an angle beside her Citroen van. Thank God the clock works in that, she thought, as she slammed her car door.

It had been quite a performance getting her car and van where she wanted them. The van was to live at the workshop. Clive had helped on Saturday evening, meeting her on his way back from Ipswich and work. She'd given him a quick tour of her latest projects in the barn, then locking and leaving her van there, she'd hopped into his Mondeo. It had been fun making a play of him being her boyfriend when he dropped her off ten minutes later at Nick's home to collect her TR7. In celebration, she'd let down her soft top, put her foot down hard on the accelerator and sped home to Woolpit with Clive on her tail in his Mondeo. But that had been Saturday and today was Tuesday.

'You'll never guess what I've just heard on the radio, Mr Clegg,' she said as she closed the heavy wooden door, threw her bag onto a workbench and drank in the calming atmosphere of the old barn.

'Good morning, Mrs Jax. On the radio? Let me think. There's a world shortage of rosewood and we're to stockpile it instead of gold? Good thing you ordered some for the quartetto tables.'

'No, no, Mr Clegg. I'm being serious. Cooper Brice has died. You know - the actor? Chiselled good looks and a hint of auburn in his hair? He is, sorry was, playing the part of a test pilot in the First World War. They've been filming over at Althorne House, where the console table got damaged. This week they were out at Orford.'

'Yes, yes, of course I remember.'

'They said on the news he was unwell during the filming and was dead by the time he got to hospital. That was yesterday, and I haven't heard from Nick. I'd have expected....' She let her words drift as her thoughts raced ahead.

'Why? Why from Nick? Was he there, Mrs Jax?'

'I don't know. I just kind of thought....'

But what did she think? Her nosey streak stirred up a whirl of questions. Was Nick all right? 'It was just over a couple of weeks ago he found Owen dead, Mr Clegg.'

'Yes, it would get to him. A second death, if he was there.'

'I'll call Clive.'

'But why not call Nick, Mrs Jax? It's Nick you're worried about.'

'He'll think I'm fussing, or nosey, or both?'

'I'm sure he already knows what you're like, Mrs Jax.'

She ignored Ron's quiet logic and searched through her bag for her phone. She didn't know what she expected Clive to say or do, but it was still before eight thirty in the morning and she didn't think he'd mind her calling.

'Come on, come on,' she breathed impatiently. 'Answer.... Hi, it's me.'

'Hi, Chrissie.' He sounded cheerful, pleased to hear her voice.

'Have you heard? Cooper Brice - it was on this morning's news.'

'He's dead. Yes, the hospital contacted us yesterday. A suspicious, unexplained death. They couldn't say what killed him but they think he'd taken something. So we're officially involved until the coroner reports back to us, and... well I was going to ask you not to talk to Nick about it. DS Stickley left an initial report on my desk. It seems Nick, along with half the cast and crew, may have been a witness and... well we don't want to compromise any investigation. So it's best not to talk to him about it yet. Not until we know why he died.'

'You said the hospital think he took something? On purpose? By mistake? Is anyone else unwell?' She listened to the silence. 'Clive, are you still there?'

'Yes, I'm still here. Now please, Chrissie, no more questions. Leave it to us. OK?'

'But....' The call went dead, leaving her thwarted, blocked.

'Tea? Ron asked, as he limped over to the kettle.

'What? Sorry, tea – yes. Don't worry, I'll make it,' she said, needing to divert her frustration.

She knew Ron wouldn't ask what Clive had said, but if he'd heard her end of the conversation, he'd already have guessed Cooper Brice hadn't died a natural death. And in reality, that was all she'd managed to learn from Clive. Any more was pure speculation.

By the time she settled on her work stool, a mug of steaming tea in her hand, she'd calmed a little and made a plan. She decided she'd send a simple text to Nick saying she'd heard the news on the radio. No questions. No comments. Any more would go against Clive's request.

'I told you I'd heard back from Balcon & Mora, didn't I, Mr Clegg?' she said, her restless thoughts gravitating to the next thing on her mind while she drank her tea, not quite ready to throw herself into her work yet.

'About the nutmeg grater and the website scam? Yes, you said you'd written to a Tony Mopar.'

'I posted the letter on Sunday. He should have received it by now.'

'That'll be a shock. I shouldn't think many of his customers track him down.'

'Nail him down, you mean. I bet he'll wriggle and squirm and try to slip away if he can. It's only in Ipswich. I've a good mind to go and face him in his lair.'

'What? Don't be silly, Mrs Jax. That may not be such a good idea.'

'The way I feel at the moment, it should be him who's worried.' Somehow it helped, beefing up her talk. For a moment it made her feel she could grab back control.

The quartetto tables took up the rest of her energy. She was thankful the legs needing replacement were slender and only required simple turning; no fancy beads or fillets. It made it so much easier to work on the lathe. There was a slight difficulty however - she was going to have to turn them from square-section stock because the legs had to be left square at both ends for mortise and tenon joints. The curved stretcher fitted into the lower end, and the upper end fitted into the apron supporting the tabletop above. There was nothing like a challenge, she thought.

'Yes, I've remembered to cut the joints before I mount the stock on the lathe, Mr Clegg,' she said when she caught his questioning look across the workshop. 'And don't forget you can make that brownish red mahogany resemble walnut if you use some ferrous sulphate solution on it.'

'Thank you, Mrs Jax, but Mrs Wimpole said she liked the colour of the mahogany, just as it is.'

Chrissie laughed and got on with her work.

By five o'clock she'd cut the replacement stretchers and Ron was giving her a hand clamping the glued joints together. She stood back to admire the series of tables, now with feet, legs, stretchers, aprons, tops and the cramps holding the pieces together, like external scaffolding.

'I thought it was going to be more difficult than it was,' she murmured.

'Luckily only a couple of the stretchers needed replacing. They look good, Mrs Jax.'

It didn't take her long to sweep up the wood shavings scattered on the floor near the lathe and tidy away her tools. She wanted to get home and check if she'd had an email back from Lester, and she also wanted to call Nick. He'd texted saying he could talk more freely after work. She checked her watch and decided to call him from her car before she set off.

'Hiya,' he said, answering almost immediately, 'Thanks for getting back to me.'

'Are you OK, Nick? I heard about it on the news, but you know that. I texted you. Hey look, this is awkward. I called Clive and he said I wasn't to talk to you about it. You could be a witness.' She waited for him to speak, alert to any nuance of stress.

'It's OK, Chrissie. They don't need witnesses. They were filming when... it happened. Two cameras running – close face shots plus slightly more distant wide angled shots, and there were several takes The cameramen say it's miles better quality than the CCTV images the police usually get to analyse.'

'What? The whole thing was filmed? So were you there, did you see what happened? No don't answer. Look, this is really difficult. Clive will kill me if I.... You'd say if you were in any trouble? You aren't being blamed for anything, are you? Like when the wall collapsed?'

'No, no. It's Priddy and Prosecco who.... Shit.'

'What? Did you just say Priddy? You never said you knew a Priddy.'

'Well I don't. Not really. She's just a girl who does props. Why?'

'Because there's a Priddy Jones using the same computer as the bastard who sold me the nutmeg grater. That's why. I suppose it would be too much of a coincidence if...? Nick? Are you still there?'

'Yeah, I'm still here.' He sounded anxious, rattled.

'Are you OK, Nick?'

'Yeah, of course. Look, Chrissie. Everyone uses first names here. Even I call the director Merlin.'

'OK, OK, it's just it isn't a common name.'

'Jones isn't a common name?'

'You know what I mean. Priddy isn't a common name. Look, it wouldn't be difficult to find out her surname, would it? You could do that for me, couldn't you?'

'I don't know, Chrissie. The filming – everything's gone crazy. No one knows what's going on. They might not even finish the film. I'm expecting to be sent back to Willows.'

She picked up the tension in his voice and backed off.

'Then best thing is to keep your head down and concentrate on your work. See you in the pub on Friday, OK? I expect if the police want to interview you they'll have taken statements by then and Clive can't have any more objections to me talking to you. But call me before if you want. Promise?'

'Yeah, sure. And thanks, Chrissie.'

She slipped her phone back into her bag and started the car. Her tyres scrunched stones as she drove the track in low gear, negotiating the potholes. This time she gazed for longer at the patch of red campion near the hedge before turning onto the airfield perimeter lane. The flowers made her think of her friend Sarah. Was it the colour of the pinky-red petals? They were much the same shade as her nail varnish.

'Sarah?' she murmured, as an idea took shape. Perhaps Sarah was the answer. Maybe she could recruit her help. What about suggesting she went along with Sarah to watch her fencing at the club in Ipswich on Thursday? Then they could drop in at the Tony Mopar address on the way back. Was it a good idea? She wasn't sure. She reckoned her plan might need a little more work.

•

It wasn't until the following evening when Chrissie caught Clive in a mood to talk. She knew he could be a little tense and distracted when he was on duty. But on Wednesday by six o'clock he was off duty and relaxing with a beer in her living room. She guessed he was mulling over the case, sorting through ideas, trying to piece everything together in his mind. But it was an internal process. Private. If she wanted him to share his thoughts, then she realised she needed to come at it laterally. Get him talking; steer the conversation.

'Do you want to walk to the White Hart? Maybe have something to eat?' she asked.

'Hmm, do you?'

'Yes. We can peep into people's gardens as we walk, see what's still flowering. Do you know I saw a bunch of red campion still flowering in the verge near work? Reminded me of Sarah. Can't think why.'

'Hmm....' He drank straight from the bottle of beer.

'And there was some purple toadflax. The flowers are kind of hooded. It made me think about another plant with hooded flowers.'

'Hmm....' He nodded but she could tell he was only half-listening.

'Monkshood. You remember the cat that was poisoned? Well I've been keeping my eyes open, seeing if I could spot any growing wild.'

Now he was watching her over his beer, the bottle close to his lips. 'Go on.'

'I've done an internet search and–'

'What made you start talking about monkshood, Chrissie?'

'I told you. The flowers in the verge near the hedge. They got me thinking about the poisoned cat. You told me it was aconitine. It's obvious I was bound to wonder what killed Cooper Brice.'

'I sometimes wonder how your mind works, Chrissie.'

She ignored his dig. 'The thing that strikes me, is if you weren't familiar with monkshood and you were looking at young plants with no flowers, you might not recognise it. You could confuse it with carrot plant leaves or some kind of herb. The police did check the garden, didn't they?'

'What? Which garden?'

'Owen and Prosecco's garden. Was there any monkshood growing there?' She watched a frown skim across his face.

'Stickley checked it out. After all, it was only a dead cat back then.' His tone seemed to justify why his DS had been entrusted with the search. 'But I'll ask an expert to take a look,' he said quietly.

'So I was right.' She wanted to punch the air but kissed him instead. 'I guessed it had to be aconitine. Cooper Brice was killed with aconitine, wasn't he?'

'But this isn't logical, Chrissie. I haven't said it was aconitine.'

'But I've guessed. I can read your face. So,' she said cosying up to him on the sofa, 'the killer tries the aconitine on the cat first, maybe perfects it a little and then slips it to Cooper. So how was it done?'

'The lab tests aren't all back yet, Chrissie.' His voice was tight, controlled.

'Was it absorbed through his skin, from his make-up or something for a cut or graze?'

'Look, I can't say. We're about to make an arrest. The paperwork for search warrants – well it's going through now. It all hangs on finalising the toxicology and the lab reports. So at the moment we've our suspicions. Strong suspicions. But if we want the charge to stick, we need facts and hard evidence.'

'How d'you mean?'

'Because, for God's sake, despite being caught on camera, and half the cast and crew seeing how it affected his speech, took away the power in his muscles, gave him gut ache and made him throw up – we need proof. Some of it could have been acting. The poison, as you suggest, is probably aconitine, but it has to be found in him, identified, quantified as a lethal level in his system, and the post mortem findings have to bloody fit in with it. We know he drank it, but we need to confirm it and prove who put it in his drink. We have to have hard evidence for it all, OK?'

'Right.' She watched him down the rest of his beer while silence washed through the room and defused the emotion.

'But why? What's the motive? Why kill the star of the film unless there's some kind of insurance payment related to the film?'

'I knew you were an accountant at heart, Chrissie. And again, to look through bank records, financial transactions, we need access.' His tone didn't invite more questions.

'If it wasn't for all the red tape, rules and regulations, life would be simpler,' she murmured.

'You mean back to the days when we could beat a confession out of the suspect, rig the evidence and not worry about miscarriages of justice?'

'No, of course not. But all that business of not being able to access juvenile records without authorisation...,' she let her voice drift hoping he'd fall into her trap.

'Yes, that turned out to be quite interesting. You know Prosecco was a talented gymnast? She could have been Olympic standard.' He looked grateful for a change of subject.

'You're kidding? What happened?'

'She had a problem with not winning.'

'But surely that's what makes a great sportsperson?'

'It all depends on how you deal with not winning. Now come on, enough questions, I thought we were walking up to the White Hart.' And with a swooping action he lifted her up and half-tipped, half-rolled her over the side of the sofa.

'Bloody miscarriage of justice,' she squealed, laughing.

'Too many questions,' he said, grinning as he held out a hand to help her up off the floor.

CHAPTER 29

Matt sat on the bench seat and held Maisie's hand. 'It's nice aint it,' he murmured as he gazed across the closely cut grass, more reminiscent of a public garden than a graveyard, and hidden from the rest of Stowmarket by the church. Beyond the rough hedge and ivy-clad lime and yew trees, the backs of buildings merged with the Victorian red-brick church hall, the library and a row of old painted cottages.

'Yeah, it's kind of peaceful.'

'It'll come alive when there's somethin' on,' Matt said, looking at the pale brickwork of the John Peel Centre, now cast in the evening shade. He caught a glimpse of the long glass windows, their shape more like a binary code to his eye than an architectural statement from a past age. He lifted his can of lager and drank, only part concentrating on the awkward tab-hole and allowing a few drops to leak onto his beard.

'There's a battle of the bands evenin' here soon. Me cousin sings country an' western and he's enterin'. He's ancient, mind. He thought I'd look cool in the wig,' Maisie said, squeezing his hand.

'Was Marilyn Monroe a country an' western fan, Mais?'

'What you on about? It's Dolly Parton, for me cousin's gig. You can't get more countr-e-e than Dolly. She's… iconic. Yeah, that's the word me cousin used.'

'Dolly? But….'

Scammin' hell, he thought, no wonder he'd messed up with Prosecco. Wrong wig, wrong look. 'But I don't fancy Dolly,' he winged. 'Marilyn's kinda younger.'

'Yeah, but Marilyn's dead.'

'Couldn't you wear a Marilyn wig on a… Dolly body, Mais?'

'Don't be weird.'

'But–'

Beep-itty-beep! Beep-itty-beep beep! He let go of Maisie's hand and pulled his mobile from his jeans.

'What's Chrissie want?' Maisie asked, leaning across and looking at the caller ID.

'Hey, watch me phone, you're spillin' your drink, Mais.'

'Why's she phonin' this late?' she whined, as she righted her can of spiced rum and cola.

'I dunno, do I? Give me a chance an' I'll see. OK?'

Beep-itty-beep! Beep-itty-beep beep! The jingle reverberated again.

'Hi, Chrissie. What's up?' he said cautiously, as Maisie nudged in closer.

'Would you believe it, but I'm at Tony Mopar and Priddy Jones' address and–'

'What? In Ipswich?'

'Yes. Is there another one?'

'No, well not I know of. Why?'

'I wanted to trap the bastard while he was in. Confront him. Ask him why he hasn't bloody answered my letter yet. But they won't even let me knock on the door. I can't get near the place.'

'What you mean? Who won't let you?' He breathed Maisie's perfume as she leaned nearer to catch Chrissie's words.

'There's a bloody policeman standing outside and he won't let me within 20 yards. He says there's no point knocking. There's no one's inside, the flat is empty. What's going on, Matt?'

'How'd I know?'

'I thought you, or rather Damon might have told the police about the scam website and they've been raided or arrested, or something.'

'What? Well it aint me. I aint informed on no one.'

'Well, Sarah reckoned it could be the reason.'

'Sarah?'

'Yes, she's here with me now. Thursday's her fencing club night. I thought she'd be useful to have around if things got nasty. But even she couldn't wheedle her way past the policeman.'

'But - what's Clive say?'

'I-I thought I'd call you first. I thought you'd be more likely to tell me.'

He felt Maisie tense. 'But why—'

'You're right. Why a policeman standing outside? It has to be more than my nutmeg grater and the scammy website....' Her voice seemed to quieten, and then he caught her words, barely audible, as if she was thinking aloud, 'Nick said.... And Clive was going to arrest.... Shit, it must be the same Priddy Jones.'

'The same Priddy Jones?' Matt gulped. Now the cat was really out of the bag.

'Yes. Why else have a policeman standing there? It has to be the same girl. They must think she has something to do with killing Cooper Brice.'

'Killin'?'

'Yes, and she's probably your Priddy Jones too, so we can add being wanted by the debt collectors to the list.'

'The list?'

'Oh for God's sake, Matt. Stop repeating everything I say.'

'But Chrissie–'

'I know what I'll do. I'll leave a note with the policeman saying please would they let me know if a man called Tony Mopar turns up. I'll leave my mobile number. That'll get them interested in the Mopar bastard as well.'

'But–'

'Thanks, Matt. Maybe catch you in the pub on Friday. Bye, now,' and she'd gone.

'But why's she thankin' me?'

'Wow, it's like hearin' news breakin'. You know, like one of them reporters talkin' to camera while stuff's kickin' off all around,' Maisie squealed from somewhere between his armpit and shoulder.

'Yeah, but Mais, she could've been in deep shit if Tony Mopar turned out to be a scammin' vicious bastard and....'

'Yeah, lucky she went with Sarah. She could've asked you.'

'What you mean, Mais?' For a moment he wondered if she was making some kind of dig at him.

'Cos if she'd asked, you'd of said yes. You're nice like that. You usually do what people ask.'

'Do I?'

'Yeah, but you can look real mean if you spread your arms and–'

'Snarl? Yeah I reckon I could block out the sun for someone.' He tried a practise snarl.

'So,' she wheedled, 'are you goin' to look for a Dolly Parton wig for me?'

•

The ramifications of Chrissie's phone call didn't sink in until the following morning. Matt had been too taken up with Maisie to give Chrissie's words more than a passing thought at the time. But realisation finally struck. Like a lightning bolt, everything fell into place.

'Oh no. Spammin' hell,' he groaned.

He'd been ambling back from a practical session on website design in the Academy's computer lab. Around him, students were talking and jostling, back packs slung over shoulders as the prospect of lunch quickened their step. He let the gaggle from the language centre pass him and sneaked through a side door into the goods and stores area. He needed to be alone. He stood rooted to the spot and tried to think.

'A policeman outside Priddy's address? Cooper dead and Priddy in the frame?' he whispered. The girl must have been arrested. It was likely there'd be a search warrant. In the films, the police always took the computer. And if the police had taken the computer then....

'Scammin' hell, Damon's key logger bug. They'll find it. I've got to warn him.'

It didn't take him more than a few seconds to grab his mobile and press Damon's automatic dial number. He had enough signal near the door.

'Damon, has Chrissie Jax called you?' The words tumbled out, his mind streets ahead of his tongue. He squirmed and shifted his weight from foot to foot as he described the police presence at the Ipswich address, and tried to explain why he hadn't called sooner.

'But I'm callin' now, aint I? I could've waited till I'm with you in Bury this afternoon.'

'So it's a DI Clive Merry I need to speak to, right?' Matt picked up the irritation in Damon's voice.

'Yeah, I reckon so, Damon. And sorry, mate.'

It was as if he'd been thrown a hot coal and he'd managed to toss it on before his fingers blistered. Damon hadn't said he'd sack him. He'd sounded annoyed, but not in a bad way. In fact he hadn't even blamed him for Chrissie being a client. Matt waited for a moment, his eyes closed as relief swept through him.

His heart rate settled and his stomach rumbled, reminding him he needed lunch. It was time he got on with the day. 'It could be me lucky Friday,' he told himself, as he wove between the maze of rooms and headed for the corridor linking the goods delivery bay with the main corridor.

'Oh DOS-ing malware. Dolly Parton!' He stopped dead in his tracks.

He'd forgotten about the wig. He didn't remember promising, but Maisie was insistent. 'Awe but you s-a-i-d,' she'd wheedled.

'But, I can't. Not here,' he muttered, recalling her words. If he was overheard by other students while he ordered a Dolly Parton-style wig, his life would become unbearable. It was too risky, not that there were many students near the storerooms. And if he called Prosecco again, he'd need another persona. He couldn't be Felix Lighter, or Leiter the CIA agent as he preferred to think of himself, nor Carl Stiltz. They weren't options.

He remembered how she'd turned sharp and become short with him last time he'd called. 'Frag. She might've blocked me mobile number,' Matt mumbled as another thought dawned. But if he withheld his number, would Prosecco answer? It was a gamble.

'Of course - Damon!'

Matt reckoned if anyone knew how to use a temporary phone number, then Damon would. He probably already used one. Burner numbers, he called them.

Later that day, after Matt emailed his advanced HTML assignment to his tutor, he rambled out to the Academy car park, pulled his scooter off its parking stand and set off for Bury and the Damon & Mora offices.

'Hi, Damon,' Matt said about forty minutes later. He trudged into the office, sweat plastering his dark sandy hair to his forehead, and his beard ruffled by his helmet.

'I thought the weather was changing and it was cooler today,' Damon said by way of a greeting.

'Not inside me scammin' helmet it wornt.'

'Thanks for calling me about the police raid. DI Merry was very interested in what I had to say. I guess we've reached an understanding.'

'Thank blog for that. I-I wuz....' The Suffolk seemed to keep breaking into his words.

'It's OK, Matt. We're cool.'

'Right.' He tried to gauge Damon's expression. Was he cool enough for burner numbers, he wondered?

'Well,' he began, 'an' I aint jannickin' but I've kinda heard about burner phones an' I reckon I got a situation to use one.'

'What the hell are you on about, Matt?'

He felt his face burn. 'It's kinda embarrassin'.'

'Try me.'

'Well....'

'An online dating site?'

'Nah....'

'I won't help unless you tell.'

'No laughin', right?'

Damon lifted his hands, his palms facing Matt in an I-give-up gesture.

'I got to buy a wig... for Maisie. Dolly Parton-style. But I can't use me mobile cos I tried last week and... well I messed up an' asked for a Marilyn Monroe by mistake. Seller got cross. Real cross an' I reckon now she's blocked me number.'

'So what do you know about burner phones and burner numbers?' Damon leaned back in in his shabby leather-effect office chair, put his hands behind his head and fixed him with his tawny eyes.

'They've got'em in America?' Matt relaxed. He sensed a tutorial.

'Yes. And they call them burners because...?'

'They're....' He saw the words as he'd read them on his computer screen, 'phones with short-lived numbers. You can delete or burn the numbers when you've done with them.'

'Yes, and now there's an app you can download onto your smart phone instead. The app allows you to use a number not connected with you and you can even choose an area code for as long as you like, for a fee. When you don't want the number anymore, you press a button to delete it, or as you said, burn the number. It will have gone forever, plus the people who could reach you on it. Then you move on to another number.'

'Awesome. An' when someone calls on the burner number?'

'It redirects to your own phone number or voicemail. And you can send text messages as well.'

'Till you burn the number.' He rolled the word around his tongue. Burn could join flame and fragment in his arsenal of techie expletives. 'Yeah, frag and burn.'

'Yes, we'll be making use of it here. But as of now, we aren't in America and the app isn't available in the UK yet.'

'So you aint got one? What can I do?'

'You can use the office number – just this once. And remember I'm listening.'

Matt reached for the cordless hand set on the trestle desk, but Damon snatched it up first.

'Just a minute. Won't the seller recognise your voice? What's the number?'

Damon keyed in the digits as Matt read them out loud from his photographic memory.

'What name shall I say?' Damon asked.

'Rad Zing. I aint used that one yet.'

'Hi, this is Rad Zing,' Damon drawled into the handset, 'I'm looking for a Dolly Parton-style wig... yeah, sure... of course.... Well, as soon as possible.' He looked at Matt for a moment, eyebrows raised. 'No, it's for my girlfriend, so a... yes, standard woman's size... that's sounds just what I'm after. So when...? No, no, I'll send my courier.... Just a sec, let me write that down... so tomorrow... yes, Saturday morning... about eleven o'clock.... He'll bring cash with him.... Well thank you.'

'Saturday mornin', eleven o'clock?' Matt winged, 'An' how much?' He read Damon's writing on the scrap of paper.

'Grundisburgh? You mean I've got to ride over to Grundisburgh?'

'She sounded nice. I can't think why you had trouble with her,' Damon said, and then grinned. 'Now come on, you've a list of names to trace.'

CHAPTER 30

Nick ambled through the pub car park. Chrissie was already firing up her TR7. He paused to watch her brake lights glow, the engine burbling gently before breaking into a throaty roar as she accelerated away. Somewhere from near the waste bins, the tinny sound of a two-stroke engine spluttered into life as Matt started his scooter. It had been a good night at the Nags Head, but none of them had wanted to linger too late, and for once a couple of beers had been enough. He felt emotionally drained. It had been a difficult week.

The shadows were closing in but it didn't feel like night-time; not yet overly dark and the temperature still mellow. He stood and rested against the side of his car and gazed up at the sky. If he gave himself permission, all his tension would drain away into the gravel and earth, and he could forget. But that would belittle Cooper's life and the blistering last performance. And besides, he had to remember what he'd said in his statement to the police. He might be called as a witness.

He let out a long slow breath. The whole film production had been thrown into chaos and everything halted. Prosecco and Priddy had been arrested and held for questioning. He'd been one of the lucky ones, sent back to Willows and treated as a celebrity rather than a traumatised eyewitness to a murder.

'So you watched him die?' Tim, one of the carpenters had said before running his tongue along a cigarette paper and rolling a mean cigarette.

'At least it wasn't Gavi,' Dave had muttered, as if that made it all right.

'Yeah, he kind of talked funny and then buckled. It was horrible. He threw up. That's when I knew he wasn't acting anymore. When his breathing changed it was obvious. I guess he wanted to but couldn't. I don't think his muscles were working for him.'

'You mean he was paralysed?'

'And you were there? Up close?'

'Well not as close as we are here, but....' And then he remembered watching the crew. How Priddy had rushed over to help, how Prosecco had hung back and screamed. How one of the cameramen had kept his camera running after Merlin had shouted *cut*. They wouldn't need witnesses, he reasoned. It was all on camera. Perhaps he could just let it all go.

So he stood in the pub car park, lingering, not ready to get into his car and drive home, but feeling the hollowness of remaining when now and then other drinkers strolled to their cars. Headlights dazzled on full beam as tyres crackled over gravel, but still he remained.

Brr brr, brr brr! He grabbed his phone, glad of the interruption.

'Hi?' he said cautiously, not recognising the number on the call ID.

'Hi, Nick?'

'Priddy? I thought you'd been... have they released you? Are you OK?'

'They couldn't hold me any longer, at least not without a charge or making an application for more time. And they didn't have enough on me for that. Thank God the duty solicitor was on the ball; otherwise I swear I'd have been there for days.'

'So who have they charged? And where are you?' The inner bleakness seemed to disperse as she drew him into her drama.

'No one. At least I don't think so. Look, Nick I'm scared. Can you talk?'

'Well yes, but–'

'I don't think I'm safe. I think I know how it was done, when the switch was made, but....'

'Are you talking about the poison? You've told the police?'

'No – the solicitor said not to say anything or make a statement until I knew the charges against me, so... I didn't say much.'

'But that's crazy. I thought you said the solicitor was on the ball.'

'Yeah, but I can't prove what I suspect, and without proof it could all be twisted to point back at me. That's what the solicitor said.'

'Right. So where are you now?'

'Standing outside my front door but I don't want to go in by myself. I know the police have been inside, searched the place, taken stuff. Would you... would you come over? I don't know who else to ask.'

'How about Tony Mopar?' The name seemed to escape from his mouth.

He waited for her to answer, and then wished he hadn't asked, as the silence on his phone chilled.

'Priddy? Are you still there? Are you OK?'

'Yes, yes. No one's come out of the shadows and clubbed me to death, yet. Look, Tony Mopar isn't. He never was. But I can't explain on the phone.'

'Well, you could come here?'

But where was here, he wondered. He couldn't offer Chrissie's spare room. Chrissie would likely kill her if she knew of her memorabilia dealings, and Clive, the DI who had probably questioned her, would be under the same roof.

'I suppose you could have my room and I'll sleep on the sofa? But it's my parent's place.'

'Thanks, but I need a shower and change of clothes. If we're talking sofas I think you'll find mine's comfortable. I'll text you my address. But I'm not going in till you get here. I'll be hiding close by. Just walk up to the front door. I'll recognise you, OK?'

He heard the fear in her voice. Genuine fear. Very different to the cool Priddy Jones with the cynical streak he'd grown used to over the past five weeks. She was in trouble; no question about that. He sensed her danger, but despite his misgivings, he knew he couldn't let her down. More to the point, it was Friday and he wasn't doing anything else. If it had been Saturday night, it could have been more awkward with Yvonne around.

'OK,' he said and ended the call, his inner emptiness gone.

As he got into his Fiesta, a tiny cell of self-preservation kicked into life. Chrissie's voice seemed to fill his car. *For God's sake, Nick. Be careful. She could be a killer.*

On the spur of the moment he copied Priddy's text message and sent it on to Chrissie.

•

It didn't take Nick long to join the A14 and head towards Ipswich. The old Fiesta ate the miles as he put his foot down hard. He reckoned the sooner he reached Priddy's flat, the less time she'd have to prepare for him. It felt safer that way. Ten minutes later he turned off the dual carriageway and drove into Ipswich along the Norwich Road, hurrying past the playing fields, seemingly dark voids in the night. The road was soon hemmed by semis built in the post-World War years. All too soon he was constrained by the speed limit, as traffic light after traffic light slowed his progress, and the town felt older as houses changed to Edwardian and Victorian terraces.

The side roads were shadowy, ill-lit, and lined with parked cars. His slim mobile felt warm balanced on his thigh, the Google map bright against the gloom inside his car

'Turn off before the road takes you under the railway bridge,' he muttered as he tried to read street names in the dark. He was familiar with the industrial estate nearby, with the IS & FSD & C Ltd premises and the skateboarding outlet. But this side, beyond the industrial estate, with its sea of houses was new to him. He threaded his way to her address, parking twenty yards away, on the other side of the road.

With the engine and car lights off, darkness filled the cab and cloaked the road. He peered through the windscreen at a small block of flats, built in the nineteen nineties, barely three storeys high and squeezed between the semis. A streetlamp cast an eerie light onto the main entrance door. A panel of buzzers and intercoms were set close by in the wall.

He scanned the narrow sward of grass between the pavement and the flats. There was no hedge, no ornamental cherry or pollarded beech tree, nothing to conceal a lurking figure. He reckoned the only place anyone could hide was around the side of the building or between the parked cars in the road.

'Right,' he murmured, as if that would summon his courage, and rested his hand on the driver's door release catch.

Bang!

Something struck the roof of his Fiesta. His heart jolted.

Rap, rap! It sounded less urgent, but on the far side of the car. His guts twisted.

'Agh!' The thing outside blocked his view through the passenger-door window. Fabric so close it pressed against the glass.

'Nick!'

'Shit!' Then his brain unfroze. 'Priddy?'

The fabric moved. He made out the murky shape of a shoulder. The form bent to peer into the car from the pavement.

'Open the bloody door. It's me,' a strident voice demanded.

'Shit, you nearly gave me a heart attack,' he wheezed, and leaned across to unlock the passenger door, his nerves shredded.

'What the hell are you doing, Priddy? You said you'd meet me at your flat's main door.' He tried to stifle the mix of scare and irritation in his voice.

She slipped into the passenger seat.

'But you didn't get out of your car, Nick. You've just been sitting here. I thought you were about to drive off again.'

'I was weighing it up, you know – assessing the situation.'

'And?'

'It looks deserted. No one lurking. There's nothing suspicious.'

'Yeah, but you didn't see me coming. Have… have you got anything with you?'

'Like what, Priddy?'

'I don't know… something to double as a weapon if….'

'Damn. I didn't think. I've left my toolbox at Willows.'

'Just watch my back for me. OK?'

'So… have you got your keys ready? You don't want to be scrabbling around in your bag for them once we're out of the car.' His confidence flowed back now his pulse had stopped sprinting.

'Yes. They're in my hand. Let's go.' She released the passenger door and got out.

Something rattled and slid as he swung his door open. Nerves fired. He froze.

'OK?' she asked.

'Yeah, I'm good. I thought I heard something, that's all.' He slipped his hand into the plastic pocket and picked out the tyre-tread gauge. He glanced at her. She didn't seem to have noticed. He sneaked it into his zipped bomber jacket.

Swiftly he locked the car and crossed the road, keeping close to her back. The sound of distant traffic blended with the silence of the night. Out in the open, the shadows now threatened. Exposed and tense, he concentrated on listening and looking. Nothing. Just their footsteps as they hurried to her flat. A quick fumble with the lock, and they were inside the building.

'Phew,' he muttered.

A movement-sensitive light blinked into life, diffusing a dull energy-saving glow. He cast around. The small hallway housed a bank of mail boxes. No nooks or crannies, no space for anyone to lurk. Even the door into each flat closed flush with the walls. A concrete flight of stairs with a metal handrail led up into darkness, the underside visible. Nick raked the gloom for danger. No crouching figures morphed from the dark. Not on the ground floor.

'Come on, I'm on the first floor,' she whispered and led the way.

A knot tightened in his guts.

Another energy-saving glow flickered into life, as the sensor picked up her movement on the stairs. Nick ran his eyes around the first floor landing. The same flush door design and a second flight of concrete steps leading upwards. Pulse racing, he stood guard while Priddy unlocked her door and switched on her lights.

They both slipped into her flat.

'There's something been left for you,' he said, bending and picking up an envelope from the floor. It was addressed to The Occupant, Miss Priddy Jones. 'Here, it looks kinda official.' He handed her the buff-coloured envelope with *Suffolk Police* in small print along the top.

'The bastards,' she muttered as she tore open the envelope and glanced at the sheets of paper. 'It's a deliberately vague list of all my stuff they've taken. And they have the nerve to call it a receipt? The bastards.'

'But what have they taken? What were they looking for?'

'Why seize my computer? This is ridiculous,' she murmured as she looked up from the list. 'They've taken my laptop, Nick. According to this, they've virtually emptied the kitchen - my spice drawer; all my dried, tinned, bottled or fresh food; my cleaning materials; everything in my bathroom cabinet. Shit, even my make-up and perfume.' Her face contorted.

She started to walk, he guessed to hide her tears. She picked up a cushion filler, its cover tossed on the floor. 'I rent the place. If anything's damaged, the landlord....'

He followed her through the flat. It was small - a tiny kitchen and living area, bedroom and bathroom; the furnishings basic, but with touches of bright colour. Ornaments had been swept off shelves and heaped in piles. Drawers were half-open, the contents rifled. Her bed, a double, had been moved and stripped, the mattress up-ended. Carpet and undelay had been pulled back.

He was shocked. 'It's like you've been burgled by someone in a hurry,' he said.

'I guess if I'd been here....' She shook her head.

'No, they were looking for something. Something hidden. What Priddy? You can't expect me to help if you don't come clean. Tell me.'

She slumped to the floor, her back against the wall. It was as if she was defeated, a broken gesture.

'Well?' He stood, waiting for her to speak, unwilling to back down. He knew he couldn't afford to appear soft.

'It's all about hero props.'

'Hero props? Is this about your memorabilia site?'

'No, no. Hero props and… poison. Cooper was poisoned. I don't know what with, but you saw, we all saw. The police think I poisoned his vodka lapsang souchong cocktail and then gave it to him in the hipflask. I guess they're searching for the poison.'

'Right… so that's why the police took anything you could have hidden it in. Now I get it. They're going to test the contents of your kitchen and bathroom. Your face creams and cosmetics. Everything. It'll take months.'

'And until then, I'm under suspicion.'

'OK, I get the bit about searching for the poison. But hero props? What's that about?'

'Don't you see, the hip flask wasn't the hero prop.'

'Because you've got it… hidden here? And they're looking for it as well?'

'No, no. You're not listening. I said, did you see the hip flask wasn't the hero prop?'

'I don't understand what you're getting at.'

'All the pilots have hip flasks. Cooper's hip flask is a more detailed piece for close up work – leather casing, silvered screw top with hinged mechanism for the stopper. It's the hero prop. He uses it. And we also use it in any close up of a pilot swigging. The other hip flasks are standard props with leatherette fabric casing and cheap polished metal.'

'So you're saying Cooper's hip flask is a hero prop because….'

'It's more detailed and authentic than the others.'

'And he's the hero in the film.'

'Yes – and that's the one I filled with the cocktail. But the one on the grass near my feet, the one Prosecco pointed at, that was a standard prop. That's the one which had the poison in it. I picked it up, handed it to Prosecco and she gave it to Cooper. The hip flasks had been switched and no one noticed, except me.'

'Shit. But you've told the police?'

'They're not going to believe me unless they find the hero flask. And even then, how can I prove it was the flask I took out for Cooper?'

'Right.'

'So the only person who knows, apart from me is….'

'The killer?'

'Yes, and the only person who could have made the swap was Prosecco.'

'Or you.'

'Then why the hell would I be telling you if it was me? No it has to be Prosecco and I think she's guessed I'll have worked out it's her. I'm frightened she's going to try and kill me next.'

'What? You're being illogical. Why would Prosecco want to kill Cooper? I thought they had a thing going between them.'

'They did, but after Owen died, it kind of cooled.'

Nick tried to make sense of it, but his head was spinning with it all.

'Let's hope the flask swop was caught on camera,' he reasoned. 'You know what they're like, those camera guys. Always shooting, playing with aperture, frames per second, different lenses. If the police have impounded all the camera chips… if they know what they're looking for, they may….' He knew it was a long shot. If Priddy was telling the truth, then it sounded as if she'd been well and truly stitched up.

'Come on,' he said, trying to sound upbeat, 'let's tidy up this mess.' He reckoned the question of Tony Mopar could wait. So far he hadn't noticed any pointers a man shared her flat.

CHAPTER 31

Chrissie read the text message as she padded downstairs. She reckoned Nick must have sent it while she was driving back from the Nags Head the previous evening, its arrival *ping* muffled by her bag and the engine noise. With Clive arriving home soon afterwards, she hadn't thought to check her phone till now.

'You're up early. You know it's Saturday?' she said, and stifled a yawn as she wandered into the kitchen.

'Yes, unfortunately I've got to work today. This poisoning case is taking off. The kettle's just boiled if you want tea.'

She wasn't really listening. Her mind was on the text. Why would Nick send an address unless he wanted her to go there or meet him? She read his message again.

'You're frowning,' Clive said and prodded the teabag.

She looked up. 'It's a bit odd, that's all.'

'What's odd?'

'This. Why would Nick text me an address? I'm pretty sure it's the same as Tony Mopar's address. I dropped by there with Sarah on Thursday night on the way back from the fencing.'

'Yes, I heard about that. It's Priddy Jones' address.' He paused and looked her straight in the eye. 'What the hell were you doing calling by at a suspect's flat, Chrissie?'

'I wasn't. At least I didn't realise you'd arrested her until we got there. I wanted to speak to Tony Mopar. He's the one who sold me the replica nutmeg grater. The fake antique, remember?'

'But that doesn't mean–'

'I told you about it weeks ago. You were too preoccupied with bigger fish to take it any further, so I asked Matt's boss to find out who was behind the website. What did you expect me to do? Nothing?'

'No, but I'd expect you not to interfere in my cases.'

'So how was I interfering? I wrote to Mr Mopar, but he didn't get back to me. I wasn't contacting Ms Jones.'

'No, but did you stop to wonder if they might be connected in some way? You just blundered up there to escalate things. Why didn't you tell me what you were doing?' His words blistered.

'And when was I supposed to tell you? You're hardly here.'

'That's not fair.'

'If you don't tell me who your main suspects are, how am I supposed to know who and when you're arresting them? Telling works both ways.'

'You expect me to tell you every piece of police information? Don't be ridiculous.'

'So now I'm being ridiculous, am I?' She knew it was a cheap line, but it flew out before she could stop it.

He hesitated. 'You're being over-hasty. Rash. And now I suppose you've sent Nick there instead.'

'What? Have you even been listening to me? I haven't sent anyone anywhere. See for yourself.' She virtually flung the phone at him and watched impatiently as he read the text.

'Nick sent this? It's her address all right, and he must have guessed or known. *Please come. P*. I assume it's P for Priddy. Did he say he was going there?'

'No, not until this.'

'Oh no, don't tell me Nick is mixed up in this as well. That's all I need to hear,' he muttered.

'What? Now you're being ridiculous, Clive. Nick sent me the message because...,' she groped for a reason, 'because.... Actually I've no idea why.'

'Quite.' The word seared through the air.

He didn't say more. He didn't need to. His face told it all - weariness, irritation, exasperation, a DI under pressure.

'Right, I've got to go, Chrissie. I'll phone later.' He grabbed his half-eaten toast and hurried from the kitchen. Moments later, the front door banged.

She stood for a second, reeling. All she'd done was pad downstairs to see if he was OK. She'd guessed he'd be working the weekend, but up and dressed before seven o'clock? Early, even for Clive on a Saturday morning. Her concern had left her with a vacuum in the kitchen and a feeling akin to being punched in the solar plexus.

She carried her mug of tea and phone upstairs, seething with the injustice of it all. But despite burying her head under the pillow and pulling the summer-weight duvet around her, sleep wouldn't come. Her mind was too active.

If Clive was cross with her, well so what, she was cross with him. And who exactly were his suspects? Prosecco was a name she'd heard bandied around. *Please come P*. Priddy wasn't the only name beginning with P.

She sat up and sipped her tea. 'But why send me the address?'

Could Nick have copied and pasted *P*'s message but not had time to add a footnote? Was something risky or bad about to happen and he'd sent it as insurance in case things went wrong? No, she decided. Her first thought was probably the most likely. 'He wants me to go to the address.'

•

Nick woke with a crick in his neck. At six foot three, he was longer than the two-seater sofa, and the cushion doubling as a pillow had forced his neck into an acute angle.

'Ouch,' he groaned and opened his eyes. 'Where the hell...?'

It all came flooding back. 'Shit!'

He swung his legs to the floor and sat up in one movement, then rested his head in his hands.

A pulse thumped between his ears. He turned his neck gingerly and scanned the room. Patterned, early morning light filtered through the thin unlined curtains. Pictures were now straight on the walls, contents returned to drawers, ornaments and memorabilia on shelves, the DVD collection stowed back in a box, covers were back on cushions and the cushions were – well he'd been sleeping on them. It was as he remembered - tidy after an hour's work late last night. Priddy had concentrated her efforts on the bedroom while he'd focussed on the kitchen living room.

'Ughh,' he moaned softly. 'What now?'

He couldn't be sure Priddy wasn't a killer, but the longer he'd spent in her company, the more he was convinced of her innocence. But he hadn't let down his guard. He'd decided to keep his phone and the tyre-tread gauge on him as he slept, and his car keys close. He figured if her technique was to poison, then the police had already cleared her flat of the means. If she intended to creep up in the night and smother him, then he was lying on all the cushions. It had been an uncomfortable night and he'd slept fitfully.

He checked his watch. Eight o'clock. It was later than he'd expected. Muted sound travelled through from the bedroom. Priddy must be awake and moving around.

Ping! A text message alert sounded from his pocket. He grappled with his jeans.

Are you OK? Any news on Tony Mopar? Chrissie, the message read.

I'm OK. No info on T M yet, he replied.

'Hi, how did you sleep?' Priddy asked, as she opened her bedroom door. 'What are you doing?'

'Nothing,' he said and slipped his mobile back into his pocket. 'I've just remembered. You haven't told me about Tony Mopar, and you promised you would.'

'What? You're still on about that? At least let me have breakfast first.'

'Great idea, except the only thing on the menu is water. Hot or cold.'

'Ughhhh... I was forgetting they'd emptied my kitchen.'

'And bathroom.' He ran his hand over the millimetre of stubble on his chin. 'Go on then; get yourself a glass of water and tell me about Tony Mopar.'

He waited. She used her fingers to rake her wavy brown hair back from her face. It struck him as a gesture of resignation, but there was no disguising the frown as she said, 'Shit, I thought you'd let that drop. Where did you get the name? And anyway, what's it to you?'

'I've heard it around. People talk. There's always gossip on set. And...,' he was taking a risk and hoped to

God Matt hadn't been mistaken, 'Owen wore a black tee shirt with MOPAR printed on it.'

'I told him that was a mistake. Someone was bound to make the connection. You know he thought it was funny?'

'Funny?'

'Yeah, the play on words. But instead of MOtor PARts, we were dealing in stage and screen parts. In other words, fantasy and memorabilia.'

'So it was–'

'Made up. Yes, a user name. We all use it when selling on the website. That way we protect our identities. Bloody fool. Owen was always taking risks.'

'But–'

'There's nothing wrong with using a cover. It's perfectly legal.' He felt her eyes mine his face. 'You thought Tony Mopar was real, didn't you? An actual person.'

'I heard the name and assumed....'

'Owen was the one who insisted on the name Tony. A reference to the Tony awards, you know - for excellence in Broadway theatres? It was like a stage name. Again, his idea of a joke.'

'Of course.' He hoped he'd hidden his surprise, but this Owen he didn't recognise. Not at all the person he'd imagined.

'So you didn't really know anything, did you, Nick? You heard a name and you're just fishing. And now I've gone and bloody told you.'

'No, I thought Tony Mopar must be a boyfriend or something. Look, I came over and helped you when you asked. I guess we're quits. Right?'

'Only if you keep your mouth shut. Unless… are you angling to join us?'

Instinct told him to play his options. 'I don't know. It depends.'

'Hmm… well it's not up to me.'

A tinkling sound burst into life from her pocket.

'A text,' she said and pulled her phone free. 'Typical,' she muttered as she read the message.

'What? What's happened?' he asked, watching her face.

'They want a possible location checked out. A crash site for Cooper! God, you'd think they'd give it a rest.'

'So they're writing in a crash scene?'

'Yeah, I guess to explain why he doesn't appear in the rest of the film.'

Nick dragged his mobile from his pocket. 'No message for me.'

'They'll have texted Lester. Knowing him, he'll probably contact you at the last minute and expect you to be there immediately.'

'Yeah, too right. So, what time?'

'Nine o'clock. Why? Are you offering a lift?'

•

Chrissie carried her empty mug downstairs to the kitchen. The initial reassurance of Nick's speedy answer had worn thin. It was barely past eight o'clock and she reckoned it was unusual to get a text reply from him so early on a Saturday morning. And why the strange phrasing, *No info on T M yet*, she wondered.

'Yet?' she murmured, sounding the T like a tut. Did the *yet* imply he was still at the address?

She opened and closed kitchen cupboards, the activity burning nervous energy. Then she took on the fridge. A faint but lingering smell of acrid sweaty foot caught her nose; a few seconds and she'd sorted the problem as she tossed a sliver of rogue gruyere into the bin.

Now what? The weekly shop? It could wait. She figured she'd be better working off her restlessness at the workshop, stripping something down, polishing something up.

Ten minutes later she was dressed in jeans and sweatshirt, car keys in her hand and ready to drive over to Wattisham for a wrestle with a bureau or a chest of drawers. She couldn't rationalise her agitation. It was instinctive, gut level, but as always the landscape soothed while she sped alongside fields of green-leafed sugar beet and earthy ploughed-in stubble. The horizon drew her eye, and then grounded her.

She saw Ron's battered old van as soon as she rattled and bumped from the rough track and into the workshop courtyard. 'I might have guessed.' she murmured.

He didn't seem unduly surprised when she opened the wooden door and stepped into the cool timelessness of the old barn.

'Good morning, Mrs Jax,' he said without looking up from marking the positions of beads and hollows along a work piece, ready to shape into a turned spindle. 'You do know it's Saturday, don't you?'

It was the same question she'd asked Clive, barely an hour and half ago. 'Yes,' she said, trying not to sound annoyed.

He made no further comment, appearing to be engrossed in his task.

She flung her bag onto a workbench and noisily filled the kettle.

'So what's bitten you this morning, Mrs Jax?'

'Nothing.'

She couldn't tell if he'd heard. 'Nothing,' she repeated, but louder.

'It doesn't sound like nothing from over here, Mrs Jax.'

It was the only invitation she needed. 'It's that bloody Tony Mopar. He's caused so much trouble. Would you believe it's turned out he lives at the same flat as one of Clive's suspects? How was I supposed to know? You can imagine how Clive reacted when he heard I'd....' It all tumbled out - her visit to the block of flats, Nick's text message.

'And now you're worried about Nick?'

'Yes, and if I drive over there and Clive finds out.... Not that I care what he thinks.'

'Of course not. But in that case Woodbridge isn't far from Ipswich, is it?'

'No, but I don't see what that's got to do with anything, Mr Clegg.'

'I thought there could be something you might be interested in buying at the auction there this morning. I think it starts at ten.'

She stared at him for a moment, wondering if he'd lost his mind.

'What? The Woodbridge Auction Rooms? But... hey, that's brilliant, Mr Clegg. I can take the new van and make a slight detour on route.'

'Exactly.'

Her day unlocked.

'Right, I better get moving if I'm going via Ipswich, Mr Clegg.'

'Good luck, Mrs Jax… and don't make any–'

But she'd stopped listening. She was as good as gone.

CHAPTER 32

'So are you comin' with me to collect the wig this mornin'?' Matt asked.

'But it's miles away. How come we're collectin' it from...,' Maisie's voice faded across the airwaves.

'Grundisburgh,' he finished for her. 'It's near Woodbridge.' He held his mobile closer.

He'd already explained about Damon's call to Prosecco, artfully skimming over the parts he'd played pretending to be Carl Stiltz and Felix Leiter, his CIA doppelganger, but for the purposes of Suffolk, morphed into Lighter.

'Ple-e-ease Mais. You got to understand I'm just the courier. See, I'll stay on me scooter, keep me helmet on and me mouth shut, while you–'

'Am I Damon's girlfriend?'

'What? No, yeah... I dunno. Look, you got to remember he's Rad Zing.'

'Rad Zing?'

'Yeah, an' you do all the talkin'. You try the wig on and make sure it fits. OK?' He baulked out of telling her she'd already seen Prosecco at the Diss auction, or that it was the wig she'd bid for and lost.

'I don't know if I can remember all them names, Matt.'

'But there's only one name to remember. Rad Zing. He's Damon.'

'Yeah, but....'

'Look, I'll be there with you. I'm ridin' the scooter, aint I?'

'Yeah, but you said you'd keep your helmet on and weren't saying nothin'. What if I get all mixed up?'

'I'll think of somethin', Mais.'

'OK. Have you paid or is it pay-on-collection?'

'I reckon a bit of hagglin' on your part. I'll get cash from the machine on the way over to you.'

'OK, see you in half an hour.'

'It might take me a little longer than that. Bye.' He ended the call.

Matt flopped back on his bed. He enjoyed it when Maisie rode pillion on the Piaggio. He relished the feel of her arms around him, but the extra weight often proved testing for the forty-nine cc, two-stroke engine to pull up the hills. Luckily there weren't many between Stowmarket and Grundisburgh. And the silver lining? He swore the scooter could almost hit a top speed of thirty-five miles per hour on a long downhill with Maisie on board, and the main bonus - Prosecco didn't get to hear his voice.

He hadn't been to Grundisburgh before. He reckoned the collection address was likely to be Prosecco's rental bungalow, and if that was the case, he knew Owen had been crushed to death under a van somewhere on the drive. It was gruesome but he was curious in a weird kind of a way. He'd thought better of sharing the chilling association with Maisie. That nugget, along with any warning of the prospect of meeting the *stuck-up bitch* who'd out-bid her for the wig, might have proved too much for her.

'Don't want her refusin' to come with me,' he reasoned. He couldn't imagine how she'd react when it all struck home, so he didn't try. In best Felix Lighter fashion, he buried the thought.

And that reminded him. How was he going to reassure her, find some way to help her remember it was Rad Zing and not Damon who had arranged to buy the wig? The answer was staring him in the face. His tee shirt. The one with:

JUMPING STILTS
Cool bounce; Awesome spring
Rad product; Leaps with zing

It was the obvious choice.

CHAPTER 33

'So where is this place? The crash scene?' Nick asked.

He sat opposite Priddy, two mugs of steaming coffee on the table and a plate of croissants between them.

'The text says to head for Tunstall and then…,' she filled her mouth with croissant and pushed her phone towards him, 'Here, read it for yourself.'

They'd stopped off at the supermarket for some supplies, but the sweet wheaty smell of bread hot from the oven had drawn them to the bakery section. From there it was only a few steps to the in-house café.

'I must get teabags, coffee, toothpaste, shower gel and…,' she said through another mouthful of croissant, 'if I nip round with my basket now, my coffee will be cool enough to drink by the time I'm back.'

'OK,' Nick said, his eyes on the message as she reached to reclaim her phone. He pulled his mobile from his pocket, entered his passcode and opened the Google Maps app. Seconds later he tapped in Tunstall on the location finder. He slid his finger across the screen, moving the map, trying to match the roads on his screen with the instructions he'd just read in Priddy's message.

'Hey, isn't this…?' he murmured as he expanded the scale, 'yeah, it's the owl nesting site.' He pictured the map on the corkboard in Nigel Grabham's kitchen. A blue coloured marker had pinpointed the same spot. It was the nesting location Ptarmigan, or was it Gull, had spotted first.

He remembered driving past the disintegrating wooden outhouses and shivered. Time, neglect and rot were almost certainly the cause, but he supposed the collapsed roofs could be made to look as if a biplane had crashed into them from the sky.

It made sense as a location, but he couldn't help wondering who in the film production team had also noticed it and seen the potential. Chrissie and he had been following back-roads to Nigel Grabham when they'd passed it, hidden, out of the way.

Ping! The slim mobile felt alive in his hand as a text alert sounded. 'Bet it's Lester wanting me there ten minutes ago.' He opened the message. 'Chrissie?'

Thought I'd drop in at address as going to Woodbridge auction for 10:00am. Are you still there? Chrissie.

'She's dropping in at Priddy's flat?' He checked his watch and replied: *On way with Priddy to check out location for crash scene for film. Think it's same place we drove past to collect your van - the owl nesting site – remember, on corkboard in Grabham's kitchen.* He tapped send, and then as an afterthought, a second text, *T M doesn't exist. It's complicated. Will explain later.*

He looked up to see Priddy hurrying towards the table.

'Right, my coffee should be cool enough now,' she said, breathless.

'You were quick. Have you got all you need?' His face burned as he closed his text messages, guiltily aware he'd just betrayed Priddy's secret. A couple of seconds earlier and his text would have been in plain view, if she'd been quick enough to look. Could he have pretended T M wasn't Tony Mopar?

Ping! He ignored the alert.

'Aren't you going to read that?' Priddy asked between sips of coffee.

'No, it'll be nothing. Hey, I've worked out where we have to go. If we head to Woodbridge and then take the main road to Rendlesham and Tunstall, we should be more or less there.'

'Great.'

'I think I've driven past it when I've been out that way before.' He gulped down the last of his coffee. 'Ready? Shall we go then?'

'We won't be the only ones arriving a little after nine. I mean, what do they expect with short notice and on a Saturday?'

Nick drove the old Fiesta, threading his way around Ipswich avoiding the northern ring road as it passed through uninterrupted residential areas. He knew the endless congestion at traffic lights and roundabouts would be hell before eventually joining the northern bound A12. Instead he chose the quiet empty roads through housing estates, and then fields and villages, cutting his way north-east to join the A12 closer to Woodbridge.

Priddy didn't say much and he was comfortable with her silence. It allowed him to concentrate on the route. He still couldn't decide if he believed all she'd told him, and for the moment he didn't dwell on the bigger question of Prosecco. Instead, the prospect of being involved in a film location from the beginning was a new challenge, and he relished the thought. He reckoned he'd be good at the planning stage.

'I like Woodbridge,' she said, as they drove through the old town.

They wove past the last muddy tidal stretches of the River Deben and headed north-east, away from Sutton Hoo and the ancient burial sites. 'I've never been round Sutton

Hoo,' he said, and wondered if he should suggest it to Yvonne sometime.

'The best stuff isn't there anymore. They've taken it off to the British Museum. Most of what you see are replicas,' Priddy murmured.

'Yeah? You sound quite knowledgeable about it.' He hoped it didn't mean she was planning more fakes. 'I'm a member of the canoeing club,' he said, changing the subject. 'If this doesn't take too long, I may call in on the way back.' He realised he hadn't dropped Yvonne's name into the conversation.

'Aren't you giving me a lift back?'

'What? Sure, but if someone else is going back to Ipswich, perhaps....'

They drove on past fields of ploughed-in stubble, before reaching patchy woods and inland sandlings with their cover of gorse and heather.

He took a right, then a left, leaving Rendlesham and Tunstall behind and followed a narrow road, barely wide enough for one car. 'It's somewhere along here. There's a hedge partly blocking your view, but you can still make out the derelict barn and outbuildings. It's not quite in the forest.' He slowed.

'There should be other cars parked around, unless there's a track or something. The text said nine o'clock and we're running....'

'Only ten minutes late,' he said, checking his watch.

'There!' She pointed.

'Can you see an entrance? Some sort of track?' Nick slowed to a crawl, and peered through the hedge.

'Just keep going, there's bound to be something. The others must've found somewhere else to park, unless…. Are you sure this is the right place?'

'Yes, definitely.'

He drove on, but there was no entrance track, just a stony rutted area in front of a galvanised metal crossbar gate, set back from the road. 'This must be it,' he muttered.

'I think we're the first to arrive. Look, there's a chain and padlock still on the gate.'

'We'll park here. It's too bad if we're blocking the gate. It's either that or the road.'

They got out of the Fiesta eager and exhilarated.

'Look at that.' Nick pointed as he traced the broken rooflines of a shed, its timbers caved in and decaying. 'I suppose if you kept the rusty corrugated panels out of shot….'

'Or removed them. Come on, let's have a closer look,' Priddy said and clambered over the gate, her excitement obvious.

'Be careful, Priddy. It doesn't look very safe. The whole lot could come down on you.'

Nick stepped onto one of the lower bars and swung his leg over the top of the gate. The extra height gave him a better view. He scanned around, trying to take it all in as he balanced. There was a dilapidated wooden barn and a series of open sided shelters for tractors and carts, now empty, barren. A long shed, probably once for chickens, and a motley collection of smaller outbuildings completed the air of desolation. Exposed beams pointed like giant gnarled fingers, and split fragmented weatherboarding lay rotting. Long grass, lush nettles and giant brambles had taken up residence. Everywhere was neglect and decay.

'The film crew will have a hell of game trying to work in this,' he muttered, enthusiasm giving way to realism.

'Come on, Nick.'

'Yeah, yeah, I'm just getting my bearings. I'm right behind you.' He was about to jump down, but something moved to the right of the barn, too fast to barely register. He looked again, focussing on the sunlight playing with shadows cast by beech saplings. A rustle of leaves, a movement of the long grass – nothing.

'Come on, Nick.'

'I thought I saw something.'

'Probably a rabbit.'

'Yeah, probably.' But he knew it couldn't be a rabbit; more likely a bird taking to the air straight from the ground, but without flapping its wings. Strange, he thought. Distracted, he half-jumped half-slid down the other side of the gate. 'Ouch!' He knocked his hip and caught his unzipped bomber jacket between the metal bars.

'Are you OK?'

'Shit.' He rubbed his leg. 'You'd think they'd have unlocked the gate for us. Hey, wait for me. Don't go in there without me.' He tugged the edge of his jacket free and hurried past the nettles.

She paused at the entrance to the long shed, then disappeared into the gloom. 'There's something–'

He heard the thud as her voice died.

'Priddy?'

Without thinking he ran after her. He didn't care about the brambles and fallen wood, too bad if they tore at his jeans. Three more strides and he was inside the long shed. The dimness hit like a blanket. He hesitated, not sure what he was seeing. 'Priddy?'

A shape sprang from nowhere. Metal pushed past and knocked him off centre. He twisted to look, but it was gone. He staggered, caught his foot and fell. Face in dirt, he caught his breath. An arm's length away he made out a form - a wrap cotton top, the limbs splayed on the ground.

A sudden thump jarred the weatherboarding.

'Shit!'

More blows pounded from outside. Each strike came louder and higher. Gritty dust filled the air.

'Priddy? We've got to get out,' he shrieked.

He pushed himself up onto one knee and crouch-crawled, stretching to grab her. An ear-splitting crack ricocheted through the hut. A wall buckled, timber fractured, corrugated roof smashed down. The hut collapsed.

•

Chrissie was puzzled. She wouldn't have been surprised if it was Matt who'd sent a confusing message, or hadn't bothered to answer a simple text question like, *are you OK*? She knew he couldn't imagine anyone worrying about him. But Nick? He was different, often too sensitive, too thoughtful for his own good.

'So why the hell hasn't Nick answered?' she muttered.

She pulled into a layby on the A12 close to the turning to Woodbridge.

'So, do I go to the Woodbridge auction or carry on along the A12 and make a right to Tunstall?'

To her way of thinking, two sides of a triangle might look further on the map, but getting lost was a damn site slower. For her, the cross-country hypotenuse would be more than likely a navigation disaster. She grabbed her phone and opened her text messages. Perhaps something had arrived from Nick while she was driving. There were no new messages.

Frustrated, she opened the morning's text conversation again, hoping for a hint or pointer she'd missed on earlier reading, something to tell her what to do.

First, she read her own message to Nick, the one she'd sent at eight o'clock. *Are you OK? Any news on Tony Mopar? Chrissie.*

Then Nick's immediate reply, *I'm OK. No info on T M yet.*

'And I sent this as I left the workshop, about eight thirty.' She read on, *Thought I'd drop in at address as going to Woodbridge auction for 10:00am. Are you still there? Chrissie.*

She studied his response. *On way with Priddy to check out location for crash scene for film. Think it's same place we drove past to collect your van - the owl nesting site – remember, on corkboard in Grabham's kitchen.*

And next the real puzzler, *T M doesn't exist. It's complicated. Will explain later.*

There was only one more message in the conversation and it was hers, the one she'd fired off immediately in reply to Nick. *T M doesn't exist? What the hell's going on? Are you OK? Chrissie.* And he hadn't answered, at least not in the last forty minutes.

'So why the hell hasn't he got back to me?'

It seemed she had a simple choice, the auction rooms or the owl nesting site.

'He's on his way to some God forsaken filming site with one of Clive's suspects. If she's already poisoned Cooper and now Tony Mopar *no longer exists...* assuming that's a weasel term for wiped out, dead... well, Nick'll be next.'

Short of him not getting back to her because of poor phone signal, everything pointed to trouble for Nick.

She started the Citroen van and eased back into the flow of traffic. Nine miles later, she turned off the A12 and took the B road direct to Tunstall.

•

Nick opened his eyes and spat gritty dust from his mouth. Specks of filth hung in the air. Rotten wood and ancient chicken droppings assaulted his nose. It took him a moment to get his bearings, take it all in.

He lay on his front, not daring to move. Danger teetered above and all around. He waited, and listened. Nothing more fell for what seemed like five minutes. Did that mean it was safe to move? Had everything settled, he wondered.

'Priddy?' he half-coughed, half-called. 'Are you OK?'

No answer. The silence took on a more sinister meaning.

A shaft of daylight penetrated between slats of shattered weatherboard and fallen beams. From where he lay, if he craned his neck, all he saw was a criss-cross of jagged timber, like a giant game of pick-up sticks. Except this wasn't a game. It was deadly. He was trapped in the bottom of a heavy pile of rotten wood and rusty metal.

Tentatively he moved his arms and legs. They seemed OK. He shifted onto his side. He reckoned he had about twelve inches of clearance. He was alive and conscious, but what about Priddy?

'Priddy,' he yelled again, his voice stronger.

He listened for a reply, a rustle, anything to suggest she wasn't dead. But there was nothing. He reached for his phone. It wasn't in his jeans. 'Must be in my jacket,' he muttered, glad to hear the reassurance of his own voice. He fingered his pockets, searching for the familiar slim shape, but all he found was the tyre-tread gauge.

'Where the hell's it gone?'

And then he remembered the gate. He'd caught his jacket on the bars. That's when he must have lost it.

A pulse hammered in his ears. His breathing came fast and shallow. Panic threatened.

'What the hell do I do?' he moaned and made a fist in the dirt. The grainy earth ran through his fingers like sand. He scratched deeper, expecting a floor of rough stones, bricks or concrete, but the only resistance was compacted sandy earth. 'Of course,' he murmured. The hut was built on the same type of ground as the sandlings heathland.

He forced himself to breathe more slowly and focussed on the debris trapping him. In front he made out the straight edge of a wooden roof strut lying on the ground; above his head, a panel of weatherboarding. He guessed it shielded him from the fallen roof. And to one side - a beam and corrugated metal speared the ground.

'She'll be on the other side of this,' he whispered as he touched the timber.

The last time he'd seen Priddy she was sprawled on the ground. He'd tried to grab her as timber and roofing-metal showered down. But she hadn't gripped his hand, didn't struggle to her feet. He remembered the dead weight of her limbs. She'd been unconscious. And now a beam and corrugated metal separated them.

He reckoned the roof truss was several metres long. If most of its length lay on the ground, then its ends would be supported by the floor. It might have been weakened by wood boring beetles, but if it hadn't shattered with the fall, then he guessed it should be strong enough for his purpose.

'I can try to dig under it, get my arm to the other side. Maybe feel if Priddy's there,' he told himself.

He pulled the tyre-tread gauge from his jacket and ran his finger across the protruding metal shaft. Not sharp enough to damage a tyre, but sharp enough for compacted sandy soil. With the gauge in one hand and a shard of wooden slat in the other, he burrowed into the earth with both hands, careful to keep close to the roof truss.

Close by, a car engine burst into life. Was someone outside? Had Merlin Leob arrived with his team? Hope leapt into his throat. 'Help,' he yelled.

He listened as the engine revved. 'Help! Someone help!'

Slowly the familiar sound faded.

'Stop! Don't go,' he moaned.

He listened. Nothing.

'Oh God....' Realisation struck. His car keys weren't in his pockets either. 'That bloody gate. Somebody must have found my keys. Shit! They've stolen my car.'

CHAPTER 34

Chrissie followed the B road to Tunstall. She didn't want to admit it, but she rather enjoyed the view from the Citroen van, the driving seat being set higher than in her TR7. Her natural nosiness distracted her as she scanned the road ahead, able for once to see over low hedges to both sides. Even as she waited at the T-junction in Tunstall, she saw the pub sign standing high on its post. 'The Green Man,' she murmured.

She took the main road through the village, and then she was past the houses, the flint walls and the church.

'Concentrate, Chrissie,' she said severely, 'you got confused here last time. There're two parts to Tunstall. Turn off immediately you're through the next one.'

She recognised the gorse and heather of the sandlings, passed the notice saying Tunstall Common, saw the trees of Tunstall Forest in the distance.

'Damn, I've gone too far. We went wrong here last time.'

She swore as she manoeuvred into a three point turn on the narrow road. 'Shit, Nick had it easy with his little hatch back. Let him try it in a van.'

This time she drove more slowly as she retraced her route and searched for the turning. She changed down to a lower gear and indicated.

'Shit!'

A blue Ford Fiesta shot out of the turning. She slammed on her brakes. It streaked past. Chrissie jolted forwards against her seatbelt. The car was gone.

'What the hell...?' Shock, relief, the image of a driver with blonde curly hair - it all flashed through her head. Half an inch further on, or a second later and she'd have been as good as T-boned. Side-impacted into oblivion.

She pulled into the turning and got out of the van. A whisper of blue paint marked her front black plastic bumper. She leaned against the bonnet waiting for her stomach to stop cartwheeling. The Fiesta had appeared so fast. If it hadn't been for the paint on her bumper, even she wouldn't have believed it had really happened.

'God, blue Ford Fiesta drivers – are they all mad?' She wanted to call Clive, ask him to alert the traffic cops and stop the crazy woman for speeding or dangerous driving. But of course she couldn't. Not after the morning's harsh words.

Her pulse slowed to its normal rate. Still slightly shaken, she got back into the van and drove cautiously along the narrow road, barely wide enough for a car.

It didn't seem familiar, but that could have been because last time she was the passenger and her eyes were glued on Nick's smart phone as she tried to get up a Google map. This time she was the driver and perched higher, eyes like saucers as she dreaded a head-on collision, and watching for old barns or anything which could be an owl nesting site. But the road was deserted and she started to relax. Even her mind clicked into gear as she reasoned Nick's car would be parked somewhere close to the location.

'Spot his Fiesta and I'll have the site,' she murmured.

She drove alongside a hedge and noticed a dilapidated wooden barn beyond the beech and hawthorn. From her slightly raised position she saw abandoned outhouses and a heap of weatherboarding and corrugated metal. She dropped to crawler speed. This was more like it. Small lumps of soil littered the road just ahead. They looked as if they'd been kicked up or shed by tyres driving from the verge.

'There!' She spotted a metal crossbar gate and saw stony rutted earth in front of it. Perhaps the Fiesta was somewhere the other side of the gate.

Curious, she pulled up and got out of the van. 'Damn, the gate's chained and padlocked,' she muttered. 'Either it's the wrong place or I'm too late.' She began to turn to get back in the van, but something glinted gold and caught her eye. Fools' gold, she thought as the yellowy-orange colour drew her towards the long grass beyond the gate. She squatted to look closer. It was no good; she was going to have to climb over.

It didn't take her a moment, and she was over the bars and on the other side. Deep amongst the long grass she made out the shape. She'd seen it before. She reached for it.

'Shit,' she breathed, 'it's Nick's phone.'

The slim metal casing felt cold in her hand. There was no doubt, she'd definitely held it before, but last time she'd been scrutinising a Google map. 'What the hell's it doing here?'

If it really was Nick's phone, then she figured she should be able to unlock it with his passcode. She remembered tapping in the numbers as he'd said them. But what were they?

She crouched amongst the brambles and long grass and concentrated, trying to recall his voice as he'd said the numbers, and the pattern she'd made as her finger moved across the keypad. She clicked the phone on, swiped her finger across the screen, waited until a keypad appeared, then made the moves.

'Top right – that's a *three*. Bottom centre – that's a *zero*. One row from top and far left column – that's a *four*. And now centre in row above bottom - that's an *eight*.'

The phone unlocked. She was in. 'Three, zero, four, eight,' she chanted, but her exuberance evaporated as the significance struck. It was Nick's phone all right, but why was it here? Had he dropped it by accident? Was it a message, a cry for help? One thing was sure, 'He's been here,' she murmured.

She scrolled through the messages he'd sent her, but there were no clues, nothing new, and her last message to him hadn't been opened. 'He never read it. Why?'

She checked for phone signal. It was dire, non-existent. 'Shit.'

A thought took shape and stirred in the depths of her mind. 'Oh God, that Fiesta I almost hit. Nick wasn't driving it, but... was it his car?' It seemed ridiculous, but could it have been Priddy driving, she wondered. And if that was the case, where was Nick? What the hell had happened?

•

Nick burrowed down and forwards, scooping the sandy earth back towards himself. He stubbed his fingers and tore his nails, but if he held the metal tyre-tread gauge like a dagger, or gripped it like a knuckle duster, he could poke and cut and loosen the compacted sandy soil. It was hot sweaty work.

'Bugger!' The rotten shard of weatherboarding he'd used as a scoop fractured against a flint. He tossed it away.

The tunnel quickly narrowed to the width of his arm. He kept it shallow, skimming under the truss, the rough wood and course earth grazing like sandpaper. If he dug deeper it felt cold and damp. Would the sides hold together? For the moment he reckoned shallow would do for the initial exploratory channel. He thrust his arm through.

He felt air and emptiness. 'Yes!' His fingertips were free. He was through to the far side of the truss. A surge of endorphins kicked in and his spirits rose.

He forced his arm further underneath. Cold unyielding soil encased his biceps and triceps, but now his wrist was through to the other side. He held his breath and strained to reach as far as he could. He moved his hand and spread his fingers. The air was cooler. He felt earthy floor and splinters of wood, the same as on his side. And Priddy? Nothing. If he was going to find her, he had to stretch in further, sweep around with his hand. For that he needed to bend his elbow, move his shoulder, but the channel didn't allow it.

He pulled his arm back and shouted through, 'Priddy? Priddy are you there? Answer me.' Foreboding mushroomed.

Brushing the dirt from his nose, he tried to look under the truss. It was impossible. All he achieved was grit in his eye. The tunnel was too narrow. More work was required. If he widened the entrance and exit, kept the channel narrow directly beneath the truss, he reckoned he'd have a wider arc of movement with his arm.

•

Chrissie leaned against the crossbar gate and considered her options. Nick's mobile didn't have any signal, and no surprise, neither did hers. If she was going to call for help or alert someone, it meant driving to Nigel

Grabham's place. He had a landline and she knew the way; a drive to the end of the narrow road and then a right turn at the T-junction. His house backed onto the forest. But he might not be at home.

'What do I do?' she moaned, torn with indecision.

A faint sound floated through the air. A man's cry? She tensed, straining to catch the softest footstep, a rustle of leaves; anything which spelled danger.

There were no more sounds. She breathed again. 'Hell, I'm out of here,' she whispered, and turned to half-climb, half-vault the gate.

One foot on the bar and the other raised to swing over, she heard a muted shout. Someone was calling. It was distant, muffled – a man's voice, and this time she'd made out the word Priddy. Had she really heard it, or was her imagination twisting sounds into familiar names, fashioning what she was thinking, what she feared?

'Answer me.' The voice, barely audible, drifted towards her, carried on a light breeze. But this time her ears were better tuned. She froze on the gate.

'Nick? Nick is that you?' she shrieked.

She sprang back from the gate and hurried towards the voice. The grass was trampled and brambles crushed close to a heap of broken weatherboarding and rusty corrugated metal. Could he have been here, she wondered, and stooped to take a closer look. She saw oblong imprints in areas of the exposed soil.

'Good God,' she murmured.

The weatherboarding and corrugated metal wasn't a random pile of building materials. When she looked more closely she reckoned it could have been a hut or an outhouse once.

'Probably been falling down for years,' she said as she glanced around, taking in the decaying lean-tos and rotten wooden barn. It was spooky.

She sensed someone was near. 'Hey, Nick! Where are you?' she yelled.

'Chrissie? Is that you? Help!' The voice was close, muffled, desperate.

'Nick?' She hardly dared believe her ears. 'Nick, I can't see you. Where are you?'

'Help! I'm trapped. The hut caved in.'

'What? Are you OK?'

And then she understood. Her eyes picked out the tell-tale signs. She was staring at the new demolition of a decaying structure. Freshly broken panels, clean looking splits in rotten wood, uprights fractured but not before loosening the sandy soil and uprooting weeds and grass.

'Has this fallen down just now, today?' She was stunned. 'Hey Nick, keep talking. Tell me what happened. I'll follow your voice.'

'Thank God you've come, Chrissie. Don't tread on any of it or pull at anything. It's unstable, dangerous.'

She picked her way alongside the panels and fallen beams, wary as she stepped over nettles and long grass. His voice kept coming. She moved back and forth, homing in closer and closer.

'I think this is the nearest I dare get. Otherwise I'm climbing on stuff. Can you still hear me?'

'Yeah, you sound pretty close. Hey, how did you know to come?'

She ignored his question. 'So, are you OK? Are you hurt?'

'I'm OK. But I don't know about Priddy. I think she may be... I don't know. She's in here somewhere.'

'What? Are you sure?'

'Yeah.'

'It's just that your car isn't here and I think I saw her driving it. In fact she nearly crashed into me.'

'What?'

'Look, it's not important. Let's concentrate on getting you out. It sounds like you're just underneath this panel. Not far to freedom.'

'Don't try and lift it by yourself. It could set everything sliding, and Priddy....'

'I'll get help. There's no bloody phone signal so I've got to drive to find somewhere. I'll try down the road where I bought the van. It's not far.'

•

Nick laid his head on the heap of freshly excavated soil. It was going to be all right. All he had to do was wait. He allowed the tension to drain from his limbs and the cold earth to calm the pulse firing through his temple. A bead of sweat ran into his eye.

But what the hell had Chrissie been on about, he wondered. Priddy driving his car? Was it possible?

Weary, but no longer desperate, he raised his head. He figured he might as well scoop more soil from the entrance to his burrow while he waited. Stripped of anxiety, each hand stroke was more efficient, less frantic than before. Methodically he widened the entrance and exit.

'Now,' he murmured and slipped his arm through as far as his shoulder. He made broad sweeping movements, raking the other side with his fingers, slow and sure.

He brushed across cotton fabric, moved his hand back to check, touched more firmly.

'Oh God, please no.'

But there was no mistaking what he'd felt. Priddy hadn't driven away in his car. Her arm felt too cold, too lifeless.

CHAPTER 35

Matt pulled into the side of the road and waited on his scooter. Maisie lived in one of the houses near the playing fields in Stowupland, barely a mile from Stowmarket, but as usual, she preferred to walk the hundred yards to his scooter, rather than have him wait directly outside her front door.

'I aint givin' them snoopy neighbours stuff to talk about,' she'd explained once. At the time it had appealed to his CIA agent doppelganger instinct, but as the weeks and months passed, he wasn't so sure.

He ran through the route to Grundisburgh in his mind while he hung around.

'Hey, Mais,' he called, spotting her in the distance. He waved.

The next few moments were spent happily eyeing up her shapely legs in her skinny blue jeans. Pink streaks highlighted her blonde hair. They matched her bubble-gum pink quilted gilet.

'Hey Matt. What d'you think? Kinda Dolly Parton enough?' She put her hand on her waist and thrust a hip towards him.

'Sure, Mais. So do you need the wig as well?'

'Yeah, course I need it. I'm in character, aint I? I'm Damon's girlfriend, right?'

'Yeah, but he aint using the Damon handle – it's Rad Zing, remember?'

'Got it.'

She settled behind him on the scooter. 'What d'you think of me top? You aint said. I borrowed it from me friend Judy. Pink's her colour. I don't think you've met her yet.'

Before he'd had a chance to answer, she'd slipped her helmet on. Thankful to sidestep the pink gilet question, he flipped down his visor and started the Piaggio.

He sped along the B roads. Maisie whooped as they zipped down slopes topping speeds of thirty miles per hour.

'Go on, go on!' she squealed when they lost pace on the hills and flat. Excitement, anticipation, the personification of pink candyfloss on the back of the scooter, he loved it.

They approached Grundisburgh from the north, slowing past the village green and then dawdling down a narrow lane. He pictured the Google earth map, recognised the Google street view with the 1960s bungalows set back behind mature shrubs. He was looking for an untidy beech hedge as he checked off the house numbers.

'Here,' he said and slowed to a halt. He flipped up his visor. 'Hey Mais, this is it. Ready?' He turned to check she'd heard.

She pulled off her helmet and shook her hair free.

'We're about right for eleven. Might as well go in, Mais,' he said.

'Yeah, but you aint stayin' out here. You're comin' too. You promised.'

'I'll be waitin' on me scooter in the drive. Just remember you're Rad Zing's girlfriend. Here....' He drew a wodge of notes from his back pocket. 'If you get confused I got it on me tee shirt under this. OK?' He tapped his denim jacket.

'Thanks. If I unzip me pink top, you show me your tee. Here,' she said and pressed closer to kiss him, caught the helmet chin guard and got his nose.

'No-o-o. You aint me girlfriend.'

'What?'

'Someone may be watchin'. Stay in character. I'm the courier, remember.'

'Right. Drive on. We've a wig to collect.' She punched the air.

He started the scooter, lowered his visor and idled onto the gravel drive. He reckoned a courier would stop at the front door, and he eased to a standstill. The sixties-styled porch, with its metal pole and slab of concrete for a roof, threw shadows.

He glanced around while Maisie jumped down from the back of the scooter. He spotted a bicycle, propped partly out of sight behind a trellis. 'Well fast,' he murmured as he took in its slender frame, narrow racing tyres, and cassette of gleaming cogs with gear shifter on the rear axle.

Maisie pressed the bell and stepped back from the door. He watched as she lowered her head, then lifted it, pulling back her shoulders and thrusting her chest out.

He figured she'd carry it off. And then another thought struck. Was he parked on the spot where Owen died? He scanned the gravel for stains.

'Hello. Has Rad Zing sent you? Are you here for the Dolly Parton wig?'

Matt recognised the voice. It sounded slightly warmer, slightly fuller than over the phone, but it was definitely the same Prosecco he'd heard in the skateboarding warehouse and talking to Priddy in the Diss Auction car park. He hunched his shoulders and kept his head turned away.

Beep-itty-beep! *Beep-itty-beep beep*! His phone sounded through his jacket pocket.

'Frag,' he muttered as he fumbled for it and read the caller ID. 'Chrissie?'

'Yeah, me boyfriend – he's so sweet. He said he was sending a courier – but I told him I got to check it fits, right? Reckoned I'd come as well.'

'OK, just wait here. I'll get it for you.'

He was catching the conversation at the front door, but a phone call? Cocooned in his helmet, it would be like trying to listen and speak into the handset under water. He cancelled the call.

Beep-itty-beep! *Beep-itty-beep beep*! The phone rang loud and clear again.

'Turn it off, answer it, do something with it, Matt,' Maisie hissed, and then like honey, 'Hey, that was quick. The wig looks amazin'. May I?'

Matt killed the call. He couldn't help but glance to watch Maisie as she pulled on the wig. Prosecco stood at the door. She looked pretty much as he remembered her, except her curly hair was wet today.

'Seems your courier's pretty busy. More jobs? More deliveries to make? Did I hear you say his name is Matt?'

'Might have done. Have you got a mirror?'

'A mirror? Believe me, it looks fabulous. Great fit.'

Beep-itty-beep! *Beep-itty-beep beep*! His patience snapped. He kept his back to Prosecco and pushed his helmet up. 'What?' he whispered, holding his mobile to his ear.

'Hi, it's Chrissie. There's been an accident. A tumbledown hut collapsed on Nick. They're getting him out now, but I think... well Clive and the police are here.

Priddy wasn't so lucky. She might not make it. Clive thinks the driver I saw who nearly hit me could have been Prosecco.'

'What? But Prosecco's here with us.'

'So how much you askin'?' Maisie's words cut into his other ear, drowning out Chrissie's voice.

'Fifty pounds.'

'What?' Maisie shrieked. 'The whole of lot 300 wasn't even fifty quid. And there was more than one wig in the lot. You're rippin' me off. I'll give you fifteen quid, max.'

'Prosecco's there with you? Are you sure? Where are you?' Chrissie sounded surprised.

'Yeah,' he turned to be absolutely sure, 'and Mais is with me. We're in Grundisburgh.' He cupped his hand over his mobile.

'What?' Chrissie's voice rose to strident pitch.

'Hey, who the hell are you? I've seen you before,' Prosecco shouted before Matt had time to shield his face.

'Fifteen quid and we'll go. It's me last offer. If you don't say yes, it'll be a tenner. What d'you say?'

'And you, little Miss Dolly, how do you know about the lot number? Are you following me as well? Who the hell are you two?'

'Right then, it's a tenner and it's time to leave,' Maisie spat the words as she pealed a note from the wodge, unzipped her pink gilet and stowed the rest inside.

Matt read the signal and opened his denim jacket.

'Hey, I've got you now! You're Matt, and you're Carl Stiltz. The weasel who called me about his fiancée.'

'Fiancee?' Maisie's voice rose to a screech, 'You stuck up bitch! Who you callin' a weasel?'

Prosecco drew herself to her full height. 'Jumping Stilts,' she said still staring at Matt's tee shirt. 'That was it, stilts with a Z. I remember you all right. You bastard.'

'Oi, watch it you bi–'

Maisie's words died as Prosecco grabbed her pink gilet, spun her around and snatched the wodge of money.

'Hey!' Matt yelled. 'That's mine.' He lurched from his scooter and flung himself towards Prosecco. His phone flew into the air, his helmet rolled on the gravel. Maisie swung a punch. Prosecco sprang away and hurdled over his helmet. Two leaping strides and she made it to the trellis.

'Stop,' Maisie screamed.

'She's goin' to get her bike. Quick, on me Piaggio!'

•

Chrissie stood next to Clive when he took the call.

'What? Let me just get that clear – a Piaggio Zip is being ridden down Grundisburgh Road by a man without a helmet and a girl riding pillion, wearing a Dolly Parton Wig?'

She watched his face colour.

'No it won't be the real Dolly Parton... and you say they're in pursuit of a woman on a racing bicycle? Stop them... I know they may not be speeding... yes, the girl cyclist may be... don't let the girl on the bike get away... no not the one in the wig, the cyclist... just arrest them all.'

CHAPTER 36

Chrissie settled next to Clive on a bench. It was the first time he'd been free enough to spend a whole Saturday with her since Prosecco had been arrested and charged with Cooper's murder. It was also the first time the nightmare of watching Priddy being pulled unconscious from the wreckage had mellowed enough for her to feel a sense of tranquillity. It could have been Nick, she kept telling herself.

'Do you realise it was only two weeks ago?'

'Hmm,' Clive murmured, and squeezed her hand.

'The Great Shed Tsunami.'

Chrissie had begun to refer to it in meteorological terms. It was easier than groping for weightier words to do justice to the horror. "Tsunami" was an unemotional label. It somehow bypassed the need to picture the scene, replay the drama or revisit her emotions. It had, after all, seemingly come out of nowhere, been overwhelming and very nearly fatal. No matter it hadn't involved water.

'It's almost as if they're able to see right into your soul. Those eyes....'

She knew he was talking about the owls.

It was her idea to come to the Suffolk Owl Sanctuary, and Clive had agreed more enthusiastically when she'd explained there'd be other birds of prey to see. She'd always considered it somewhere holidaymakers and day-trippers visited. Not her sort of place. But since the Great Shed Tsunami, she'd become curious about owls. She reckoned she owed it to them to pay an entrance fee, make a donation, find out more. They'd saved one life, maybe two. She needed to understand what is was it about owls that drove Nigel Grabham to go to all the trouble of fixing cameras around their nesting and roosting site. She sat close to Clive, dusk falling, and began to realise.

'Look, Clive. Is that a kestrel? I think it's recognised its keeper.' She pointed.

'It could be. But kestrel, hawk, falcon? Don't ask me. Now owls – I've got the shape of the head, beak, eyes. It's a kind of photo fit.'

They watched the keeper take the magnificent bird from its display perch and onto his gloved forearm and fist, the tether swinging like a long festoon.

'It must be time to go back to their cages,' she said as a second keeper gathered an equally magnificent but small barn owl from the neighbouring perch.

'Yes, display time over, job done, off duty. I know what that feels like.'

They watched the keepers walk side by side, tethers looped and swaying as they headed for the aviaries.

'It's almost like a changing-the-guards ceremony,' she murmured. 'It's strange how you think of a falcon or eagle as a bird of prey, but somehow an owl... well your first thought is its eyes rather than its beak or talons.'

'And the large head.'

'I think it's the way they look at you full on.'

'Yes. Don't you think the face makes you want to give them human qualities?'

'Like wisdom? I guess the feathers half hiding the killer beak help with that concept. It's funny how the more owls you see the more fascinating they become.'

He didn't answer. She guessed he was somewhere in the case, tying up loose ends, puzzling over some of the details.

'Thank God for Nigel Grabham,' he said under her breath.

'And owls,' she added. 'Who'd have guessed he still had cameras set up despite the end of the nesting season? And if I hadn't gone to him for help, and he hadn't returned to the Tsunami site with me, how long, if at all, would it have taken before he realised what he'd captured on camera?'

'Or we'd realised there were cameras and whose they were. Hell, they were well hidden. Thank God Prosecco hadn't spotted them.'

'I doubt it would have crossed her mind to look for them. Barn owl nesting sites? It wouldn't have been on her radar.'

'She had other things on her mind.' Clive's voice hardened, as if enough had been said.

Chrissie ignored his tone. 'Without Nigel's images, would anyone have believed it was possible? I mean, Prosecco leaping at the side of the hut on her jumping stilts?' For a moment she pictured the rotten wood. Weeds, fungi and wood boring beetles had continued what the wind and rain had started. It wouldn't have taken much to bring it all down, just some well-placed high impacts.

'You're forgetting we found where she ditched the stilts. Forensics have matched up wood splinters from the hut, clothes fibres and spots of Priddy's blood.'

'You never said about the forensics.' She tried not to get distracted as her thoughts ran on a different track. 'Do you think Nick being there was part of Prosecco's plan?'

'No. She'd only sent Priddy the text message to go there. No one else. And she'd made sure Priddy wouldn't realise it was from her. It's easy enough to get hold of these pay-as-you-go phones and then ditch them. I think she planned to ambush her, kill her with a blow to the head, and then bring the hut down as if it had all been some tragic accident.'

'But Nick turned up too.'

'Right, and that complicated things. His car was parked right next to the gate. Abandoned cars get reported. Eventually someone would have come sniffing around. She had to ditch it. That's why she drove it away, and then hid it down one of those forest tracks. The one where she'd left her bicycle.'

'And she nearly crashed into me.'

'Yes, and if you remember, you told everyone it was Priddy driving. Luckily there's some of the Fiesta's paint on your bumper, otherwise no one would have believed you. You'd make a hopeless witness.' He squeezed her hand.

'Yes, I know. But I'd never seen Priddy before. I just assumed….'

'That's the trouble. You make assumptions, jump to–'

'That's not fair, Clive.'

He fell silent.

But he was right. She knew she jumped to conclusions. But so had Prosecco. She'd assumed she'd left Priddy for dead and Nick as good as dead. She'd probably even chosen the location because there wasn't any phone signal and there'd be no chance of them summoning help.

'Friends weren't on her radar either,' she murmured.

'What's that about friends?'

'Prosecco hadn't reckoned on me.'

'Well no, you're hardly predictable.' Clive leaned closer. 'Come on, they're closing here. It's time we made tracks.'

She stood up and walked with him past the vacant perches. Perhaps it was the evening light, or talking about Prosecco, but her mind spun back as they ambled alongside the wooden hut-like aviaries. For a moment she saw the segments of weatherboard being lifted; Nick dazed and blinking as he was helped from the wreckage; Priddy, hair matted with blood and covered in dust and dirt.

'Are you OK?'

'Yes, of course I'm OK. Why shouldn't I be?' she said, and pushed back the image. 'But there's loads you haven't told me, and I still don't get it. How can you be so sure Prosecco will be found guilty of Cooper's murder?'

He didn't answer for a moment. He seemed more preoccupied with unlocking his car and waiting for her to get settled in the passenger seat before driving slowly out of the car park.

'We must be the last ones to leave,' he said mildly.

'Hmm,' she murmured, not sure whether to wait for him to say more or push him to answer.

'I suppose it's several things,' he said, eventually breaking the silence when she failed to press for more.

'Priddy is pretty shaken up by the attempt on her life. It seems she's decided her best chance of staying alive is to be open with us.'

'You're answering in riddles, Clive.'

'Not at all,' he said as they drove away from Stonham Aspal and headed for Woolpit and home. 'I didn't know there were such things as hero props until Priddy explained.

So it wasn't until we got all the digital footage from the camera crew that we realised the flasks had been swapped. Thank God for digital cameras. One of the cameramen was shooting before the scene got under way. You know, playing with light exposure and camera angles.'

'Hey, stop teasing me. Explain properly.'

'Well it was obvious, if you knew what to look for. Priddy took out the hero hip flask for the shoot. It's caught on camera when they were setting up the take. The flask which Prosecco gives to Cooper is the bog standard prop. I don't think he complained because he wanted to get at the vodka.'

Chrissie wasn't sure if she was following but she wasn't going to let on, not with his slightly perverse mood.

'And that's enough evidence to convict her?'

'Well, there's plenty of circumstantial evidence. Our expert found monkshood growing in her garden out at Grundisburgh. And she must have prepared some because we found it in a bottle marked oil & vinegar salad dressing in her kitchen and with her prints all over it. Also of course there was the cat. So opportunity, motive….'

'Motive?'

'You're forgetting she didn't like "not winning". She'd set her sights on Cooper, but I suspect Owen wasn't jealous enough and she unleashed her cold fury on him.'

'And you think Prosecco killed Owen as well?'

'Yes, he'd been unwell because she was giving him poisonous wild mushrooms and then encouraging him to take the cleansing bleach miracle cure stuff. Again, it's all circumstantial evidence. But she did something like this before, when she was a kid.'

'Really? Is that admissible?'

'Probably not. I guess she tried the monkshood out on the cat first, and it died.'

'So it gave her an idea?'

'Yes, I think she put the dead cat in the cat carrier and squeezed it under Owen's parked van. She probably even told him he'd reversed over it and asked him to rescue it. He couldn't just drive the van away without injuring it more, and so I guess he jacked it up.'

'But I thought he'd texted Nick saying he was going to change the oil.'

'I know, but it doesn't make sense. I think he was too ill and it was obvious he hadn't even touched the oil sump.'

'But....'

'The cat was the excuse to get him under the van. I think she kicked the jacks out of the way and he was crushed under the oil sump. Then she used a broom to push the cat carrier and dead cat out. At least we've got that as evidence, and the expert's opinion about the jacks not having spontaneously failed.'

'So she had opportunity. And you think she was the one who sent the text to Nick using Owen's phone and saying he was going to change the oil?'

'Yes, although I can't prove it.'

'But that implies she'd planned it for days.'

'Exactly. It's an example of cold, slow burning rage. But as I said, she has a history. We're waiting for the legal team to decide if we've got enough to charge her with Owen's murder as well. We've definitely got enough to make Priddy's attempted murder stick.'

Chrissie shivered. 'And Cooper?'

'With Owen out of the way, Cooper more than likely tired of her, so I figure she turned her fury on him.'

As Clive drove along the small twisting roads, he talked more freely about the case than she'd heard him speak for weeks. She'd craved answers but he was swamping her with information. It must be the release of tension, the relief at having solved what had become a high profile case. Or was it the result of spending down-time with the owls, she wondered.

'I thought Nick said it was Owen, not Prosecco who was the one into jumping stilts, but I suppose he was too unwell for that too,' she finally murmured.

'We've made some enquiries. It seems it was Prosecco who was the jumping stilts enthusiast, and it makes sense. She was a past gymnast.'

'Of course.'

'Sorry,' he said. 'I've been a bit mean over these past few weeks, haven't I?'

'No, not really. It's nice when you share with me. But you know I can't help wondering about things. And when I've only got some of the facts, then I jump to—'

'Conclusions.'

'No, I was going to say, make assumptions.'

She listened to him laugh, a kind of happy chuckle. It brought back memories of a much earlier conversation, weeks before the filming had really got underway.

'There was me,' she said, 'thinking you police were watching out for Gavi Monterey cycling around the county in her Lycra. And all the while it was Prosecco on her racing bike you should've been watching.'

'If she'd worn some Lycra we might have noticed her.' She caught his wry smile.

'I know, most cyclists are pretty anonymous around here,' she murmured, happy and relaxed at last. It must be those owls, she decided. Those wise old owls. Remarkable.

CHAPTER 37

Matt clumped up the outside wooden staircase with Maisie close on his heels.

'You brought the lager?' he asked.

'Yeah, I been sittin' on it, aint I?'

'What you on about, Mais?'

'It's been under me seat. It'll be real shaken up by now.'

He paused on the small platform at the top of the stairs and glanced down at the gravel drive with its assortment of cars and his scooter. 'I don't think Nick'll mind. He don't drink lager.'

'Then we should've brought some real ale. No, on second thoughts, some wine. It is a kinda flat warmin' do aint it?' She stopped on the last-but-one step and caught her breath. 'Hey, that metallic blue car looks awesome down there.'

Before Matt could say anything, the door swung open and Nick stood grinning as he blocked their way.

'Hiya. You made it!'

'Course we made it. Wouldn't want to miss out on seein' your new place.'

'Well don't hang around outside. It probably isn't safe if too many people stand on the staging. Come on in.'

'Right, mate,' Matt said. It was invitation enough. He hurried through the doorway into a long room in the eaves over the double garage below. The sloping ceiling and low sidewalls made him gravitate towards the centre of the room.

'You didn't say it was an attic,' Maisie squealed as she followed him in.

'I heard that, Maisie,' Nick said. 'I see it more as a one-room-bedsit-opportunity. Or in estate agent speak, a bijou lodger let.'

'A little gem,' Sarah said, appearing as if from nowhere. A feathered cut shaped her sleek black hair. Matt guessed it made it all the more easy for her to slip her fencing helmet on and off. He focussed on her campion red nail varnish.

'I didn't know you had a garage loft for stayin' in, Sarah.'

'No, Matt. I didn't. But when Chrissie told me about... well about Nick, I thought he might as well make use of,' she took a deep breath, 'well what I call The Garret.'

'The Garret?'

'Yes, Maisie. Hey Chrissie, hi!' She dodged around Maisie and hurried to the doorway.

'The thing is,' Nick said leaning closer to Matt, 'it's my own. I don't have to pay much rent and I get to maybe have the band up here for a practice.'

'She said that were OK?'

'Yeah, it was one of the first things I asked when she offered it to me. In fact they'll be arriving soon.'

'Cool – d'you think she's after Jake. Better warn him, mate.'

'Got all the mod cons, I see,' Chrissie said walking over. 'Hi.' She gave Nick a hug.

Matt left Nick to Chrissie and wandered through the room to inspect the instant hot water dispenser. 'It's great.

An' he's got a microwave an' a small fridge,' he murmured to Maisie, who'd drifted alongside.

'Don't it make you want to leave home, get a place of your own, Matt?'

'What? DOS-in' hell, Mais. Why'd I do that when I can hang out here?'

'Yeah, but this is stuck out in Woolpit, Matt. It's easier you bein' in Stowmarket.'

He was about to say something about not always needing to be close to the Utterly library and computer labs, but he knew he'd be lying.

'Yes, there's a much nicer shower he can use downstairs in the main house.' Sarah's voice drifted across the room.

'D'you think she fancies Nick?' Maisie whispered in his ear.

'What, Mais?' his thoughts now caught between two tracks.

'So you think it's Sarah? Don't tell me Nick fancies her?' she squeaked, her strident tone cutting through the air.

For a moment the sound in the one-room-bedsit-opportunity quietened.

'So how is Priddy recovering?' Chrissie's words filled the space.

'Yeah, she's going to be OK. But, she's a main witness so Clive's advised me to stay away. It was only a month ago, remember.'

'So it's Priddy then?' she cupped her hand to his ear this time.

'How'd I know, Mais? Hey Nick, how long you got the replacement car for?'

'I think three months. But Clive says the police will probably keep my Fiesta until after the trial.'

'Clive should be along shortly. You can ask him if they compensate for impounding evidence.'

'I doubt it. Hey Chrissie, have you decided if you're bringing a case against the selling site through the Trading Standards Regulator?'

'I'd like to against Lester, but… I think I'm going to let it all drop. It's all… I don't know, I think we need to….'

'Move on?'

'Yes.'

Matt pulled the tab off one of the cans. A Vesuvius of foaming lager shot into the air. He bobbed over it, gulping and licking to consume the eruption.

'Hey watch out, Matt.'

'Yeah, yeah. I know, this aint a pub.' He gazed around at his friends. He understood them. At least he thought he understood them. But someone like Prosecco? How did that happen? Had any of them seen it coming? 'Why?' he murmured under his breath.

'Why what?'

Chrissie must have amazing hearing, he thought and ignored her question.

'Why what?' she repeated. It was obvious she wasn't going to let up.

'Well, why? Why did Prosecco… I mean what kicked it all off?'

'The Olympics.'

'What?'

'The Olympics. She was a frustrated gymnast. She had the potential to compete on the world's stage. And then all the hype of the London Olympics, the TV coverage, and then more weeks with the Paralympics. It destabilised her, released her suppressed anger. It was simply a matter of time before she found targets to turn on.'

'Is that what Clive said?' Nick asked.

'Yes.'

'So what you sayin'? Exercise is dangerous?'

'Yes, Matt. If they ask you to join the next Olympic squad - just say no.'

'Sounds like one of your tee shirts,' Maisie squealed.

The end.

63861292R00185

Made in the USA
Charleston, SC
15 November 2016